LIKE NEVER BEFORE

He had not missed the spark in her eyes when she first saw him, and there was no mistaking her passionate response to his kisses. She may be furious with him for leaving her, but she was still physically attracted to him. This was something her traitorous body could not deny. He would use her attraction for him to his advantage.

Whistling, Greg walked out to his car. He would win her back any way he could. There was no playing fair when there was something he wanted. Danielle would be his again, and this time he would not let her go. This time she would be his wife.

Greg showered and got ready for bed. His last waking thought was of Danielle. Her not throwing him out of her house was a good sign. All he had to do was bide his time. As long as the love and the passion were still there, they could work on the rest.

Also by Sylvia Lett

Perfect for You

Like Never Before

Sylvia Lett

Dafina
BOOKS

Kensington Publishing Corp.

http://www.kensingtonbooks.com

DAFINA BOOKS are published by

Kensington Publishing Corp.
850 Third Avenue
New York, NY 10022

All Kensington Titles, Imprints, and Distributed Lines are
available at special quantity discounts for bulk purchases
for sales promotions, premiums, fund-raising, and educa-
tional or institutional use. Special book excerpts or cus-
tomized printings can also be created to fit specific needs.
For details, write or phone the office of the Kensington
special sales manager: Kensington Publishing Corp., 850
Third Avenue, New York, NY 10022, attn: Special Sales
Department, Phone: 1-800-221-2647.

Dafina and the Dafina logo Reg. U.S. Pat. & TM Off.

ISBN-13: 978-0-7582-1980-0
ISBN-10: 0-7582-1980-6

First mass market printing: April 2008

10 9 8 7 6 5 4 3 2 1

Printed in the United States of America

This book is dedicated to my wonderful children: Michael and Courtney Lett.

Michael, my handsome teenager, you have turned into a thoughtful and caring young man. Strive to be the best person you can be. Kindness is not a sign of weakness. Don't look for a role model. Be one!

Courtney, "Lexi," my beautiful little warrior princess, you seem to always know when I need a hug or an "I love you Mom." Your thoughtfulness and compassion never cease to amaze me. Seeing life through your eyes is an amazing gift.

I love you both very much and I am proud of you.

Mom

Acknowledgments

I'd like to take a moment to thank some very special people in my life. To my mother, Mattie Willis, you have always had faith in me. Mine has faltered from time to time, but you were there to see me through it. You encouraged me to follow my dream of writing. I love you, Mom.

To my sisters and brothers: C. Earl, Johnnie, Liz, Val, Sam, and Bessie, what can I say? Being the baby of the family is no easy feat. You guys set the bar pretty high for me and I hope I haven't disappointed you. Your continued love, support, and encouragement keep me focused and strong. I love you all.

Chapter 1

Danielle was inserting the key in the door when she heard the telephone ring. By the time she maneuvered her way inside, amid boxes and packages, the answering machine clicked on. She gave way to exhaustion, dropped everything on the sofa, and collapsed against the soft cushions.

She waited for the machine to click off before she got up to hit the message rewind button. Beep. "Hi beautiful, it's Randy. Let's get together this weekend. I have tickets to the Ranger game."

"Not in this lifetime." She shook her head and laughed. She was not up to a wrestling match with handy Randy, the human octopus. Randy Howard was a nerdy professor who attached himself to Danielle at a party about six months ago and now she couldn't seem to shake him.

Beep. "Hi, it's Liz. Dinner has been changed to 7:30. See you then." Beep. "It's Randy again. I guess you're not home yet. I'll try you again later." Beep. "Danielle, it's Victoria. Don't make any plans for Saturday three weeks from tomorrow. I'm planning a surprise birthday party for Lawrence at the club. Call me next week and I'll fill you in on all the details." Beep. "Randy, again.

Danielle, if you're there pick up. Danielle. Danielle, I guess you're really not there. I'll call back later." Beep. "Hi. Long time no talk to. It's Greg. I'll be in town this weekend and I'd really like to see you. I'll give you a call back either tonight when I get there or tomorrow." Beep.

She stopped the machine abruptly. Her hand shook as she hit the rewind button. Danielle pressed the fast forward button until she got to Greg's message. She played it again, and slowly sat down on the couch.

The last thing she needed was a blast from her past in the form of Greg Thomas. Danielle didn't think she would ever see or hear from him again. Their four-year roller coaster romance ended when he moved away two years ago.

She and Greg met at college. They were in a criminal justice class together, but had yet to be introduced. The two of them were thrown together at a party. Danielle's date was with Mark, who later became Greg's then-best friend, Adam. Adam saw the sparks between the two of them and stepped aside. Greg drove her home and they became inseparable.

Greg was tall with a medium build. His shoulders were broad with well-defined biceps. He was sexy and gorgeous from his dark, wavy, short hair down to his designer loafers, with the greatest pair of legs and ass Danielle had ever seen.

He was an avid runner, golfer, and tennis player. Dreamy, brown eyes filled his handsome, copper face, and his voice was a deep bass that could melt snow in the middle of January.

After graduating from college, they continued to date exclusively. Danielle went into corporate law, working for Masters, Lockhart, and Rivera.

Greg went into criminal law. He was offered, and accepted, a job from the very prestigious firm of Wentworth and Carlton even before graduation.

He proposed six months later. They were at the Masters' private nightclub on a Saturday night, when the disc jockey mysteriously cleared the dance floor. Greg placed a chair in the middle and led Danielle there. Dropping down on one knee, he asked her to marry him.

There had been well more than two hundred people present at the time, including some of her family and friends. She happily and tearfully accepted and sealed their engagement with a kiss. Amid applause and best wishes, the D.J. played a special song for them and they slow danced. Greg was the most romantic guy she had ever met. That had been one the happiest moments of Danielle's life. Their special night would be implanted in her memories forever.

They were engaged for two years. Every time they made it close to the altar, something would happen to sideline them. Danielle and Greg postponed the wedding twice before Danielle finally broke off the engagement. From that point on, it became an on again off again relationship. It continued that way until Greg was offered a job in Oregon. He asked Danielle to go with him, but by this time the relationship was already in shambles and she refused. Greg left town and they had had no contact until now.

Danielle paced the room in agitation. She was not sure she wanted to see him. Her betraying heart did a flip-flop at the thought. Her head knew she should stay away, but her heart wanted to see him again.

Danielle was a beautiful and successful corporate attorney. She had everything most people would kill for monetarily, but her life was still incomplete. Her dream was to marry Greg and have a family. Those plans changed when the man she loved walked out the door and left the state for greener pastures.

* * *

Greg showed the smiling flight attendant his ticket, and she directed him toward the front of the plane. After stuffing his gray designer carry-on bag and his briefcase in the overhead compartment, he folded his six-foot frame into the small seat.

He vaguely listened as the flight attendant gave crash instructions, but he couldn't concentrate on what was being said. He had flown enough to recite the spiel by heart.

Greg leaned back in the his seat and closed his eyes. In a few hours, he would be home. His first stop was to see Danielle.

He had not seen the love of his life in almost two years. Those years had been lonely ones for him. Sure, he had gone out with other women during his stay in Oregon, but none of them held his attention for long. He slept with a few of them, but no one could make him forget about Danielle. To his way of thinking, there wasn't a woman alive who could accomplish that feat. He and Dani were the end game. He would bet his bank account on it.

Her image was forever embedded in his mind and his heart. He could still see her twinkling gray eyes and flashing bright smile when she was happy or excited about something.

Greg could also remember her sad eyes when he told her he was leaving town. She tried to hide her feelings behind a smile, saying she was happy for him, but he could see the tears in her eyes and hear it in her voice.

He didn't realize how lucky he was to have her until he left. Greg was motivated by money and power, and he ended up leaving the only woman he ever loved for his career.

He knew now what was important to him, and that was a future with Danielle. Now he had to make her believe him, and believe in him, again. Greg wondered what her reaction would be when he appeared on her doorstep. Would she be overjoyed or would she be angry and resentful? His only other hope was for her to be alone when he got to her place. What would he do if she wasn't alone? Would he leave and come back another time or would he just walk away? No! There was no way he would walk away again. This time he was playing for keeps. He would do whatever he had to do to win her back.

He peered down at his watch, and then he closed his eyes again. His mind drifted back to the last night he and Danielle were together. They went out to their favorite Cajun restaurant for dinner and then back to her place. They sat around talking for about an hour, before things heated up and they ended up in bed.

Their last evening together was the most incredible night of his life. They made love into the wee hours of the morning and Greg slipped out of the house before she woke. He couldn't face saying goodbye to her again. It was better for him to leave without seeing her pain.

Danielle was sound asleep when the doorbell chimed. Rubbing the sleep from her eyes she looked over at her clock and swore.

Who in the world was ringing the doorbell at 1:00 A.M.? *If this is not a life-threatening emergency, it will be when I'm finished with them,* she thought to herself.

The doorbell continued to ring. She frowned. It sounded like someone was leaning against the bell.

Exasperated, she threw back the covers and bounced out of bed. Not bothering with the light, she cursed as she stubbed her toe on the end table. Her fumbling fingers found the lamp and she switched it on.

Danielle limped to the door and peered out the peephole. Her face went white and then red as she saw her unexpected visitor. She didn't know whether to throttle him or hug him.

Furious and fuming, she yanked open the door. She opened her mouth to spew out all the venomous thoughts that were on the tip of her tongue, but with eyes wide in disbelief, she was pulled into Greg's strong, capable arms and kissed soundly. She resisted only for a moment, before she melted and returned the heated kiss.

Starving for the taste of her, his tongue plunged into her mouth. He explored all the hidden treasures he had left behind. His hungry mouth plundered hers again and again.

Danielle was breathless and on fire as she eagerly returned his kiss. Her mouth met his and she hugged him to her, never wanting to let go. If this was a dream, she didn't want to wake up.

Firm hands molded her body to his and she shuddered when one hand covered her breast. Bold, warm lips slid smoldering kisses and nibbles down her throat, then traveled back up again to reclaim her parted lips. Danielle pressed her trembling body closer to his and her arms went around his neck.

When he finally lifted his head, they were both breathless and panting. She took a shaky step backward and fumbled to close and lock the door behind her.

Danielle leaned against the door for support, while taking several deep breaths to calm her frazzled nerves and to clear her head. Still gasping for air, she smoothed down her rumpled nightshirt and clasped her hands in front of her to still their trembling.

"Tell me I'm not dreaming," she whispered, as she stared up at the man in front of her. She blinked to make sure he wasn't an illusion.

"It's not a dream, sweetheart. I'm real, and I'm here." The beguiling smile on his lips caused her stomach to do a cartwheel.

God, those dimples sure started a fire inside her.

"Okay. You are very real. So, what are you doing here?" Danielle asked, running her shaking fingers through her disheveled hair.

"Why wouldn't you think I'm real? Were you dreaming about me?" His hand caressed her cheek. Danielle took a step back to break the connection. "I dream about you, too, baby. I hope it was as hot as the ones I have."

A tattletale blush stained her cheeks and she ducked her head to avoid eye contact. "More like a nightmare," she mumbled, as her eyes narrowed on him. "You didn't answer my question, Greg. Why are you standing in my living room at one o'clock on Saturday morning?"

"My plane got in late and I couldn't wait to see you." She stared blankly at him. "I came here straight from the airport."

"But, why did you come here? Why didn't you go home and call me at a decent hour? Like, ten o'clock or twelve o'clock. Or never," she sarcastically added.

He ignored her retort, and took a step forward. "Dani, there is so much I need to tell you. I missed you."

Danielle backed away, putting more distance between them. She protectively hugged her arms to her body. She had to move a safe distance away, so her traitorous body would not end up back in his arms.

"Wasn't it a bit presumptuous of you to think I'd be here alone? Or, that you would even be welcome here. What were you going to do if I had company?" she snapped. "I could have a man upstairs in my bed."

"The way you responded to me, if there is a man there, he's very lacking in the lovemaking arena. From what you're wearing, I doubt that's the case. Do you have a man in your bed?" he asked, as his eyes slid up the staircase.

"No," she reluctantly admitted, "but that's not the point. The point is, you should have phoned first. You can't just drop in here when the mood hits you. What would you have done if I had a man in my bedroom?"

"I don't know what I would have done," he admitted, meeting her angry gray eyes. "I didn't think that far ahead. I'm sorry I dropped by without calling first. If I had called, would you have answered the phone? Would you have let me come by to see you?"

She guiltily turned away without saying a word. They both knew she would have made some excuse not to see him.

She stepped away before his hand could touch her flushed cheek. "It's still there, sweetheart. All the fire, and the passion."

Danielle closed her eyes and moved farther away from Greg, breathing in deeply to calm her rapidly beating heart. It was the wrong thing to do. She knew it. But his cologne filled her nostrils and her senses. The fragrance was even more intoxicating than the man who wore it.

"Don't," Danielle pleaded, turning her back on him. He came up behind her and caught her arms. He pulled her against him and held her. Greg slowly turned her around to face him. His head lowered. Just as his mouth touched hers, Danielle extricated herself from his arms and moved away from him. "I'm not falling for this again. I refuse to go down this road again."

"There is no escaping the way we feel. I put three states between us, and it still wasn't enough. I still want you. I crave you like the air I breathe. It has always been you, Danielle. I dated other women. I even slept with a few of them, but they weren't you. I touch you and we both melt. I kiss you and we ignite. I see you and I can't stop wanting to take you in my arms. You are my one and only."

"Don't do this to me! Not again." Her eyes pleaded with him. "If you care anything about me, you will just go. We can't just pick up where we left off. I can't do it, Greg. It was too painful for both of us. What did you expect to happen tonight? Did you think you could come here like nothing ever happened and I would just fall into your arms and into bed with you? Maybe a friendly romp in the sack for old-times sake before you go traipsing off to Oregon again? It's not going to happen. I refuse to let you back into my life or my bed. I've learned my lesson the hard way."

"I don't know what I was expecting," Greg softly confessed. "All I knew was I had to see you. I didn't come here for a one-night stand. You were never that. I'm not visiting. I've joined the legal firm of Lebowitz, Jacobs, and Shapiro as a partner. I'm here to stay, Dani. I realize what I lost, and I want it back. I want you back. I will do whatever it takes to get you back in my life."

"Why, now? Has it taken you almost two years to decide, 'hey, maybe what I had wasn't so bad after all?' So now, you want me back. Should I feel honored by your revelation? I am not a boomerang. I will not keep coming back to you because you say you want me. I was doing fine without you and I will continue to do so. Why couldn't you just stay in Oregon?" she angrily asked.

"Because you are not in Oregon. I missed you, and I missed my family. Dallas is my home. This is where I grew up. They say you can't go home again. That's garbage. I belong here and we belong together." He took a step toward her and then stopped. "I know money is not the most important thing in the world. I gave up the one person in the world who meant the most to me. You. I walked away from you and it was the worst mistake of my life." He closed the distance between them.

His words touched a chord deep inside of her. She

tried to fight back the tears, but they silently coursed down her cheeks.

"Stop." She held up her hand to ward him off. "I can't do this." She wiped furiously at her wet cheeks. "I can't go through the roller coaster ride again. I made the decision to get off when you left. I am not getting back on."

"All I'm asking for is a chance. We can take it as slow or as fast as you want to. Just give me the chance. We can get it right this time." His eyes pleaded with her for forgiveness, but Danielle was not yet ready.

She turned away from him. "It's too late for us," she began. "Have you forgotten what it was like between us after the engagement? We became two entirely different people. The honesty and trust went right out the window. I can't go back to that. I want more for myself. I deserve more." She held up her hand to silence him. "No, please let me finish. I can even tell you when our relationship began to go downhill. When Michael died, you became the center of my life. I would have fallen apart any number of times had it not been for you. You were my rock, my pillar of strength. I let you take control of my life. I became dependent on you instead of standing on my own two feet. And yes, it took John's cruelty to make me see I was a puppet and you were pulling all the strings. It took a while, but I finally opened my eyes and I didn't like myself very much. The more I tried to take control of my life again, the more you resisted. You were so used to me letting you run my life and making all the decisions and plans for us, you couldn't handle me being strong and independent again. The minute I stopped letting you have your way all the time and standing up for what I wanted, you would become furious with me. Your own insecurities came between us. You couldn't take me not agreeing with you. You were not only manipulative, but chauvinistic as well."

"Have you forgotten the sex, Dani? It was wild. It was spontaneous and it was steamy."

Danielle closed her eyes to keep from meeting his penetrating stare.

Greg continued. "I will never forget that part of the relationship. I have dreams about how hot you were in bed and I wake up in a cold sweat. I wake up feeling for your warm body in bed next to me, but you're not there. I dream about that last night we were together. It was the most incredible night we ever shared."

Danielle's face flushed and she tried unsuccessfully to hide her face from him. He raised her chin so he could look into her eyes.

"We were meant for each other," Greg pleaded. "I have never felt about anyone the way I feel about you. You are in my blood and you have always been in my heart. I know I screwed up our relationship. I was a real jerk and I have no excuse for the way I treated you. My only defense is a weak one. I was insecure. What male wouldn't be? Two wealthy socialites raised you. How could I hope to compete with that? I come from a poor broken home and I was just getting on my feet when we met. I had a long way to go before I became established. You already had everything most people work all their lives for. You lived in a mansion with servants, shopped at the best stores, and were heir to a fortune. How could that not intimidate me? How could I compete with what you already had? What could I give you?"

Danielle shook her head sadly. "The only competition was in your head. All I ever wanted was a husband who loved me, and a family of my own. The rest could come later if it came at all. No amount of money can buy love or trust. You knew about the Masters before we started dating. You knew my life story. Before my mother came looking for John Masters we were dirt poor, too. My mother worked harder than any one person I know. I remember where I came from and I will never forget it. I have no intention of going back there, but I will always remember. How could you think those things were so important to me? They are just things, Greg. They don't own me. I own them. I would have lived anywhere with you. Your past and the fact that your parents were not wealthy never mattered to me. Your mother is a terrific person. She raised seven children alone after your father ran out on her. I have nothing but the utmost respect for her. You were what mattered to me. I was more concerned about you and the future than our past. I had faith in you, apparently more than you had in yourself. I knew you would be a successful attorney. I never had any doubts about your success, but even that wasn't enough for you." She paused to catch her breath. The conversation was draining her. "Okay, enough with the walk down memory lane. What's the point in rehashing the past? There's nothing we can do now to change it. Life goes on."

"Does it? What I've been doing hasn't been living. I've been, existing. I haven't moved on. I can't. Have you? Can you?" When she made no reply, he changed the subject. "I wanted you to know I'm back. I also wanted you to know how I feel. You will always be in my heart, Danielle. Always. I didn't mean to upset you."

"Funny, but I seem to recall it was one of your specialties. Today has not been a good day for me, Greg, and I'm tired." Danielle sighed, emotionally spent.

"I hate to ask, but can you put me up for the night? I'm tired too and I don't want to risk driving to Duncanville tonight."

Her suspicious eyes flew to him. His look was sincere and his eyes were drooping. He looked genuinely tired and she knew if something did happen to him, she would never forgive herself.

"This goes against my better judgment, but the

spare bedroom is down the hall, to your left. The bath-room is to the right. Goodnight. Oh, and don't even think about sleepwalking. My bedroom door will be locked."

"For your protection, or mine?" he asked, with raised eyebrows. She ignored his comment and con-tinued walking. "Danielle?" She stopped in the door-way to her bedroom, but didn't turn around. "Thank you. I'll go get my overnight bag from the rental car." He paused. "By the way, I like your T-shirt. At least I know subconsciously, you are thinking about me."

Once inside the safety of her room she looked down at the red nightshirt. In bold letters it read, "Lawyers are people too, almost." The shirt had been a gift from Greg, after she passed the bar exam. It was her fa-vorite sleep shirt. She wore it because it was comfort-able, not because it reminded her of Greg. At least that's what she kept telling herself.

She plopped down on the bed. She was too wound up to sleep. Danielle tossed and turned most of the night. It was unsettling having Greg right down the hall. He was so close, yet so far away. It was close to 4 o'clock when she finally drifted off.

Greg watched the door close behind her. Danielle was even more beautiful than he remembered. Her face was devoid of make-up and she was wearing a rumpled nightshirt, but to him, she was still the sexi-est woman alive. He felt every curve of her luscious body when she was in his arms.

He had not missed the spark in her eyes when she first saw him, and there was no mistaking her passion-ate response to his kisses. She may be furious with him for leaving her, but she was still physically at-tracted to him. This was something her traitorous body could not deny. He would use her attraction for him to his advantage.

Whistling, Greg walked out to his car. He would win her back any way he could. There was no playing fair when there was something he wanted. Danielle would be his again, and this time he would not let her go. This time she would be his wife.

Greg showered and got ready for bed. His last waking thought was of Danielle. Her not throwing him out of her house was a good sign. All he had to do was bide his time. As long as the love and the passion were still there, they could work on the rest.

He woke bright and early and cooked breakfast. Cooking for her was something the old Greg would never have done, but he had grown up a lot in the past two years.

He walked to her bedroom door and stood there. Raising his hand to knock, he changed his mind and let his hand drop. Instead, he went back to the kitchen and made a pot of coffee and waited for her.

This was also a step in the right direction. The old impatient Greg would never have waited. He would wake her and cajole her to the table because it was what he wanted. He was very time conscientious and rarely waited for anyone.

He peered down at his watch to note the time. He chided himself for his impatience. Looking for some way to pass the time, Greg went to the front door and got the newspaper.

Chapter 2

Danielle woke to the heady aroma of frying bacon and brewing coffee. She yawned and her stomach growled, reminding her of the small salad she ate for dinner last night. Her mouth watered thinking about breakfast.

It only took her a moment to remember the handsome, sexy houseguest down the hall. She could not shake the image of Greg in the kitchen cooking breakfast only wearing an apron. The fact that he was cooking at all puzzled and amazed her. The Greg she knew did not cook, do dishes, or laundry.

She shook those thoughts from her head as she forced herself out of bed. Danielle stalled facing Greg for as long as she could. She combed her hair and stared at her reflection in the mirror. She still looked the same. The only difference in her appearance was the once long curly locks were replaced by a shorter more sophisticated style. Her brown hair rested easily on her shoulders.

Dressed in a blue short set, she gathered up her courage and left the room. She found Greg sitting at the table drinking coffee and reading the Sunday newspaper.

She quietly stood in the doorway observing him. Much to her annoyance he still looked great. Two years had not changed him a bit. He short wavy hair was still intact. He could have at least had the decency to have a receding hairline. He did not even have the beer belly she wished on him.

Greg was handsome in a red polo shirt and red and black cotton walking shorts. He looked up when she entered the room and laid the newspaper aside. She noted he had been looking at the stock market section with avid interest.

"Good morning. I considered waking sleeping beauty with a kiss, but I thought better of it. I didn't want to risk getting my face slapped so early in the morning." She could not resist his warm smile. "How about some breakfast? I made all your favorites."

"Why did you fix breakfast for us and why are you still here?" she asked, eyeing him suspiciously. "I thought you'd be on your way to your mother's house by now." She made a cup of hot chocolate and sat down at the table across from him.

"Wishful thinking no doubt. Still not a morning person I see. I wanted to do something nice for you for letting me stay here. I also wanted to see you before I left. Why do you have to question everything? For once, just accept it. It's breakfast without strings." He pushed the chair back and came abruptly to his feet. "I'm sorry I imposed on your hospitality. If you want me to go, I will. I'm hungry and there is enough food for two, but I will leave if you want me to."

Danielle weighed her words carefully. "You don't have to leave yet. Please stay and have breakfast with me," she relented. "There is no way I can eat all this by myself." Her hand waved over the abundant feast he had prepared.

He sat back down, but continued to watch her closely. "So, how's the family?" he asked, sipping his coffee. "Is Jack still trying to run your life and his? It must keep him very busy, unless Karen has him on a short leash."

She shot him a murderous glare. Folding her hands on the table, she met the amusement in his eyes. He was purposely goading her and she knew it, but she refused to play along.

"Funny. My father and stepmother are both fine. He's not trying to run my life." Danielle's denial fell on deaf ears. She took a sip of hot chocolate, determined not to let Greg draw her into the old argument of theirs. "Once you were out of my life, he was content."

"Let's face it, Dani. Jack was and probably still is, the center of your world. He can do no wrong in your eyes, whereas I could do not right. You bent over backwards to please him."

"Why do you have to do that? Why are you always comparing yourself to Jack? It was never a contest. The first ten years of my life, I didn't know who my father was. When my mother died and left me with Jack and Karen, I didn't know what to think. My whole world was turned upside down. Finding out he was my father meant everything to me. You know what, why am I explaining this to you? You will never understand. You don't know what it feels like to be completely alone in the world. I can't talk about this with you, Greg. What are we?" She quickly got to her feet.

"Sometimes getting back the things we lose is not as difficult as it may seem. Oftentimes, it is worth taking a chance."

"Are we still talking about my father?" she asked, meeting his serious expression. She knew he wasn't talking about her relationship with her father.

"If that's the way you want it. Danielle, things are not always black or white. As a lawyer you know this, but on a personal level you never apply it."

The conversation was getting them nowhere, so

Greg changed the subject. He did not want to fight with Danielle about her father. He wanted to enjoy this time with her.

During the meal, they discussed old friends, relatives, and business acquaintances. Danielle caught him up on what some of their friends were doing now, at least the ones with whom she had kept in contact. They talked about everything, except their past relationship. The subject was taboo and they both knew it. They talked instead for what seemed like hours about nothing in particular.

They were still sitting at the kitchen table chatting when the doorbell rang. Danielle excused herself and left the room.

Peering out the peephole, she rolled her eyes heavenward and then stared at the closed door. Cringing, she quietly leaned against the door, hoping against hope the unwanted visitor would go away. She jumped when he knocked on the door.

Why now? Why anytime? Frowning, she braced herself for what was to come and opened the door.

"Sweetheart, I was beginning to think you weren't home. But I saw the rental car outside and knew you should be here," said Randy, pushing his way inside. He kicked the door shut with his foot. "You can run my sweet, but you can't hide. You have company in from out of town? So who's visiting us?" he asked, looking around the room.

"Yes, I do have company. It's none of your business who that company happens to be. What are you doing here? Why didn't you call first?" she asked, annoyed. "What is it with people these days? The polite thing to do is call, then wait to be invited over."

"Like that would have really happened, sweetheart. This way is much better. So now that I'm here, what are we doing today? We could take in a matinee, or better yet, we could go to the dollar movie. Then we can come back here for a long hot soak in your whirlpool and then a little horizontal hula to finish off the day?" he winked at her while suggestively, gyrating his pudgy hips.

Danielle gritted her teeth at his crudeness, but then almost laughed at how ridiculous he looked. Shaking her head, she stared at the imbecile in front of her. Randy was the type of person who would take "go to hell" as a maybe.

She moved around the coffee table to put an obstacle between them. He followed in hot pursuit, like she knew he would. One lap. Two laps. Danielle stopped in midstride and held out her hand to stop him from getting any closer.

She walked back over to the door and opened it. "Randy, you saw the car outside. I have company. Get out. Greg and I spent last night together and we are spending the day together. Just for the record, we would like to do it alone in case we want to get naked and do the horizontal hula, as you so tactfully called it. I have tried to be nice to you. I have tried to spare your feelings, but you leave me no choice. I want you out of my home. Now goodbye. Have a good day and have a nice life. Without me in it, of course. Leave!"

In the blink of an eye, Randy closed the door, but he was standing on the wrong side of it. He had Danielle pinned between his body and the door. She pushed at his massive chest, but he would not budge.

"You expect me to believe you have a man here, sweetheart? Miss Touch-Me-Not-Roberts, I don't think so. Something with batteries, I would believe. In which case, you could still be in complete control." She turned red at his comment and shoved him again without any success. "Sweetheart, I'm beginning to wonder if you would know what to do with a real man, if you had one in your bed."

"Believe me, she knows," said the deep masculine voice from behind them. Danielle's face flamed and

Randy looked over his shoulder. With his attention diverted, she ducked under his arm and moved behind Greg for protection.

This was the perfect opportunity for her to get rid of Handy Randy for good. All she had to do was play her cards right, lie a lot, and hope Greg went along with her.

The two men stared each other up and down and then looked at her expectantly. Greg was taller and in better shape, but Randy outweighed him by about twenty pounds. In a fight, there would be no contest. Greg would wipe the floor with him.

"Randy Howard, meet Greg Thomas, my fiancé," she lied, without batting an eye. Moving from behind Greg, she moved between the two men, who both stared at her like she had two heads.

"I don't believe it. This is the first I've ever heard of this guy. I thought you were seeing someone named Eric or Derek or something like that," said a disbelieving Randy, pushing his black plastic glasses up on his nose. "I've met all the competition and I'm a little disappointed in your taste in men, but I guess you can't do much better than me."

Danielle had to suppress a giggle at the expression on Randy's face. Regaining her composure, she smiled up at him. "I was dating Derek, but we broke it off. Greg came back into my life and swept me off my feet again. You see, we were engaged several years ago before Greg moved away. He's back now and last night we got back together. We are even talking marriage," she smiled, putting her arms around Greg's waist. "I guess this means I'm off the dating circuit. Don't worry. There are nine more eligible bachelorettes for you to meet. I am a one-man woman and he's the man I've chosen to spend the rest of my life with. It's better that you find this out now rather than later."

Her eyes pleaded with Greg to corroborate her story

as she leaned into him and gave him a light peck on the lips. Greg pulled her closer and covered her mouth with his in a heart-stopping, hungry kiss. Their audience was forgotten as her mouth met his. Danielle swayed into him and reveled in his every touch. Remembering the man watching them, Greg set her aside.

Randy looked on, horrified and speechless.

Greg could not resist pouring salt in the wound. "I'm not so sure yet about the rest-of-our lives bit, but a couple of months will do for me. You see, I didn't exactly propose marriage. Dani must have misunderstood me in the heat of the moment. All I wanted was to move in with her. You know how some women are. You sleep with them a couple of times and they are ready to put the noose around your neck. You probably know what I mean. A stud like you," said Greg, smiling down at Danielle's flushed face.

She turned her back to him and slyly stomped his foot. After hearing his grunt of pain, she grinned in satisfaction.

"Sure, I know what you mean. That's why Danielle and I didn't date much. I'm just not the marrying kind. I like to love 'em and leave 'em. Isn't that right, sweetheart?"

She cringed visibly every time he called her sweetheart. "How should I know? I never slept with you," she hissed, between gritted teeth. "I never even went out with you."

"Only because I knew you were the marrying kind and I didn't want you to get too attached to me. I like to play the field myself," Randy said leaving.

Danielle slammed the door and whirled around to face Greg. She wanted to knock that big silly grin off his face. "You sleep with them a couple of times and they are ready to put the noose around your neck," she mimicked, advancing on him.

"Danielle, 'sweetheart,' what happened to your

sense of humor? Actually I think it just walked out the door," Greg said bubbling over with laughter. "What happened to your taste in men? I didn't know you went for the nerdy type. Come to think of it, I didn't know you dated geeks at all. He is some piece of work. Where did you find him, the want ads or nerds 'r' us? I guess after me, no one else could compare," said Greg, blowing on his fingers and then polishing them off on his shirtsleeve.

She picked up a throw pillow off the sofa and hurled it at his smiling face. He caught it before it hit its mark and sat down on the sofa laughing.

She was stacking dishes in the dishwasher when the doorbell rang and Greg was hanging up the phone. "Can you get that?"

"Sure, 'sweetheart,'" he yelled, imitating Randy's nasal drawl. She cringed. He was not going to let it go quickly.

Danielle hurriedly dried her hands on a dishtowel and headed for the living room. There she found Liz still in Greg's arms.

"It's so good to see you Greg. Are you visiting?" Liz asked, smiling up at him. She turned when she heard Danielle. "I see we have a lot to talk about later. I just dropped by to see if you wanted to go shopping with me, but I can see you have your hands full."

"To answer all your questions, I just got back last night. I'm not visiting. I'm back to stay. I'm glad at least one person so far is happy to see me back in town," said Greg, smiling back at her and then looking over at Danielle. "Danielle was kind enough to put me up for the night."

"You were kind enough to let him spend the night?" Liz flustered, glancing at Danielle. Danielle shrugged her shoulders knowing she would explain everything to Liz later. "You are kidding, right. Well, you two are consenting adults. It's none of my business. I am happy to see you, Greg. I'm glad you're back. We'll have to get together sometime so you can meet my husband, Gabe. You two have a lot in common. Male chauvinism at its best for starters. Danielle, call me later. I want explicit details. All I can do now is dream about it anyway." She protectively rubbed her tummy.

"Believe me, it's not what you think. He slept in the guest room," Danielle said furiously and tried not to blush.

"Sure he did," Liz smiled, winking at Greg. "That would have been my first guess. Let me fantasize okay. That's all I can do right now. Well, I've got to run. Don't do anything I've done." Her eyes strayed down to her huge stomach. She breezed back out the door before they could stop her.

"Subtle isn't she," Danielle said, turning around to meet Greg's laughing eyes. "Don't even think it."

"Think what? Hey, there's always time for a horizontal hula." Danielle elbowed him in the ribs before walking away. "Liz is one in a million. Some people never change. I hope she never does. I'm glad you have someone like her in your life. True friends are priceless. I'm going to get out of here, so you can do whatever it is that you need to do today. I told Mom and Travis I'd see them in about an hour. Of course, Mom is cooking a big lunch for us. All the family is coming over. That should be interesting. I haven't seen or talked to Marie in over a year and am not looking forward to it. Leo got out of prison a couple of months ago. I don't know what to say to him. Denise and her family drove in from Arizona this morning. Paul has joined the Air Force and is home for a few weeks before he's being sent to Germany? We have a lot of catching up to do. I'll bet that by five P.M. we are fighting and I'm ready to get out of there. Will you have dinner with me tonight?"

Greg moved forward a few feet to be directly in

front of Danielle. He took another step closer and she took a deep breath.

Big mistake, she thought: The scent of his cologne was intoxicating. He reached out and caught her fidgeting hands before she could move away. Danielle felt him tremble when their hands touched.

"I'm not asking you to marry me, yet," he teased. "All I'm asking for is dinner? Nothing more. Nothing less. I can't pretend that I don't want to make love to you right here, right now, but I won't rush you into anything." He brought her hand to his lips and she shivered as his lips touched her heated skin.

"I'll be ready by seven," she whispered.

His eyebrows shot up in humor.

"For dinner," she quickly amended.

Greg winked at her and she turned beet red. "Unfortunately for me, I know what you meant. Thank you again, for letting me stay last night. The next time, and there will be a next time, will be a night to remember for both of us. That's a promise." He kissed her flushed cheek, lingering a little longer than necessary. "I'll see you at seven."

Anxiously she watched him pick up his bag and leave. Danielle sat down on the sofa at a loss. She wasn't sure how she was supposed to react now that Greg had pushed himself back into her life.

She promised herself when he moved away that their relationship was over for good. He was out of her life and she was determined to move on. The promise was easy to make with him living out of state. Out of state, out of mind. So much for promises now. Greg was back.

Danielle spent the rest of the afternoon trying to forget about Greg. She cleaned her house until it was spotless and then ran several errands.

To keep herself busy, she worked out in her weight room and then went jogging. Nothing seemed to help.

Two years had not changed him. Greg was tall with a medium build. His shoulders were broad with well-defined biceps. He was still as sexy and gorgeous as she remembered.

She berated herself for thinking about him. She did not want to see or think about Greg Thomas. There was no way she would let him back into her life.

As punishment for letting him invade her thoughts, she pushed herself to run an extra mile.

When Greg pulled the black Bonneville into the driveway, the front door flew open and his mother came out to meet him. He jumped out of the car and swung her around happily.

"Put me down," scolded Doris Thomas smiling and trying to catch her breath. She let Greg kiss her cheek and said, "Baby, I am so glad you're home."

"Me too, Mama," said Greg, hugging her again and kissing her cheek. "You are a sight for sore eyes."

"Welcome home, Bro," Travis smiled, embracing him.

He returned his younger brother's warm embrace. "It's good to be home. I missed all of you. I guess that's why I'm back. Where's that beautiful wife and baby of yours?"

"Inside," Travis said, leading the way. "I may be a little biased, but Brianna is the most beautiful baby in the world."

They sat around the kitchen table laughing and talking about old times. As usual, Marie and Leo were both running late for lunch. So, like in the old days, they started eating without them.

"Well if it isn't Mr. Perfect," said the sarcastic voice from the doorway. "Did you miss us so much, you just couldn't stay away?"

"Hello, Marie. It's good to see you too." Greg was determined to not let his younger sister get to him. For his mother's sake, he would not let her goad him into an argument on his first day home. He took a deep breath and he counted to ten. Marie continued to pick at him, but he refused to take the bait. He wasn't about to force his mother to play referee. She finally shut up and sat down at the table.

Leo showed up when everyone was finished eating, he said a cordial hello to Greg, fixed himself a plate, and left the room. Greg was overjoyed he didn't choose to dine with them.

He promised himself, he would try and keep the peace. Dining with Leo and Marie would be a challenge for which he wasn't quite sure he was ready.

When Travis told Leo to remove the cap in their mother's presence, Leo flew into a fit of rage. He told Travis he was a control freak like Greg and he didn't take orders from anyone.

Greg calmly got up from the table, snatched the cap off Leo's head, and threw it in the garbage can. Leo went for Greg and Travis had to separate them. Greg went to the den to calm down and Leo stormed out of the house vowing not to come back until Greg left.

Greg spent most of the day with his mother and Travis catching up. He unpacked some of his clothes in his old room before taking a short nap.

Greg was getting ready for his date with Danielle, when the phone rang. Ignoring it, he put on his jacket and left the room. He was on his way out the door, when he heard his mother's voice. He stopped and walked back into the house.

"Greg, it's for you. Mark's on the phone." She was smiling as she held out the phone to him. Kissing his cheek, she left the room.

"Dr. Mark Sanders, what's up?" Greg asked, smiling into the receiver. He was planning to call his best friend tomorrow. Mark was the first one he told, when he decided to move back.

"Not much," said the friendly voice. "When did you make it back? Aren't you a week early? Just couldn't stay away could you?"

"What can I say? There's no place like home. I got back last night. Are you busy tomorrow? If not, let's get together for a drink or something. I have plans tonight." He was not in the mood for a Danielle lecture from Mark.

"That must be a record even for me. You're back one day and you have a date. You are way too obvious, Thomas. Tell Danielle I said hello. I'll see you tomorrow night. I hope you get lucky tonight," Mark laughed before the phone went dead.

Staring at the receiver in his hand, Greg smiled as he replaced the phone. He couldn't get anything past his best friend. Mark knew him better than anyone.

So do I, my friend. So do I, but I don't think it's going to be that easy. Danielle and I have a long way to go before we get to that point.

Chapter 3

About 5 o'clock, Danielle took a nice, long, soothing soak in the whirlpool. She stood in front of her closet for about ten minutes trying to decide on an outfit. Her business suits were too stuffy and no nonsense, and most of her dresses were either too plain or out of season.

She decided on a black silk dress with short sleeves and what seemed like a million and one tiny buttons down the front. The waist was fitted with a wide band around it, and it stopped just below her knees. She took out black snakeskin pumps to wear with it. She laid the dress on the bed.

She was standing there in bra, slip and pantyhose when the phone rang. Sitting down on the bed, she picked it up.

"Hello," Danielle said, taking off her large black and gold earring and laying it on the bed beside her.

"Hello, yourself," said the excited voice on the other end of the line.

Dani smiled into the receiver. "Jeff, where are you? When are you coming home? I miss you, cousin."

"I miss you, too. We're in Las Vegas and we will

be home Friday night. I've got someone here who wants to say hello."

"Danielle. Hi. It's Alissa. How are you?" asked the warm friendly voice. "Long time, no talk to."

"Alissa, I'm fine. How are you? I'm so glad Jeff found you. He was driving Liz and me crazy talking about you. Just tell me you are back together."

"I can do better than that. I hope you're sitting down," she said breathlessly. "Jeff and I were married about an hour ago."

"You're kidding," she laughed. "That's wonderful news. I'm so happy for you both. He loves you so much. Welcome to the family."

"Thanks Danielle. Your blessing means a lot to both of us. I can't wait to see you again. Here's Jeff."

"Congratulations, Jeff. I'm so glad you found her. I'm glad to see you were not crazy enough to let her get away a second time. You made a wise choice."

"Are you kidding me? She is now tied to me for life. I think I made a wise decision as well." She could hear the happiness in his voice.

"Did Liz tell you about the party Saturday night for Uncle Lawrence? Aunt Vickie expects the whole family to be there."

"Unfortunately. We'll be there. I'm not so sure they will be in a partying mood when they find out about my marriage to Alissa. Forget about my alien family for minute. Tell me about you and one Mister Gregory Thomas?"

"Your sister has a big mouth. She's like a sieve. She can't hold water. You can't take her anywhere and you can't tell her anything."

"It's that twin ESP we share," he laughed. "I felt her vibes." Danielle joined in the spontaneous laughter. "Quit stalling and give me the scoop. What's going on? He spent the night. You two sure don't believe in taking things slow."

"Look who's talking about taking things slow? You haven't seen Alissa in three months and you married her."

"You can't throw me off the subject that easily," he teased. "So, was the magic still there, Danielle?"

"You tell me," she shot back. "I guess it was since you are now a married man." She got up from the bed and sprayed perfume on her wrists and between her breasts.

"Ha ha, very funny. Just don't quit your day job. You wouldn't make it as a comedienne. Okay, seriously, how did things go with you guys?"

"As well as can be expected. I couldn't believe he was standing in my living room. And to answer your other question, we are not taking things fast. Greg slept in the guest room. Nothing is going on with us, but we do have a date for tonight at seven."

"Then I hate to break it to you, but he should be ringing your doorbell in about thirty seconds."

Danielle looked down at her watch. "Then I guess I'd better get dressed. I love you guys. Take care and have a marvelous honeymoon."

"I'm not leaving the bridal suite until necessity demands it," Jeff laughed. "We will see you Saturday night. Have fun tonight. Don't do anything I'm going to."

Before she could put the phone back on its cradle, the doorbell rang. "Oh, no!" She pulled on her short purple robe and went to the door. Peering out she saw Greg and a dozen long stemmed white roses. Smiling she opened the door and waved him in. "They're beautiful. Thank you. Sorry, but I'm not quite ready."

He handed her the bouquet of flowers. "That depends on what you have in mind. You look perfect to me." She ducked her head as heat rushed to her face. "I'll find something to put those in while you finish dressing or undressing, whichever you prefer. It's your choice."

She handed him the roses making sure not to touch him. He was breathtaking in black Dockers, black and dark blue striped shirt, and casual black leather shoes. The top two buttons of his shirt were open to reveal a thin gold chain around his neck. Coarse black hairs on his chest peeped through the lower button.

Danielle pulled her eyes away from him and made a dash for her bedroom. "There's a vase under the kitchen sink." She felt his eyes on her retreating back as she left the room.

Ten minutes later she felt back in control of her emotions. The clothes made her feel less vulnerable and the buttons made her feel safe.

She found Greg sifting through her album and CD collection. She studied him. He was still easily the most attractive man she had ever seen.

He turned and caught her staring at him. His eyes rose in question, but he apparently thought better of mentioning it and let it pass.

"I can't believe you still have all these," he said pointing out several disco albums as well as 45 records.

"Hey, disco is making a big comeback. I love the golden oldies, the disco era, and the Motown sound, which is my favorite if you recall."

"I recall. I remember the talent show at Hope House when you did your own rendition of the Motown sound. In fact I don't think anyone will ever forget it. You won the first place trophy. I still have the video. You were pretty incredible, not to mention, sexy and alluring."

"We won the first place trophy. You were pretty good yourself, Thomas. Those skin-tight pants and that afro wig looked pretty cute on you."

"We had some good times, didn't we?" He caught

her hand and gave it a squeeze. "And some not so great times."

"Yes, we did. Oh! I almost forgot. I had a good excuse for not being ready when you got here. Jeff and Alissa flew to Las Vegas and were married a couple of hours ago."

"That's great news. I can't believe they waited this long. Have they been together all this time?"

"Not exactly, but to make a long story short, Alissa left shortly after you did. She received a full scholarship to a fashion merchandising school in New York. So she left. They continued to date for about a year and then slowly drifted apart because both were too stubborn to move. About three weeks ago Jeff went to New York looking for her and the rest you know. They are due back in Dallas on Friday."

"I'll have to give him a call when he gets back. We all had some fun times. I'd love to see him again."

"How about coming with me to a party at the club in three weeks? It's Uncle Lawrence's birthday and they are having a big bash to celebrate. It should be a lot of fun."

"Is the whole clan going to be there?" he asked tentatively. She knew he was referring not only to Jack, but also Danielle's cousin, John.

"Yes and no," she hedged. "Dad and Aunt Karen are still in England visiting her parents, but John will be there. I'm sure seeing you will be as much a thrill for him as it will be for you."

"You realize putting John and me in the same room will cause World War III. If he comes at me, he will lose. I won't start a fight with him, but I won't walk away from one either."

"I can accept that. I'd like to take things slow. I don't want to rush into anything."

His eyes moved over her in a soft caress. Greg could

not resist the urge to touch her. He caught Danielle's hand and tugged her forward.

"And I appreciate your honesty. It's a date for Saturday night." He smiled at her. "It is a date right," he teased. "We'd better get going. We have reservations at Reunion Tower for 8 o'clock."

Dinner was delicious. Danielle had stuffed flounder, wild rice and new potatoes. Greg ordered the seafood linguini. He selected a bottle of white wine to accompany their dinner. The table for two was bathed in candlelight. Their view of the Dallas skyline was spectacular.

Greg talked about his family get-together being as awkward as he knew it would be. Marie was still the same spiteful witch. Leo wasn't exactly a reformed criminal—only a hardened one. Denise's two children were noisy little outlaws who were driving everyone crazy. The only normal people were his mother and his brothers, Travis and Paul.

They were almost finished with their meal when Danielle spotted Drew and a female companion coming their way.

"Hello, Danielle," Drew said smiling down at her.

She returned his warm smile warily as she looked from him to Greg. "Hi Drew. It's nice to see you again. Small world. Oh, I'm sorry. Drew Murray, Greg Thomas."

The two men sized each other up, shook hands, and exchanged hellos. They both looked back at Danielle.

"This lovely lady is my cousin, Regina," explained Drew. "She flew in from Houston this morning to surprise me for my birthday."

"Hi, Regina. It's nice to meet you." Danielle held out her hand to the other woman. "Happy birthday, Drew."

"Thank you. We'll let you two get back to dinner. I'll call you later in the week about Friday night."

Danielle flushed under Greg's straightforward stare. At least he had the decency to wait until they were out of earshot.

"What's Friday night?" he asked, casually taking a bite of his baked potato. "This is delicious. You should try it."

"Drew and I have a date on Friday." He instantly became quiet and withdrawn. "You see. This is why I didn't mention it. You have no right to get angry with me. I don't owe you an explanation. I don't owe you anything. I am not going to drop all my plans because you popped back into town."

He slowly picked up his fork and speared a piece of linguini and popped it into his mouth. She watched him chew angrily.

"I didn't ask you to," said Greg harder than he meant too. "Your food is getting cold."

She sat back and watched him devour his food.

Greg paused, looked up, then added, "Is there a problem? You're not eating."

"You are the problem. You bounce back into my life and we are suddenly back together again. One date does not a relationship make. Is this how it's going to be? Do I need to check with you before I make any plans of my own?" Danielle asked coming to her feet.

"I guess this date is over." He put down his fork again and looked up at her. "It must have been something I said," he mumbled, dropping money on the table and getting to his feet.

She sat fuming, while Greg paid the tab and in silence they took the elevator down to the parking garage. They had reached an impasse much sooner than either of them anticipated. They broke their own record. Before it had at least taken them two dates to get where they were now. The drive home was long and quiet.

The minute the gray Volvo stopped in the driveway,

she jumped out of the car, slammed the door, and went inside. She locked the front door behind her and leaned against it.

Greg sat there a few minutes before following her. When he tried the door, he was not surprised to find it locked. He knocked softly on the door. "Dani, please open the door. I'm sorry. I was wrong."

She hesitantly opened the door, but did not allow him to enter.

"I didn't mean for this evening to turn out like this," Greg apologized. "May I please come in?"

Stepping back, Danielle waved him inside. "I'm not going to argue with you. You have no rights where I'm concerned. I can date anyone I choose." She walked to the sofa and sat down. "Why are we bothering?" She ran her fingers through her hair in frustration. "Haven't we learned anything from the past?"

"I'm hoping we've learned a lot. I was jealous. I admit it. I kept picturing you in that guy's arms, in his bed, and it drove me crazy. I can't bear to think of you with another man. I know there have been other men while I was away, but I can't bare to think about you with any of them."

She didn't bother correcting him. Greg had been her first lover and there was only one guy after him. She didn't dare tell him that. The first lover part he knew about, but as passionate as she was with him, would he believe she hadn't been with anyone else?

Danielle had only recently began to date again. But so far, there was no one special in her life. There was no man she wanted to make love to, no one other than the man sitting next to her.

Maybe she wanted him so much because she had been abstinent for so long and he was familiar. No, that couldn't be it either. She craved his touch. She couldn't tell him that, either.

"I met Drew last night at a dinner party," she admitted, turning to face him. "We haven't even gone out yet."

Greg sighed in relief and pulled an unresisting Danielle into his arms and held her close to his heart. She relished his nearness and lay back in his comforting arms. Warm lips nuzzled her temple and strong fingers raised her chin. Their eyes met before his mouth tenderly covered hers in a heart-stopping kiss. She wound her arms around his neck and returned the heady kiss. Her lips parted and her tongue met his in an erotic dance.

Slowly Danielle leaned backward until Greg's body was covering hers. Large, sure hands caressed her tingling body from head to toe.

Danielle was so caught up in the moment that she did not notice the top of her dress was unbuttoned to the waist until the cold air hit her bare flesh.

The dress was pushed from her shoulders and Greg's warm lips pressed hot kisses to her throat before leaving a fiery trail down her neck. When his mouth covered her breast through the thin lace red bra, she moaned in pleasure and held his head there.

With shaky hands, she unbuttoned his shirt and pulled the ends from his pants. Trembling fingers raked through the coarse dark hair on his chest and she pushed the shirt from his shoulders.

His body trembled against hers when she caught his nipple between her teeth. Her bra, panties, followed his shirt to the floor.

Danielle shuddered with need when his hands slid under her dress to her bare thighs. She held her breath as his hand traveled upward. She gasped and surged against him when he slid one finger inside of her. The wetness was instantaneous and Danielle convulsed against him.

He nibbled at her breast, until they were hard pebbles. His mouth devoured one breast before moving on to perform the same rite to the other one. He licked and sucked until she closed her eyes and bit her lip to keep from crying out from sheer ecstasy.

Expertly, he played her like a master pianist plays a piano. He knew exactly which chords to strike to make the most beautiful music. Her body moved in unison with his magical fingers and she softly cried out as her release came, again.

She opened her eyes to see Greg smiling down at her. His lips brushed hers and she watched in a daze as he brought his wet fingers to his lips and tasted the essence of her eruption.

She was even more shocked when he levered himself off her and moved down her body and settled himself between her still quivering thighs. Danielle lunged forward with the first initial touch of his mouth replacing his fingers.

She almost forgot to breathe and more than likely would have vaulted off the couch had he not been holding her legs down. Her mind silently screamed for him to stop, but her body was begging for more.

Danielle thought she would die from the pure bliss his skillful mouth was causing. Her toes curled into the sofa cushion and her trembling hands grasped his hair.

What he was doing to her was torture and magical at the same time. This time, she did scream when her body convulsed as she reached yet another pinnacle of pleasure. Panting and exhausted, she collapsed on the sofa. She watched him raise himself off her.

Danielle stared at him in longing and didn't know what to think when he picked up his discarded shirt and buttoned it. Disappointment showed on her face and desperation showed in her pleading gray eyes.

Her body was on fire and burning for him to take her. She was past all rational thoughts of saying no. Her body and mind were screaming out for him to continue.

"Stay with me." She held out her arms to him and

he pulled her close. "I need you, Greg. Make love to me. Don't leave me like this. I want you to make love to me," she pleaded with eyes glazed with passion.

"I think we should slow things down a bit. I don't want there to be any regrets. I know I'm the first to introduce you to a different kind of lovemaking. I'm glad I was the first. Call it a gift from me to you," Greg said kissing her stunned lips. "I rushed you and I'm sorry. I shouldn't have taken unfair advantage of you like that. I think we should slow things down a bit. We have all the time in the world."

Her mind and body screamed, please take advantage of me! I need you so much right now. Make love to me.

"What about you?" Danielle asked, coming unsteadily to her feet and looking down at his protruding zipper, proof that he wanted to make love to her.

"A cold shower can do wonders for the male anatomy." He silenced her with a kiss. "I'll call you. Sleep well, princess."

She regrettably watched him leave. Danielle still could not believe what she let happen. Locking the door behind him, she leaned against it smiling.

Greg leaned against the closed door, trying to get his body and mind under control. He took several deep breaths. His body was on fire. It took every ounce of willpower to walk out the door. He had Danielle exactly where he wanted her, and he walked away.

It's more than sex, Dani. I love you. I will use whatever trick necessary to make you see that. We belong together. One cold shower coming up.

He drove straight home and headed for his bathroom. He took a long, cold shower and he got ready for bed. Lying awake that night, his thoughts were on Danielle. He remembered every inch of her responsive body. She had responded to his every kiss and caress. She had been his for the taking. Damn!

One day Danielle, we will be together. That is a promise. I'm not looking for just a lover. I want a wife. I want you.

Chapter 4

Sunday was a quiet and peaceful day for Danielle. After church, she ate lunch with Liz and Gabe. Lunch turned into an interrogation about her date with Greg. Her cousin wanted all the juicy details.

The following week was hectic. With her father on vacation, Danielle ended up taking half his workload. She was buried under contracts and negotiations from dawn to dusk. Her workday consisted of working lunches and dinners while going over contract disputes.

Victoria called to inform that her uncle's birthday party was to be a formal affair and a surprise to Lawrence. The festivities were to begin at 8 o'clock. She was to bring a gag gift only to the Lawrence Masters roast.

By Tuesday she had digested almost a pack of Rolaids. She briefly talked to Greg, and Drew phoned to confirm their date for Friday night, which she hadn't had time to even think about.

Danielle got his telephone number in case something came up. The way things were going right now, it was a very real possibility.

Her week went from bad to worse when she inherited the client from Hell from Jack. The client's name was Bobby Mike Durant. Mr. Durant was not pleased Jack had sent him a woman lawyer and even less pleased that she was black. He was so insulting the first day that she walked out on him.

Frank Lockhart phoned him and took him out to dinner to smooth things over. He let Durant know Danielle was one of the best and smartest lawyers in the firm. He somehow talked Durant into calling her.

He apologized to her and rescheduled their appointment. They spent a strained couple of days revising and changing his latest contract to open a new store in the Irving area.

When they finally agreed on the changes to the contract, she was relieved to see the last of him. Danielle thanked God Jack would be back in time for the final negotiating.

She had met a lot of people who thought like Bobby Durant during her years working for Masters, Lockhart, and Rivera. Danielle had developed a thick skin.

It was around 7:00 A.M. when Greg took the elevator up to the twenty-seventh floor. He felt a warm feeling of pride and joy at having his name on the front door. For him this always seemed like a distant dream. Now he knew dreams really came true. If this one did, then there was hope for him and Danielle.

He unlocked the door and went inside to the offices of Lebowitz, Jacobs, Shapiro, and Thomas. He closed the door behind him, locked it, and went to his office. He smiled at the gold letters on the door that read, "Greg Thomas."

Setting his briefcase on the large oak desk, he walked over to the window and looked outside. The downtown Dallas view was one to behold.

It was good to be home. Watching a homeless man

go through a trash bin, he said a silent prayer for his success. He hated to see anyone living like that.

Before he left town, he had made it a practice not to give them money, but to buy a homeless person breakfast or lunch at least twice a week. It was only a small act of kindness, but it made him feel good to be giving something back.

He left his office and went into the break room. He made a pot of coffee, poured a cup, and went back to his office.

He picked up one of the case files on his desk and read over it. It was a divorce case. Sandra Blake was suing her husband for divorce and complete custody of their two children. He read over the list of assets and whistled in appreciation. Richard Blake was worth more than $20 million. Sandra wanted half of everything, plus $20,000 in monthly child support. She filed for divorce after catching her husband in bed with a male employee at his computer company.

This was a pretty cut and dried case. Greg was sure Mr. Blake would give her anything she wanted to keep from being exposed in public.

Greg picked up the next file. He was reading over it, when a brief knock sounded on the door. He came to his feet and walked over to answer the door.

"Good morning," Jacob Lebowitz said, extending his hand. "Welcome aboard, Greg. Have you read over the files I left for you?"

"Not all of them. The Blake case seems pretty cut and dried. The Hanson case could go either way."

"That's the same conclusion I came to. Well, don't make plans for lunch today. All the partners are taking you to lunch. For the first week, I want you to assist Ben Shapiro just to get an idea of how we do things. After that, you are on your own. We are having a staff meeting in my office in an hour so you can meet everyone. I'll see you then."

An hour later, Greg was introduced to all the staff. His assistant was Tara Martin, a lovely dark-haired, paralegal. She was about twenty and fresh out of college. Her face reflected eagerness to learn and she seemed to exude energy.

Greg knew instantly they would work well together. She was the perfect assistant for him because he was always on overdrive.

He picked up the phone and he ordered a bouquet of flowers for Danielle. He reached for the next file and leaned back in the black, overstuffed, leather chair.

By Tuesday, Danielle was running on pure adrenaline. She was eating take-out Chinese food when her paralegal/assistant, Valerie, gave a brief knock and entered the room carrying a beautiful floral arrangement. Smiling, she put the flowers on Danielle's desk.

"Read the card," said Valerie excitedly clapping her hands. "They are gorgeous. Who sent them?"

Danielle was smiling as she opened the card. It read, *You are always in my thoughts.* Smiling she replaced the card and sniffed the flowers.

"Well?" asked her anxious assistant eyeing her suspiciously. "Spill it. Who sent the flowers? Don't make me take the card."

"His name is Greg Thomas. He's an old friend who recently moved back to Dallas. Is there anything else you want to know?"

"Is there anything else you want to tell me? From the dreamy look in your eyes, I'd say he's more than a friend. I'm off to lunch. I'll see you in about an hour. I'm having lunch with my hubby today. Miracles never cease."

Danielle leaned back in her chair smiling. Thinking

of Greg lately seemed to always bring the same silly grin to her face. Picking up the phone, she dialed his number.

"Lebowitz, Jacobs, Shapiro, and Thomas, how may I direct your call?" asked the crisp no nonsense voice of the receptionist.

"Greg Thomas, please." She leaned back in her black leather chair and spun around to look outside the window.

"Greg Thomas's office. This is Lisa, how may I help you?" said the soft friendly voice. "I'm sorry. Can you hold one moment?" She was put on hold. "Sorry about that."

"Greg Thomas, please. Tell him it's Danielle Roberts calling." She spun around in her chair and picked up the blue felt tip pen on her desk.

"One moment please, Ms. Roberts. He's on a call, but he asked if you would hold a moment."

She opened up the Solitaire game on her computer and played while she waited. Laying the phone down, she hit the speak button and forgot about the call as she played.

"Hello, beautiful," drawled the sexy voice. "Where have you been all my life and what took you so long to find me?"

"Hello yourself. I've been in plain sight. You were too distracted to notice me. Thank you for the flowers. They are breathtaking." Danielle smiled, while toying with the telephone cord.

"You're more than welcome. Beautiful flowers for an even more beautiful lady. Are you still swamped?"

"That's an understatement, but I do have a breather for the rest of the afternoon. My last appointment for the day was canceled. Why, do you have something up your sleeve?"

"I wish I had the time, but I have a luncheon to attend, and from there I'm in court the rest of the afternoon. I'm taking you to lunch on Thursday, so mark your calendar. Will you be home later? I can give you a call."

"Yes, I'll be home." She tried to hide the disappointment in her voice. "I think I'll skip out a little early. I'll talk to you later."

"Count on it, beautiful." Greg's intercom buzzed. "A lawyer's work is never done. I'll call you later."

Danielle's next case was a bit different. Her client was Marty Uribe. He was a famous gay clothes designer. He had her draw up a partnership/ prenuptial agreement for him and his lover, who was also a designer. They were opening a new chain of boutiques in the Oak Lawn area.

At about 3 o'clock, she went by her parents' house to check on things and go for a swim before going home. When she arrived home, there were four messages waiting for her.

Beep. "Danielle, it's Valerie, please call me as soon as you get this message." Beep. "Danielle, it's Frank. Tom had a car wreck and I need you to meet with his client on Friday. Call me when you get this message." Beep. "It's Valerie again. Tom's client is only in town for the weekend. He's headlining at a local comedy club on Saturday and Sunday night. So Friday was the only time he had available to meet. Frank wants you to meet with him since he is going out of town on business tomorrow morning." Beep. "It's Frank. I left the folder with all the information in it with Valerie."

Well so much for a personal life for the next few weeks. She dialed Drew's number and was greeted by the answering machine.

"Drew, hi. It's Danielle. I'm not going to be able to make it Friday night after all. I have to meet with a client. I'd love a raincheck. Give me a call."

She then dialed her office and had Valerie give her the client's name and phone number. The client was none other than the chauvinistic, crude, rude comedian

Jerry Weaver. His act, if one could call it an act, consisted mostly of women bashing and off-color jokes.

Silently Danielle wondered what she had done in another lifetime that was so horrible. Being saddled with Jerry Weaver was more punishment than anyone deserved.

She left four messages for the bag of hot air before finally giving up. She left the office to meet Greg for lunch.

Danielle was at Pappadeaux's when Greg arrived. She was wearing a navy blue pantsuit and low-heeled pumps. Greg wore a charcoal gray business suit and tie. He looked every inch the professional.

"Hi," he smiled, hugging her and kissing her cheek. "Where have you been all my life beautiful lady?"

"Waiting for you to grow up and get over the 'me me' stage in your life," she retorted returning his smile.

"I guess it was a pretty long wait." He laughed, brushing a strand of hair from her face. The brief contact left them both wanting more. "It's nice to know you waited."

"Right this way," said the hostess, leading them to a table. Greg pulled out the chair for her and took his own seat. "Your waiter will be right with you."

"So, how's your day going?" he asked, opening his menu.

"So far so good. How about you? Working on any interesting cases?" She scanned the menu quickly. She already knew what she wanted. Her favorite was fried crawfish and a loaded baked potato.

"I do have one, and that's a bit over the top. There is no such thing as an open and shut case. There is always room for doubt." He waved the discussion away. "Do you have plans for later? I could show you my briefs." They both smiled at his play on words.

"I've seen your briefs. Don't quit your day job counselor. Unfortunately, I'm with a client tonight. It was the only time he could meet with me. I'm not looking forward to it."

"What about Saturday night?" He took a drink of his soda. "I'm free as a bird all weekend. We could get together and reminisce about old times."

"Sorry, no reminiscing for me, I have a date," she confessed, waiting for the other shoe to drop at her disclosure.

"Let me see if I can guess who the lucky man is. It can't be Randy. We ditched him. It must be Drew," he sarcastically replied.

"Yes. It is Drew. Greg, we share a past. I'm not ready to give a relationship with you another try. It came close to destroying both of us the last time. I think we should take things slowly and see where that leads us."

"We can't very well do that dating other people. I know who and what I want. I guess you're not convinced yet."

"That's a first," she snapped, glaring at him. "When you left, you didn't know what you wanted."

"Neither did you," he shot back. Greg took a deep breath. "Can we not get into this right now? I was looking forward to having a nice lunch with you, not a debate."

They ordered and ate, making idle meaningless conversation. They both knew they had to keep their conversation on neutral ground or it could turn ugly very quickly.

After lunch, he walked her to her car and they went their separate ways. Greg wanted to kiss her, but he decided not to. He was still fuming about her date with Drew.

Greg called her that evening and apologized for his behavior. They talked for about an hour before she had to hang up.

* * *

Danielle was in the office bright and early Friday morning to go over the Weaver file. It was a simple ten-page contract, written with a lot of little loopholes that an inexperienced lawyer could have accidentally overlooked. She jotted down several notes on her legal pad and inserted all of it into her leather portfolio.

When she returned from lunch, there were three messages from Mr. Weaver. He was arriving at DFW airport at 6 o'clock and he wanted her to pick him up. The second message said to book him a room at the most expensive hotel in the city, and the third one said to have a young beautiful female masseuse waiting at the hotel.

Danielle bristled at first. Then she smiled. Danielle wished she could see his face when Pierre, the masseuse arrived and ordered him to strip for his massage.

Danielle did however make reservations for dinner at 8 o'clock at a nice elegant restaurant in North Dallas. She arrived at his hotel room at 7 o'clock and was greeted by a smiling half-dressed Jerry Weaver. He waved her inside.

"You must be Ms. Roberts. I'm Jerry Weaver, in the flesh," he quipped. He held out his hand and she hesitantly took it. "I don't bite Ms. Roberts. May I call you Danielle? Please have a seat. Would you like something to drink?"

"No, thank you." She sat on the couch crossing her legs in front of her. " I hate to rush you, but our dinner reservations are for 8 o'clock."

He gave her the once over from her red business suit down her shapely legs to her matching red pumps. Whistling in appreciation, he left the room smiling.

Danielle came quickly to her feet. She did not have a good feeling about this. Jerry Weaver was a creep and she was sure the evening would go downhill from here.

A few minutes later, he emerged wearing surprisingly enough, a two-piece black suit. He was not exactly what she expected with his boyish good looks. He was short and stocky. His sun-bleached blonde hair reached his shoulders and blue twinkling eyes lit up his round face. His only jewelry consisted of the gold wristwatch.

Danielle had almost decided his stage demeanor must be an act. They chatted pleasantly during a fabulous lobster dinner, which she paid for with a company credit card.

After dinner, they went over the contract. He was very impressed by all the loopholes she found. On the drive back to his hotel, the real Jerry Weaver began to emerge.

"So tell me Ms. Roberts, who did you sleep with to get a cushy job like yours?" Danielle was so shocked that she momentarily took her eyes off the expressway. "Lady, are you trying to kill us?"

Regaining her composure, she slammed on her brakes to avoid hitting the red Mercedes in front of them. She glared over at the man seated next to her. Her eyes shot venom at him.

"What did you say?" she asked, angrily gripping the steering wheel and counting to ten. Relaxing her grip, she let out the breath she was holding.

"Which partner did you have to sleep with to get your job? That's usually how it's done isn't it? A gorgeous, intelligent, black female lawyer in a male-dominated profession? You work for one of the top law firms in the state. What man in his right mind would turn down a little brown sugar on the side?"

Danielle was livid. It took all her self-control and willpower not to reach over and slap the smug look off his face.

He put his hand on her shoulder and squeezed gently. Since she didn't object, he moved his hand downward.

"Mr. Weaver take your hand off me or I swear I will

stop this car in the middle of Central Expressway and put you out."

His hand slid lower and Danielle slammed on the brakes. The traffic behind her came to a screeching halt and the car behind her almost crashed into them.

"Are you nuts?" he yelled at her. "You could have killed us. I am reporting this to your superiors. You can't tease a man and then say no!"

"Tease you!" she shouted back. "Where did you get the idiotic idea that I was trying to tempt or tease you? Your ego has no bounds. I am not interested in sleeping with you. I not only find you revolting, but you are rude and disgusting as well. I would rather bed down with a pack of dogs than sleep with you. At least with them I would only get fleas. If you touch me again, you will be showing up for tomorrow night's show with a black eye. I am not a fringe benefit. Do you get my drift?"

She took her foot off the brake and set the car in motion. Her face was flushed with anger and she had never been more insulted in her life.

Danielle was still furious when she dropped him off at the hotel and drove home. After taking two aspirin, she went to bed. Surely, things couldn't get any worse.

Danielle was reading over a contract when Valerie buzzed her over the phone. Drew was on hold. He called to confirm their date. They talked a while longer before Danielle had to answer another call.

Maybe this was the new beginning she was seeking. Just maybe, Drew could fill the empty void in her life left there by Greg. She tried not to think about him anymore. This of course, was easier said than done, especially, when he kept turning up at the same places she frequented.

Whenever she saw him with another woman, a little

piece of her died inside. Their eyes would meet and she would turn away. It was getting harder and harder to deny her feelings.

Drew was at her doorstep promptly at 7 o'clock. They finally agreed on Creole food. Danielle suggested Creole Cuisine, her favorite seafood restaurant. The atmosphere was friendly and they played New Orleans style music and some soft jazz.

Chapter 5

Greg was sitting at home feeling sorry for himself when the telephone rang. He picked it up and stared at the caller ID several seconds. Hitting the talk button, he put the phone to his ear.

"Hello," said the disinterested voice. He rose from the chair and walked over to the window. Peering outside, he watched the cars passing by.

"Greg, hi," said the excited friendly voice. "It's Debra. I heard a rumor you had moved back. If it's true, why haven't you called me?"

Greg rolled his eyes heavenward. He was not in the mood to deal with another ex-girlfriend right now.

"Hi, Debra. Yes, it is true. I moved back a couple of weeks ago. I've been busy settling in. What's up?" he asked cordially.

"I'd really love to get together. I haven't seen you in, what two years? I know this is short notice, but are you free for dinner tonight?"

"As a matter of fact, I am," Greg said, smiling secretively. "Give me your address." He jotted down the address and the directions. "I'll pick you up in forty-five minutes. Dress semi-casual. I have the perfect restaurant in mind."

Greg hung up the phone and picked up his keys and left the house. While driving the short distance to Debra's apartment, his thoughts were on another woman. He was hoping Danielle and Drew were going to the same restaurant he was taking Debra to.

Steeling himself for her reaction, he rang the doorbell at her apartment. The door opened quickly and Debra launched herself into his arms. Greg caught her, and, after a brief hug on his part, he set her away from him much to her chagrin.

"It's so good to see you." She beamed, looking him up and down. "You're still as handsome as ever. Are you as naughty as ever?"

"It's good to see you too Debra." He laughed, not bothering to answer her question. She was as straightforward as he remembered. There was nothing meek or mild about her. "You look great as always."

He eyed her short red low-cut mini-dress in appreciation. It hugged every curve of her very fit body. Debra was always very self-conscious about her appearance. Everything she wore was short, tight, and seductive. She craved attention and dressed to obtain it. Her once-long hair was now short and chic. Her skin was a deep brown and her eyes were the color of midnight. Long thick lashes flirted at him.

"You like?" she asked, slowly turning around to give him the full effect of the outfit. "I wore it just for you."

Greg's eyes couldn't help but admire her. If he thought the front was low cut, the back deep v-cut stopped just above her hips. There was no way she could be wearing underwear.

"It's definitely you Debra." He smiled. Not leaving anything to the imagination is definitely you, he refrained from saying. "Shall we go?"

They sat in the bar chatting while they waited for a table. Debra caught him up on everything and everyone they knew. She seemed to know everybody's business.

His eyes strayed to the door from time to time to see if Danielle and her date were coming. A slow secretive smile spread across his lips when he saw them walk in.

He was only half listening as Debra prattled on and on about everything and nothing. He couldn't seem to take his eyes off Danielle and Drew.

"Thank you for bringing me here. This is one of my favorite restaurants," smiled Danielle, touching Drew's arm.

"I'm glad you approve. The line isn't too long, so maybe we won't have a long wait. I hope that's not the case. I'm starved. I made reservations this time."

"Drew, party of two," said the hostess. They stepped up. "This way please." Putting his arm on Danielle's waist, he guided her in front of him.

Danielle and Drew were being led to their table, when she spotted Greg with Debra Nelson sitting at the end of the bar. He was engrossed in something his date was saying and didn't see her.

She felt something painful squeezing at her heart as she watched the ex-lovers. Her footstep faltered. Danielle tore her eyes away from the laughing couple and followed the waiter to the table.

"Are you all right?" asked an observant Drew following her line of vision. "Isn't that your friend?"

"Greg's not my friend, but yes, that's him and the wicked witch of Oak Cliff," Danielle said, opening her menu with an angry snap.

She didn't want to think about Greg and Debra. Debra Nelson was Greg's high school sweetheart. They had been dating pretty hot and heavy when he and Dani first became study partners in law school. Debra became enraged when Greg broke up with her and started dating Danielle.

"So, what do you recommend as an appetizer?" asked Drew changing the subject. "Let's try two items?"

"Definitely the fried alligator. It's wonderful. The crawfish is awesome as well." Her mouth began to water just thinking about it.

The fried alligator was cut into bite size pieces, battered, and deep-fried. A spicy red sauce accompanied it for dipping.

The waiter took their order and she looked up to see the hostess leading Greg and Debra toward them. She turned pale as they stopped at the table next to hers.

Surely this was a bad joke. *They are not about to sit across from me. Surely this town isn't this small! Why me?*

It was bad enough seeing him from afar with another woman, but to have them seated across from her was more than she could tolerate. As if that wasn't bad enough, Debra turned to face her and smiled a triumphant smile.

"Hello, Danielle. I haven't seen you since you stole my boyfriend," she smiled, linking her arm through Greg's.

"Hello, Debra," she responded politely. "Looks to me like you have him back now. Congratulations. Debra Nelson, meet Drew Murray. Drew, you've already met Greg."

They all exchanged hellos, while Danielle tried to avoid any eye contact with Greg. An uncomfortable silence fell before Greg ushered Debra away from the table.

When he pulled the chair out for Debra, Danielle's eyes met his. He winked at her as he took the seat directly across from hers.

Danielle averted her gaze. *I can't believe this is happening. Surely this is not a coincidence. Maybe he made a copy of my planner or something. Just maybe it's wishful thinking on my part.*

Throughout the evening, each time she looked up,

Greg was staring at her with hunger in his dark eyes. First, she spilled her water. Then she almost spilled her drink. Excusing herself from the table, she went to the ladies room to collect herself.

She was reapplying her lipstick, when Debra sauntered in and sat her purse down on the counter next to Dani's.

Danielle ignored her, hoping against hope she would just disappear like the bad dream she was. No chance of that happening in the continuing saga of Dani's life.

"Danielle and Drew—how sweet. It's like seeing the black version of Ken and Barbie." Debra laughed. "I have to give you props. You have great taste in men. Although, what they see in you, I'll never know. I lost Greg once to you. It won't happen again. I'll do whatever is necessary to make sure I keep him this time."

"He's all yours. I have no designs on him. You are more than welcome to Greg. That is, if he wants you."

"I saw the way you looked at him. You still love him, but I have news for you, girlfriend. This time I'll win."

Danielle put her lipstick in her purse and turned to face her nemesis. Crossing her arms over her chest, she smiled sweetly.

"Didn't you already try that once, with a fake pregnancy. It didn't work then and whatever game you try to play won't work now. Greg is too smart to let someone like you trap him. I didn't walk back into his life. He walked into mine. He didn't want you six years ago, Debra, and I seriously doubt he wants you now. Lonely men resort to desperate measures and I'd say you are about as desperate as he can get. If you do manage to get him into bed tonight, remember he will be pretending it's me. You see Deb, my house was the first stop he made when he came back to town. You are now and always will be an afterthought. Greg is only using you to make me jealous, and guess what? It's not working. I know he has no interest in you. Why do you think he brought you to my favorite restaurant? Do you think it was pure coincidence that I was here with a date? You're a lot of things, but naïve isn't one of them. Why would he want the woman who slept with his best friend while engaged to him? Have a nice evening." Danielle left the seething Debra glaring at her back.

"Witch!" Debra yelled as the door closed behind Danielle. She heard something hit the door as she walked away.

Drew stood when she came back to the table. Danielle sat down and picked up her menu. Concentrating on it was a lost cause with Greg watching her every move.

"If you want to go some place else we can," said Drew breaking the uncomfortable silence. "This can't be easy for you."

"No, it's not, but I'm a big girl. With Greg back in town, we are bound to run into each other from time to time. I will learn to deal with it."

"I saw sexy Debra follow you to the ladies room. Did I miss flying fur or did you manage to keep your cool?" he smiled as he inspected her. "No scratch marks. I'd say you handled the situation pretty well."

"She tried to goad me, but I gave her a piece of my mind and walked away." Danielle closed her menu. "Let's forget about Greg and Debra and enjoy our meal. I'm ready to order if you are."

The tension was so great Danielle and Drew barely spoke ten words to each other over the rest of the meal. She barely tasted the delicious food. She was so tense and wound up, relaxing was next to impossible.

They were halfway through dinner when Drew's beeper went off. He went to return the call, while

Danielle had the waiter box up the remainder of their food.

"Sorry to end our evening, but I need to take you home and get to a client site. They are experiencing some major problems."

They talked all the way home. Drew kissed her cheek, promised to call her again and was gone. Danielle stood by the door watching the car drive away.

She hoped Greg's evening ended as abruptly as hers did. The thought of him with Debra went all over her.

"Thank you for dinner," said Debra trying to pull Greg inside her apartment. "Would you like to come in for dessert?" Her hand moved up and down the buttons on his shirt.

"As inviting as that sounds, I think I'm going to pass this time. I'm glad you called. It was good seeing you again."

He lowered his head to kiss her cheek and she turned her head. Her mouth met his. Greg tried to pull away as her arms went around his neck and she planted a hungry inviting kiss on him. He extracted her arms from around his neck and gently pushed her away.

"Have a seat," she said unwilling to let him call an end to the evening. She had her own ending planned and it did not include him going home tonight.

Against his better judgment, he stayed and sat down on the couch. When she excused herself, he knew it was time to go, but he didn't leave.

Greg could almost read her mind. Please don't let her try and seduce me tonight. I am not in the mood. Dani and her date left too abruptly. What if they are at her place? What if she let Drew make love to her? He got angrily to his feet and paced the room. I should go over there. No, if I go over there and he's not there,

I will look like an idiot. Either way I would look like an idiot. I have to be patient. You're kidding Thomas. Patience is not one of your strong points. You want what you want when you want it.

Greg didn't have long to wait or wonder before Debra reappeared wearing a see through black lace teddy. There was nothing left to the imagination as usual with Debra.

Wow! Okay, how do I get out of this gracefully without coming off looking like a jerk? Debra is a very beautiful and sexy woman, but she's not the woman I want.

Debra had a great body. She would have to have one in her current line of profession. He found out from Mark that she quit her job in the hospital-billing department to be an exotic dancer.

Those implants certainly looked worth every penny. Money well spent in Greg's estimation. He was sure it wasn't her money, though. He wondered what man paid for them. Debra was a user.

"I thought you deserved a proper welcome home," she smiled seductively walking toward him. Her arms went around him and she kissed him. Greg didn't resist or respond. Debra pulled back and looked at him in question. "I wonder what Danielle and her boyfriend are doing right now. Drew is a very handsome guy. I know what I'd be doing with him right about now. I'd rush home to take him straight to bed."

Greg couldn't mask the jealousy, which sparked in his eyes. Debra knew which buttons to push with him and she seemed to enjoy it.

"Danielle is not you, Debra. She's a little less obvious. She doesn't bed every man who buys her dinner."

"Are you sure about that? People change. I'm sure she hasn't been moping around over you the past two years. I wonder how many men have been in her bed and between her almost white thighs."

"Some people change and some don't. You're one of those who should. Vulgarity isn't appealing. It's a turn off. You're right, Deb. A lot can happen in two years. I grew up. The two years away from her made me appreciate what we had."

"Past tense. She didn't look to me like she wanted to pick things up again. She told me in the ladies room she wasn't interested in you. Danielle gave us her blessing. She's with Drew now."

"Is that the reason you followed her into the restroom, to get her blessing. People say a lot of things they don't mean in the heat of the moment."

"People also do a lot of things in the heat of the moment," she purred, brushing her body against his suggestively. "Forget Danielle. She's not worth the trouble."

"Good night, Debra," said Greg, taking a step away from her. "It's been real and it's been fun, but it hasn't been real fun. See you around."

"Leaving so soon," she pouted. "I was hoping to at least get a rise out of you." His hand caught hers before it made contact with his crotch.

"Next time, leave at least a little something to the imagination. Danielle would have." He released her hand and walked out the door. He laughed when he heard the crash on the other side of the door.

Danielle lay in bed flipping through the channels with the remote. She was trying unsuccessfully not to think about Greg and Debra the human barracuda. She knew Debra would throw herself at him the minute they went back to her place. Would he accept her offer?

Will he take her to bed? Why shouldn't he? She had not exactly given him any reason not to. It would be her own fault, Danielle reasoned.

She hopped up from the bed and paced the room. She unconsciously gnawed on her French manicured nails.

What if I've sent him straight into her bed? Will I be able to handle it? Do I want him back? What a silly question. Of course, I want him back, but I can't go down that road again.

She fell back on the bed in exasperation. Turning off the television, she closed her eyes and tried counting sheep. It didn't work. She sat up again.

The phone rang and she debated picking it up. Curiosity won out and she hit the talk button.

"Hello," came out in a breathless whisper. She eased back against the headboard and pulled the sheets over her.

"Hi," said the deep voice. "I hope I'm not interrupting anything. Are you alone or should I call back later?"

"If you were interrupting something, I wouldn't have answered the phone." Danielle smiled into the receiver and propped a pillow behind her back.

"Can I come by?" he asked hopefully. "I would really like to see you. We have some unfinished business."

As tempting as the thought was, Danielle knew she had to be strong. If he came over they both knew where it would lead.

"I don't think it's a good idea." Her heart was pounding with need, but her head was now in charge. "I thought we agreed to take things slow."

"You agreed to take things slow. I want to take you to bed." Greg didn't mince words or beat around the bush.

"What happened? Didn't Debra strip for you?" Danielle laughed softly. She could see the scene playing out with Debra excusing herself to get more comfortable and probably coming back in the room wearing only a smile.

"Jealous?" he asked. She could see the smile on

his face. "Does it bother you to think of Debra and me in bed?"

"Maybe a little," she admitted, grudgingly. "I guess if you were in bed with Debra you wouldn't need to come see me tonight."

"You're not only beautiful, but you have brains. The thought of you with Drew drives me crazy. The thought of you with any man drives me nuts. Danielle, my feelings for you have not changed. If anything, they're stronger."

"Greg, don't," she pleaded, fighting to stay in control of her emotions. "I can't handle this right now. Please slow things down a bit."

"If I make them any slower, we'll both be crawling. I don't want Debra or anyone else. I want to make love to you. I've always wanted you. Think about how hot we were together. It wasn't good Dani. It was great. Think about it and have a good night. Sweet dreams, princess."

Danielle held the phone to her chest. Her breathing was heavy and labored. She was fighting against the temptation to call him back and tell him to come over. For the next couple of hours, she reached for the phone, but stopped herself each time. She had a restless night, finally getting to sleep in the wee hours.

Chapter 6

Danielle was cooking dinner when the phone rang. She looked at the caller ID and let the answering machine pick it up.

Thank you God for caller ID. I don't know what I would do without it. Yes, I do. I would let the answering machine pick up all my calls.

"Danielle, if you're there pick up." She walked over and picked up the phone. "Hello, beautiful." Danielle smiled as she always did while talking to Greg. "What are you doing for dinner tomorrow night?"

"No plans. So what do you have in mind, Counselor?" She opened the oven and checked the lasagna. Grabbing the potholders, she turned off the oven and removed her meal.

"How about we have dinner at your place? I'll bring dinner with me. You are only responsible for dessert."

"This sounds a little dangerous to me. Can I trust you to be a good boy and keep all appendages to yourself?" She took the salad out of the refrigerator.

"I'm always good. I can't promise to keep my hands to myself, but I can promise only to go as far as you let me."

"So what are you bringing for dinner?" she asked,

changing the subject. Danielle sat down at the table with her dinner.

"It's a surprise. Trust me. What's for dessert?" Danielle could almost see the smirk on his handsome face.

"Obviously not what you're thinking, Thomas, so you can wipe that smile off your face. It's a surprise. Trust me," she mimicked.

"A can of whipped cream or a jar of honey would be good," he teased. "Chocolate syrup also works very well."

"Get your mind out of my bedroom, Counselor." She laughed, biting into her lasagna. "If you are planning to wine me and dine me and . . ." She stopped abruptly realizing what she was about to say. Her face flushed and she heard nothing but laughter on the other end of the phone.

"And you think my mind is in the bedroom? Danielle Roberts Masters knows a dirty limerick. I'm shocked. How long has it been?"

"How long has what been?" She knew what he was asking, but she wasn't sure she wanted to answer the question. "Let's not go there. If I answer your question, you will have to answer mine. I'm sure I've been celibate a lot longer than you have."

"Okay, we won't go there," he agreed, "even though my answer might surprise you. Oh mighty Danielle of little faith."

"So is dinner to be a casual affair?" She hit her forehead with her hand after the statement was out of her mouth. She shouldn't have used the word *affair*. It left her wide open for another sarcastic retort from Greg.

"Nothing is casual with us sweetheart. Let me just say the way you dress will give me a signal as to how lucky I will get. If it's easy to take off, I will assume I'm getting very lucky."

"And I suppose you will come naked because you

will be ready to sweep me off my feet and take me straight to bed," she teased.

"Thanks. I needed that visual right now. When I sweep you off your feet and carry you to bed, are you naked?"

"You are hopeless," laughed Danielle. "So how long has it been? Do I detect a note of sexual frustration in your tone?"

"Almost a year," he admitted. "Okay, we'd better change the subject or I will need a cold shower."

"Thanks. I needed that visual," she mimicked. In her mind, she pictured him naked in the shower with rivulets of water running down his muscled chest to his flat stomach to . . .

"Danielle, are you still there? What are you thinking about? You got awful quiet there for a minute."

"Yes, I'm here," she croaked fanning her hot face with her hands. "I'm just picturing you naked in the shower. The visual is still there. I'll see you tomorrow night."

"Why wait? Since we're pretty damn close to having phone sex, I can be there in thirty minutes or less for the real thing."

"Down boy. We are not having phone sex. What time can I expect you tomorrow night?" she asked changing the subject.

"Don't knock it if you haven't tried it, Roberts. What time can you expect me to do what?" he laughed. "How is 7 o'clock?"

"Works for me. I'll say goodnight. My dinner is getting cold and I'm getting hot. Good night, Greg."

"Remember what I said about the way you're dressed. I'll take my cue from you. It's either red light or green light."

Smiling, she replaced the receiver. She finished her dinner quickly and took a nice long relaxing shower.

* * *

Danielle studied her reflection in the mirror. She changed clothes a total of five times. She wasn't sure what message she wanted to send this evening. Dani took off the navy blue wrap-around blouse and tossed it on the bed. Too easy to take off. *I don't want him to think I'm easy.* She stared at the black slacks she wore. They zipped in back. *Okay he takes me in his arms. He distracts me with a kiss. His hands slide down my hips and he has easy access to unzip my pants.* Dani paced the room. *This is his fault for putting these thoughts in my head. He's messing with my head.* Smiling wickedly, she walked to her closet. *I think I should return the favor.*

Picking up the black low-cut blouse with the thousand and one pearl buttons, she slipped it over her head. She twirled in front of the mirror smiling victoriously.

Okay, Mr. Thomas, what message am I sending you now? Low-cut may mean yes, but all the buttons is a definite no.

She brushed her hair together and pinned it on top of her head. *If I pin it up, it gives him a clear path to nuzzle my neck. If I leave it down what does that mean? It's a simple dinner and I am now overanalyzing every single thing.* She released her hair from the clip and brushed it out. *Down it is.*

Leaving her room, she walked down the stairs and went into the kitchen. Pushing open the double doors to the formal dining room, she surveyed her handiwork.

The table was already set for two. Two candles and a flower arrangement adorned the table. She dimmed the lights and turned the radio control to jazz.

She was nervously pacing the living room when the doorbell rang. Trying to calm her racing heart, she wiped her sweaty palms on her slacks and opened the door.

Greg had his hands full carrying two large brown

bags with one of her favorite Mexican food restaurants name printed on them. She held the door open for him and stepped back for him to enter.

"Hello beautiful," said Greg, leaning over and dropping a chaste kiss on her cheek. Her head turned and his lips touched hers. When she didn't pull back, he brushed her lips again.

"Hi." Stepping away from him, she closed the door behind them. "The food smells wonderful. Tell me you bought chicken quesadillas and fajitas."

"You'll have to wait and see. It's a surprise." She followed him out to the kitchen where he set the bags on the counter.

He took her in his arms and his mouth covered hers in a tender kiss. Her arms went around his neck and her lips parted beneath his. His tongue plunged into her mouth and she gladly accepted the offering. Her tongue mated with his as she melted against him. They came up for air before their mouths fused together in another fiery kiss, which left her tingling from head to toe.

"I'm starving," said Greg, tasting and teasing as his lips left a trail of hot kisses on her neck and down her throat. "If you don't intend to be the main course, I'd suggest you get the plates and I'll unpack everything."

"I'm still weighing my options," she smiled saucily. "I suppose we do have to eat first. We will need our strength for later." Danielle winked at him as she left the room.

She returned breathing in the heady aroma of Mexican spices. Placing the plates on the counter, she opened the containers. Her face lit up with joy.

"Ooh, beef and chicken fajitas, quesadillas, and stuffed jalapénos." Her smile lit up her face. "A man after my heart."

"You'd better believe it," he teased. "That's not all I'm after, but I think I can wait until after dinner."

"Have a plate." She slapped the plate into his stomach. They fixed their plates and carried them into the formal dining room. "This is wonderful," said Danielle, savoring a bite of a stuffed jalapéno. She held it to his lips. "You should try this."

"No, thank you," he smiled, moving her hand away from his lips. "You eat it. I don't do jalapénos."

"I thought you liked things hot and spicy." Smiling she leaned across the table and waved the pepper in front of his mouth.

"That's hot, sweetheart, not spicy." He caught her hand and took a small bite. Greg immediately released her hand and picked up a glass of water.

"What's the matter? I thought you could handle anything thrown your way. Is it too hot for you?" she asked innocently.

"A bit," he said clearing his throat. "So what's for dessert?" He set his plate aside. Putting both elbows on the table, he took her hand in his and brought it to his lips. He kissed each fingertip, causing her to shiver in desire.

Her gray eyes darkened at the touch of his lips on her soft skin. She knew what he wanted and she wanted it also, but she was not ready to take that step.

"Not what you're thinking, Thomas. I bought strawberry cheesecake. Cool your heels and I'll go get it out of the fridge." Removing her hand from his, she went to the refrigerator and took out the cheesecake. She set it on the table in front of him. "As I recall, this is your favorite."

"It looks wonderful." He watched her slice the cake and place a piece on a plate for him. "Did you make this?" He laughed at his own sense of humor. They both knew it was a rhetorical question.

"Ha ha ha. No, I didn't make it. You know, one day I might surprise you," said Danielle, shaking the cake cutter at him. "It might also surprise you to know I do turn on the oven occasionally. *Cooking* is not a dirty word with me anymore."

After dessert they adjourned to the living room. They sat on the sofa staring at each other. Danielle saw the hunger in his eyes that mirrored her own.

"How about a movie?" Danielle suggested springing to her feet and moving away from his nearness. She flipped through a stack of DVDs.

She tensed when she felt his hands on her shoulders. He turned her around to face him. Greg took the DVDs out of her hand and put them on the shelf. Taking her hand in his, he led her to the sofa.

"Relax. I don't bite . . . much." He brought her hand to his lips. "I didn't come here tonight thinking I would get lucky. I came to have dinner and maybe snuggle a little with a beautiful woman. I'm in no rush, Dani. I meant it when I said we could take things as slow as you need me to. Waiting is not one of my strong points, but I'm learning."

"Yeah right. I know you, Greg. You are so full of it. So where is your overnight bag?" she asked smiling up at him.

"In the front seat of my car," he laughed, "but I meant what I said. I came prepared just in case you decided to speed things up by ripping my clothes off and ravishing me."

"In your dreams, Thomas." She punched him in the arm. "You are as obvious as Debra."

"I'm going to pretend you didn't bring her into our conversation at an intimate moment. And just for the record, in my dreams you're wearing black leather and five-inch heels."

"Okay, stop." Danielle roared with laughter. First of all, I don't own any black leather or five-inch heels."

He turned and lay back on the sofa pulling her with him. Her breasts were pressed against his chest. Her eyes turned a smoky gray and her body reacted instinctively to his. Her nipples hardened and she felt a tingling sensation in the pit of her stomach.

"Pity. You don't know what you're missing. I know what I'm getting you for Christmas. What size shoes do you wear?"

"Size seven," said the throaty voice. She lowered her face to his. Nothing could have stopped her from fusing her mouth to his. Her lips parted and her tongue danced a tango with his. Greg's hands moved up and down her back in a soft caress. Their tender kiss turned passionate within a matter of seconds. Greg molded her to him. Danielle moaned in pleasure as she felt Greg's hands on her bare skin.

"Sweetheart, we'd better stop right now before this gets out of hand. I'm not sure how much more of this I can take."

"It's already out of hand," whispered Danielle, as she unbuttoned his shirt. She felt his shudder as her mouth traced a pattern on his chest. Her tongue circled his nipple. "Stay with me tonight."

"Are you sure?" he asked, caressing her cheek. Coming to her feet, she held out her hand to him. Greg caught her hand and kissed it. His cell phone suddenly rang, taking them both off guard. Greg ignored it. "It will go to voice mail." It stopped ringing and immediately began to ring again.

"Maybe you should answer it," Danielle said, as he pulled her into his arms and kissed her. "I'm not going anywhere."

"Neither am I," said Greg shaking his head. "I want you. I've always wanted you." He led her toward the stairs.

Danielle's phone rang. They both stopped and stared at it. Someone was determined to ruin their evening.

"I have to get it. It might be important." She reached up and kissed him. "It'll only take a minute."

His arms were around her waist as he followed her to the telephone. When she picked up the phone, Greg nibbled at her neck. "Hello." His hands moved from her waist to her breasts. She bit back a moan of pleasure as he teased her nipples into hard pebbles.

"Danielle, it's Travis. I need to speak with Greg," said the agitated voice of Greg's younger brother.

"Just a minute." She placed her hand over the receiver. "It's for you." Danielle stilled Greg's roaming hands and turned to face him. Giving him a quick kiss, she handed him the phone.

"Hello," said Greg, frowning into the receiver. He pulled Danielle against him and planted a kiss on her cheek.

"Greg, it's Travis. I'm at County General. We had to rush Mom here about an hour ago. They just informed me she had a light stroke."

"I'll be there in half an hour." He hung up, buttoning up his shirt. "I've got to go. My mom has been rushed to the hospital. I'll call you when I know something." He kissed her and rushed out the door.

Greg was on pins and needles as he drove to the hospital. He couldn't even fathom his life without his mother. He prayed all the way there.

He parked his car and rushed into the emergency room. He immediately spotted his brother and made a beeline for him.

"How's Mom?" Greg asked with a heavy heart. His heart was pounding in fear as he waited for his brother's answer.

"She's stable and resting comfortably," Travis said. "We were talking and all of a sudden she keeled over. Mom scared ten years off my life." The two brothers sat down in the waiting room chairs. "The nurse said she would come out and let us know when we can see her. Relax, big brother. She's going to be fine."

Please God tell me I didn't come home to bury my

*mother. She has to be okay. She's a fighter and a survivor.
Please help her get through this, help us all get through
this. I truly can't believe it's her time to go. We need her
so much. She's the glue that holds this family together. If
and when Danielle and I walk down the aisle, I want her
to be there to see it happen. She has to be there. This is
what she's prayed for, and what I've prayed for. I can't
lose her.*

An hour later, Greg breathed a sigh of relief when
the nurse led them back to his mother's room. She was
awake and alert.

"I'm sorry I gave you boys such a fright," said
Doris Thomas holding out her hands to her sons. They
both took her hands too choked up for words. Greg
and Travis both hugged her and kissed her cheek.

"Some people will do anything for attention," Greg
teased past the lump in his throat. "Mama, don't you
ever scare us like that again."

"Greg's right. I'm the one who almost had heart
failure."

"I'm sorry, Travis," said Doris, squeezing her
younger son's hand. "I should have told you both I've
been on heart and high blood pressure medication for
the past two years. I didn't want to worry you boys."

"Mama, how can we not worry about you? We love
you," replied Greg, taking her other hand in his and
kissing it

Greg and Travis sat around talking as they waited
for their mom to be admitted to the hospital. In her
private room, they made sure she was comfortable and
sleeping before they called it a night and went home.

Greg called Danielle when he got home to let her
know his mother's condition. She asked him if there
was anything she could do to help. He thanked her for
caring and they talked for about an hour before he said
goodnight.

He and Travis both called in sick the next day and

ended up at the hospital bright and early. They hung around the hospital most of the day. Marie came by and stayed for about an hour.

Greg was livid Leo didn't bother to show up. Marie assured him she told Leo what happened. There was no excuse for him not being there.

Chapter 7

Her dress was a deep purple strapless Rayon, Marty Uribe creation. The top was low-cut and hugged her chest and waist. It flared out at her hips in a ducktail. The skirt of the dress was straight and stopped just above her knees.

The dress was totally out of character for practical Danielle. In the past, she wouldn't have dreamed of buying or wearing something like this.

She finished dressing for her uncle's birthday party as the doorbell rang. Slipping her feet into purple leather pumps, she went to answer the door.

"Hi. Come in." She stepped back for Greg to enter the house. "I'm actually dressed and ready to go. Can you believe it?"

"I've gotten used to you greeting me in your slip and robe, but I have to admit this look is much better. You look fantastic." Greg let out a whistle of appreciation and produced a bouquet of flowers from behind his back.

"They're beautiful," she smiled in surprise taking the flowers. "I'll go put them in a vase and some water."

Greg followed her out to the kitchen. He said nothing as he watched her take a vase from the cabinet and add water. She arranged the flowers and sat them on the kitchen table.

Catching her hand, he twirled her around to get a better look at the outfit she was wearing. She wore a single diamond pendant necklace around her neck and matching earrings. Greg was wearing a black double-breasted suit, white shirt, and a bright paisley bow tie. He could put any male model to shame in his present attire.

He could do that dressed up or undressed. Greg had a natural sex appeal. He held out his arm to her and, smiling, she put her arm through his.

The valet opened the door to help her out when they arrived and took the car keys from Greg. Hand-in-hand they took the elevator up to the fifth floor.

A smiling Jeff met them at the door. Her face lit up as Jeff swept her off her feet in a bear hug. Still smiling, he sat her back on her feet and kissed her temple. He proceeded to push her at arms length so he could get a good look at her.

"You look great. I can see having this guy around agrees with you. Is that a sparkle I see in those beautiful gray eyes?" She elbowed him and he kissed her again and shook hands with Greg. "It's good to see you again, Greg. Welcome home."

"Thank you. It's good to be home. It's good to know I was missed by at least two Masters family members."

"Did I miss anything?" Alissa asked, coming toward them. "It is definitely good to be home." Alissa and Danielle embraced each other fondly. "Dani, it's so good to see you again. Greg you're as handsome as ever."

"Congratulations, Mrs. Masters. I wish you two the best," Danielle smiled giving her hand a squeeze.

"Yes. I hear congratulations are in order," Greg smiled, kissing Alissa's cheek. "It's good to see you and Jeff back together."

"Come on in. Liz and Gabe are at a table over by the bar. You guys should have seen the priceless look on John's face at my announcement that Alissa and I were married. A picture is worth a thousand words, and I made sure the photographer Mom hired has it on film," Jeff laughed, leading them over to the table.

They found Liz and Gabe in a world of their own. Gabe's hand was on her stomach feeling the babies kick. He had a dreamy doting expression on his face. Leaning over he kissed his wife tenderly.

Danielle's heart almost stopped when Greg turned to look at her with the same dreamy expression in his eyes. She turned away from him guiltily and shook off the feeling of dread she had been having all day.

"Cut it out you two. You are going to give my wife ideas," Jeff joked. "On second thought, please continue. I kind of like the idea of bouncing twins on my knee."

"Just what you need. One more child to raise," Danielle teased. "Please at least wait until Jeff grows up."

"That could take a lifetime. Twins," Alissa shrieked. "Keep talking like that and I'll have you fixed. Don't say the word *twin* in my presence." Ignoring her comment, he pulled her into his arms for a steamy kiss.

"Hi guys," Liz laughed. "Greg Thomas, this extremely loving and attractive man is my husband, Gabe Giovanni."

The two shook hands and exchanged greetings before they all sat down at the large table. They were all laughing and talking when John sauntered over to the table with a drink in his hand. He glared at each of them. His wife, Rebecca was close behind him and not thrilled to be at the party.

"Well, well, well. Look at what the cat drug in." He raised his drink in salute to Greg. "Danielle, you look like a million bucks, though you're worth quite a bit more. Is that the attraction, Thomas? Is that what keeps

you coming back? I'm pretty sure it's not her person-
ality. Did you happen to dress her tonight? She looks
great, but we both know this isn't her style. She has no
style. How does it feel to sleep with an heiress?"

Danielle was used to her cousin's anger toward her.
She ignored him whenever she could. He would
never get over his father giving half the family fortune to Jack. John also refused to acknowledge Jack
as his uncle or Danielle as his cousin. He was a blue-
blood snob.

Greg was about to come to his feet, but Danielle
caught his arm and gave it a slight squeeze. He caught
her pleading look and tried to relax.

"He's not worth the trouble," she whispered caressing Greg's arm. "Ignore him and maybe he'll go away."

"I guess this is the United Nations table. We have a
Black, a two-thirds black," he emphasized, smiling at
Danielle, "a Mexican, oh excuse me, it's Hispanic now
isn't it, Alissa. I suppose I must be politically correct,
and then there's my favorite brother-in-law, Gabe the
Italian gangster. So what is it with this family? You
can't stick to your own race? Dear sweet Liz probably
has never dated a white man. Why not Liz? Why can't
you stick to your own kind?" asked the slurred voice
of John Masters.

"Look in the mirror, John. If you are any indication
of what the rest of my kind are like, then you've just
answered your own question big brother."

"Jeff, we know what your attraction is to this little
jalapéno pepper." Jeff jumped to his feet with murder
in his eyes and Rebecca stepped between the two
brothers.

"John, stop it," Rebecca pleaded trying to hide her
embarrassment. "You are embarrassing yourself as
usual."

"Hey Becky, if you sat down, then we'd have the
t.p.t.," said John cruelly. "For those of you who have

no idea what I'm talking about it stands for 'trailer park trash.'"

No one saw Richard walk up until he punched his older brother. Richard lifted him up and sent him sailing through the air.

"Here they come," said Dennis Graham, the youngest son of Lawrence and Jack's cousin, Pamela. He turned off the lights and they waited.

"Surprise!" everyone yelled in unison. They proceeded to sing happy birthday to a surprised Lawrence.

Lawrence laughed and turned to his smiling wife, Victoria. Opening his arms, she stepped into them and kissed him. After thirty-five years of marriage, she had only managed to surprise him twice. This made the third time.

Danielle and Greg danced to almost every slow song the D.J. played. Being together again felt right for both of them.

They were in their own little world and Dani conceded this was where she belonged. She never stopped loving Greg and probably never would.

In her eyes, he was everything she had always wanted in a man and more. Maybe he had changed. Just maybe he wasn't still the same manipulative bullheaded chauvinist he used to be. Maybe they did have a chance.

"All right Thomas, you've got one chance to prove to me what a wonderful man you are. You have to convince me I can't live without you," Danielle said caressing his stubbed cheek. "This time, we do things my way."

"Dani's way has a nice ring to it. I'm liking it more and more with each passing moment." His lips brushed hers lightly.

"OK, everybody!" voiced Victoria. "It's time to cut the cake so gather around." They all returned to the large table and took a seat. Victoria placed the cake cutter in her husband's hand. "Don't forget to make a wish." He took it and leaned over and kissed her.

Danielle hoped she and Greg would one day be as happy and in love as Lawrence and Victoria were. Was it possible to find and hold on to that kind of love anymore?

"I have everything a man could wish for." His hand caressed her flushed cheek. This brought out a lot of oohs and ahs. Lawrence raised his champagne glass. "I would like to make a toast." Everyone raised their glasses. "To my beautiful wife Victoria, who is always in my thoughts, and my son Jeff and my new daughter-in-law Alissa. I wish you the best of luck in the future. May the two of you experience the kind of love and friendship in marriage that Victoria and I share. To the newlyweds. May you add to your union many healthy grandchildren for me to bounce on my knee in my old age."

John snickered and slammed down his glass, refusing to toast the newlyweds. Lawrence glared at him to remain silent. They watched him push himself up from his chair and stalk out the front door. Everyone seemed to sigh in relief at his departure.

"Did I happen to mention that you look stunning tonight?" whispered Greg twirling Danielle around the dance floor. She smiled up at him happily.

"Yes, but feel free to tell me again." She smiled up at him stroking his cheek, "and again, and again."

"You are the most beautiful woman in this room and you have a body to die for." His arms tightened around her waist. "I would like nothing more than to take you, right here, right now, but I'm afraid it would shock everyone." He nibbled on her neck, sending chills down her body. Her arms pulled his head closer to hers.

"This place is too public for what I want to do to you. How about my place?" she whispered seductively. "I don't want an audience. I want you all to myself." Her lips brushed his in invitation and she nibbled at his ear. Danielle held out her hand to him and he caught it. "Let's go say goodnight to everyone." They went in search of the guest of honor, to say goodnight, before they made their hasty exit.

Jeff came over to the table to get Greg to solve a sports trivia debate he was having with one of his cousins. Danielle watched them walk over to the bar.

"Liz, where's Uncle Lawrence?" Danielle asked searching the room for her Aunt and Uncle.

"He had an overseas phone call. I think it was Uncle Jack wishing him happy birthday. Are you guys leaving?" she asked smiling knowingly.

"Yes, we are." Smiling, Danielle sat down in the chair next to her. "Things are definitely looking up for us. I know Greg's only been back a short time, but it feels so right. It almost feels like he never left. I never stopped loving him. He has always been my one and only true love."

"Leaving so soon?" asked the hateful voice behind her. She didn't have to look around to know John had returned. "Just can't wait to hop back into his bed can you? You can't leave cousin, it wouldn't be the same without you."

"Nice of you to say so, John. It wouldn't be the same without you either. It might actually be pleasant for a change. You stay and I'll go. Have a nice evening. I intend to."

"You are a fool, Danielle." She turned around to face him. "This guy is going to break your heart again."

"Am I to take this to mean you care what happens to me?" She laughed without humor. "Please give me more credit than that. You can't stand to see anyone happy, can you? Not Jeff, not Liz, and especially not me. Get over it. I'm happy. Greg is back in my life. Deal with it." She turned her back on him again.

"You can't trust him. He cheated on you once and

he'll do it again. You weren't woman enough to hold his attention." Danielle's head shot up at his accusation.

"That's enough, John." Liz glared at him. "Why don't you go play in traffic or something? Don't do this. Not here and not tonight.

"Greg never cheated on me," she denied hotly. "You are a liar. You will say and do anything to hurt me, but you know what. It's not going to work. Just because you are miserable doesn't mean the whole world has to be."

"No it's not enough, Liz. It's time she knew the truth about the love of her life. He's a liar and a cheater. See for yourself how faithful he is. He slept with my wife."

Danielle looked down at the pictures John dropped on the table in front of her. All color left her face and tears came to her eyes.

Through a blurred vision, her trembling hands picked up the photos. She closed her eyes to clear them and tried to blink away the tears, instead they dropped onto the pictures.

In the first photo, Rebecca was wearing a see-through teddy and was pulling Greg into a hotel room. Next he had her pinned against the wall with his body and he was taking her clothes off. The last one was the two of them in bed.

Hurt and angry Danielle dropped the pictures back onto the table. Her heart was breaking and her world was crumbling down around her again.

Before John could retrieve the incriminating photos, Liz grabbed them. Her hand covered her mouth and her eyes flew to her best friend's pale face.

"Oh God! Why did you do this to her?" she hissed, throwing the pictures in his smiling face. "You are despicable."

Witnessing the scene, but not being able to hear what was being said, everyone chose that particular moment to return to the table. Rebecca reached them first.

She spotted a picture near John's foot and slapped him. She tried to pick up the scattered photos before anyone else could see them.

Not realizing what it was she was picking up, Greg bent down to give her a hand. When his eyes flashed on the first photo, his eyes went quickly to Danielle's tear-stained face and his heart stopped.

He knew in that moment he had lost her again. Her face was devoid of any expression except for the tears rolling silently down her pale cheeks.

Greg took one look at John's smirking face and instantly knew the source behind the pictures. Without further thought, he lunged at John. Slamming him against the wall, he broke his nose and busted his lip before Gabe and Jeff could pull him off the object of his contempt.

Richard took all the photos from Rebecca's trembling hands and announced to the crowd of people the party was over. He ushered them out the door, before things went any further. After closing the door on the last guest, he returned to the table.

"Danielle, I'm sorry," cried Rebecca, wiping at her own tears. "I thought I destroyed all the prints and the negatives so nothing like this would ever happen."

"Obviously you were wrong. You see Becky there's a wonderful new thing called double prints," John sneered wiping the blood from his cut lip and bloodied nose.

Danielle continued to stare into space. This wasn't happening. This could not be happening. It must be a dream. That's it. She was having a nightmare and soon she would wake up. Just a few more minutes and she would wake up. Greg couldn't have slept with Rebecca. Not her Greg. He wouldn't do that to her. She knew in her heart he loved her.

"Why bring them forward now John? You know as well as I do this happened before we were married.

I'm filing for divorce," said Rebecca. "I've had it. When you get home, the children and I will be gone." She turned her back to walk away.

"What is going on here? What happened to everyone?" asked Lawrence walking up to the table. He looked from one to the other, but no one answered. Richard was about to rip up the pictures, when Lawrence grabbed them. After seeing who they were, he did rip them up.

"Richard where did these come from?" he demanded. He didn't need to be told as all eyes turned to John. "John, are you responsible for this? Answer me? How dare you embarrass the family in this way? This is a private matter between you and your wife. But you didn't do it to get back at Rebecca did you? No. You did it to hurt Danielle."

"Rebecca and Greg cheated and they were caught. Danielle's an intelligent woman, I think she can do the math without my help." He turned to a speechless Greg. "Welcome home, Daddy." With that parting comment, he left the room.

"It's not true," cried Rebecca, watching Greg and Danielle. "She's not Greg's daughter. I swear she's not."

Everyone watched in silence as he left the club. Rebecca also bolted from the room and Richard went after her. Danielle's blank gaze met Greg's confused expression.

"Can we go someplace where we can talk?" Greg pleaded, pulling Danielle from her chair. "Please."

"I have nothing to say to you," she said, angrily jerking her arm from his grasp. "Get away from me."

"There's an office in the back," Lawrence suggested pointing in the direction of the office. "Danielle, I think you should hear him out."

Wiping her eyes and regaining her composure, she followed Greg into the next room. Stiffening her spine, Danielle walked over and looked out the office window, turning her back on him.

She felt his presence close behind her, but couldn't face him just yet. It still hurt too much. Every time she closed her eyes, she could see Greg in bed with Rebecca. He not only had an affair with her, but he had a child with her. Lexi was his daughter.

She blinked several times to keep the tears at bay, but without luck. They fell anyway, wetting her face. She angrily wiped them away with the back of her hand.

"Tell me why?" Danielle turned around to face him. All her pain and anguish were staring him in the face. "Is Rebecca the one who taught you that little trick you did to me last weekend? When exactly were those pictures taken? I know it was years ago, but when? When did you sleep with her? Correction, when did you have sex with her?" Danielle cried wiping furiously at the tears, which kept falling.

"About four years ago," said Greg gazing down into her teary eyes. "It didn't mean anything to either of us. It just happened. It's in the past, Dani. Let it go. We have a future to think about."

When he tried to touch her, she took a step backward and his arms fell to his side. She couldn't bear for him to touch her, not now.

"When four years ago?" He remained silent as if weighing his words carefully. "It happened while we were engaged didn't it? You slept with her while you were making plans to marry me." From the pained expression on his face, she had her answer. She shoved him away angrily. "So tell me Greg, was it worth it? Was one night in Rebecca's arms worth the risk of losing me?"

"No, it wasn't. I only slept with her once. It happened during one of our many break-ups. Technically, we were not together. Danielle, we have a chance for a new beginning. We can make a fresh start. Let the past go. I can't change what happened with Rebecca. If there was something I could do to make it up to you, I would do it in a heartbeat. Don't let my past mistakes ruin our future. Nothing is worth losing you."

She couldn't believe what she was hearing. Danielle stared at him aghast. He wanted her to forget the whole thing like it had never happened. He wanted her to forget the fact that he had betrayed her. How could she ever forget?

"Let it go! I trusted you. I believed you when you told me you loved me, that you wanted only me. I believed every lie you ever told me. I gave myself to you, body and soul. I gave you everything and you threw it back in my face by sleeping with Rebecca. How could you do that to me? To us? John hated you because of me. It had nothing to do with me, but everything with the fact you slept with his soon-to-be wife." Danielle paced back and forth, unable to look at him anymore and not wanting him to see her cry again. "There is no going back this time. I can't trust you. I don't know if I can ever believe anything you say to me. You are right, we did have a chance for a new beginning and you destroyed it."

"It will never be over for us." He grabbed her and held her at arms length. "This is only the beginning. You can trust me. Dani, we weren't even together when I slept with Becky. You gave me back my engagement ring. You told me it was over. I admit what I did was dumb and it was stupid. I can't take it back. If I could, honey, I would. We belong together, Dani. I love you and I know you love me, too. I can see it in your eyes when you look at me." She wrenched away from him and glared up at him with flashing gray eyes.

"Then tell me what you see now? Do you see the pain, the hurt, the humiliation I felt out there? I made a fool of myself. I was ready to give you another chance, to give us another chance. I was ready to go to bed with you. I guess you were right two years ago when you said love is not always enough. It wasn't enough to keep you here and it wasn't enough to keep you faithful. I'm not enough for you. You've proved that yet again. What happens if some other woman catches your fancy? Are you going to just fall into bed with her too without giving me a second thought? What's the old saying 'fool me once shame on you, fool me twice shame on me'? I won't let you make a fool of me again. We have nothing left to say to each other."

"I swear to you, Dani, I wasn't unfaithful. We were not together when this happened. You shouldn't condemn me for something that had nothing to do with you."

"I don't believe you. I can't. If I were you, I'd find Rebecca and Richard and make sure they don't skip town with your child." She hugged her arms to herself in a defensive gesture. "Please go!" Danielle screamed losing complete control. "Just get out of my life and stay out this time! There is no room for negotiations this time, Counselor. It's over. I can't do this anymore."

"I know you are upset and once you've calmed down you'll feel differently. The past doesn't matter. Only the future is what matters. Our future. I'm not giving up on you again. I'll go for now, but I will be in touch. Just for the record, there's no way she could be my child. John is lying to hurt you. Lexi is not my daughter." Even as he said the words, he wasn't sure if it were true or not. He would have to talk to Rebecca to be sure. What if this child was his? What then?

When the door closed behind him, Danielle collapsed on the sofa and cried. It was over, again. So much for dreams and happily ever after. For some reason her dreams never came true. Fate cruelly always seemed to spoil what little happiness she found.

She thought back to about eighteen months ago,

when John asked her to babysit for Lexi. Dani had been more than a little surprised. He said he and Rebecca were going out of town, and Clint was spending the night with a friend.

Come on, Dani, you and Lexi have a lot in common. More than you know. It'll be fun. Who knows? Maybe one day . . . His words had trailed off.

She also remembered Rebecca's shocked expression when she went by their house to pick up Lexi. She was nervous and uneasy. She had tried to talk Dani out of keeping the little girl. Dani could never figure out why.

"Now I know why," she whispered to the empty room shaking her head. "You knew this day would one day come didn't you, Rebecca. You knew John would eventually tell us."

Minutes later, Jeff found her sitting on the couch hugging her knees to her chest. The tears were still rolling silently down her cheeks.

Without saying a word, he sat down next to her and pulled her into his arms. He held her until the tears finally stopped.

"Do you want to talk about it?" She shook her head no. "That's okay. Take your time. I'm not going anywhere." He pulled her back into his arms. "I could kill John for this. Honey, don't let what happened four years ago ruin what you and Greg could have now. No one is perfect. I'm a fair judge of character and my gut tells me Greg loves you. He came back because of you."

"I don't know what to believe anymore. He said he slept with her during one of our break-ups. I don't know if I believe him. What if Lexi is his daughter? This creates so many new problems. How can I look at Lexi and not think about how she got here? Every time I close my eyes, I'll see those damn photos of him and Becky. John and Becky deliberately let me fall in love with Greg's little girl. They let me become attached to Greg's child. It was all part of John's master plan to destroy any happiness he thought I might have. He set me up to be hurt. What did I ever do to him to make him hate me so much?"

"I don't have the answers to any of those questions. As for Greg, don't make any hasty decisions just yet. Give yourself some time to get over the shock. You have to realize, sweetie, you and Greg had a pretty rocky relationship. I know that doesn't excuse what he did, but half the time I didn't know myself if you guys were together or apart. He's a good guy, Danielle. He made a huge mistake. Now he has to pay for it. So will Becky and, most importantly, so will Lexi if she is his daughter. You can't believe anything John says. Lexi didn't ask for any of this. Her little world is about to be turned upside down and you may be her one saving grace. We both know Greg is not going to just let this go. If Lexi is his daughter, he will always be connected to Becky." Dani looked up at him with tear stained eyes. "You can help to keep this situation from getting out of hand. I know you are hurt and angry, but please think long and hard before you make any decisions about the future. If you push Greg away again, it just might be for good this time."

"I don't know if I ever really had him. Maybe it's for the best that I've found this out now, before our relationship went any further. I was ready to give him another chance. I feel like such a fool. I must look a mess. I can't go out there looking like this."

"We are family. We all know what this has done to you," Jeff said raising her chin with his finger. "Come on." He held out his hand to her and she caught it. "Alissa and I will give you a lift home."

Facing the group of people in the next room was the hardest thing she had ever done. Danielle couldn't stand the looks of pity. She said her goodnights and left the room quickly.

Jeff and Alissa offered to stay awhile, but she declined the offer. Danielle wanted to be alone with her thoughts.

She ignored the message button blinking on her answering machine while she got ready for bed. She didn't want to talk anymore tonight, so she turned the ringer on her phone off. She heard the answering machine click on several times, but she rolled over in bed not at all curious as to the caller.

Chapter 8

Greg furiously paced back and forth relating everything that went on to his friend. He could not believe what had happened tonight. He had such high hopes for tonight and for his and Dani's future.

John Masters was going to pay for hurting Danielle. He would get even with him. Somehow, someday, he would make him pay for what he had done.

Mark stared at his best friend not saying a word. He really didn't know what to say. He knew how much Greg loved Danielle and he wanted him to be happy. He didn't necessarily think Dani was the right person to make him happy, but if she was what Greg wanted, then so be it. He viewed her as all fluff and no substance.

"So what are you going to do now?" Mark asked sipping his rum and coke. "Do you think there is a chance this is your child?"

"No, I'm always careful, but I have to know for sure," he said downing the drink. "If it's not, then Dani and I may have a chance." He paused and sat down. "If she's my daughter, I lose the woman I love. How's that for a trade off? We were so close to getting back together. I still can't forget the look on her face. She was heartbroken. I have never seen her look like that before. What if I've really lost her this time? What if she doesn't forgive me?"

"Greg, not to sound callous," said Mark facing him, "but do you realize how many times you've stood right in this spot saying the same thing. Danielle always forgives you. She loves you. Don't give up on her. In the meantime, what are you going to do about Cousin John? I have some friends who could rough him up a bit."

"No. John Masters is mine. I have some friends in the police department I can call. I'll have them run a check on John's license plate to see if he has any outstanding driving or parking tickets. With his arrogance, I'm sure if he has them, he hasn't paid them. I'll see if I can get a warrant issued for his arrest. I can see the headlines now."

"That's all you're going to do?" Mark asked fixing himself a drink. "That's kid's play. I have a friend at the IRS. You want to have him audited just say the word."

"Let's do it. All's fair in love and war and John Masters has declared war. I am not finished with him by a long shot," vowed Greg.

Danielle heard the next day from Liz, John had moved out of their parents' house and Rebecca and the children had moved in with Richard. To avoid any scandal, John had flown to Mexico to obtain a quickie divorce.

Greg left several messages on her answering machine, but Danielle refused to call him back. Instead of answering her phone in the evenings, she let the machine pick up.

True to his word, Greg called a few friends down at the police station and they found several unpaid parking and speeding tickets John had never paid. He then called the newspaper to alert them; John Masters was being arrested.

Greg and Mark stood in the background smiling as they handcuffed an angry John and read him his rights.

Two hours later he paid the fines and was released. But it didn't matter. Greg felt satisfaction in knowing John had been embarrassed in public.

Dani continued to refuse all of Greg's phone calls, but he vowed not to give up on her. He would get through to her no matter how long it took. He would wait for her to forgive him.

He glanced down at his watch. *Time to meet Becky and Mark at the hospital. In a few days I will know what my next move will be. Maybe I should leave Dani alone, at least until we get the test results back. Then I can plan my strategy. If Lexi is my daughter, I could lose Dani forever. If she's not my daughter, we may have a chance.*

An hour later he stood in Mark's office pacing angrily. Becky was a no-show. He dialed his office to check his messages. He had his secretary patch him through to the deputy who was delivering the legal papers to Becky this morning.

"We're here now," said Becky, stepping into the office leading Lexi. "You can call off the S.W.A.T. team. There was an accident on the freeway."

Greg turned at the sound of her voice. He was momentarily stunned as he saw Becky's daughter for the first time. She was beautiful like her mother. Her complexion was lightly tanned and she was wearing a red and white sundress. There was a matching hat on her head. Her long dark hair hung loosely down her back. A pair of twinkling brown eyes lit up her small heart-shaped face.

Greg looked for traces of mixed heritage in her and

found none. He didn't really expect to see any. He knew Becky didn't sleep around.

"I'll go make sure a room is available and we'll get started. I'll be right back," said Mark, leaving the room.

Fifteen minutes later, they were all leaving Mark's office. He told them he would put a rush on the test results.

Greg decided to stay away from Danielle until he had the results of the tests. He already knew what they would tell him, but he wanted to show Dani the proof.

Again, Danielle tried to put Greg out of her thoughts. She didn't want him in her mind or in her life. Things always were complicated when Greg was around.

Her father called to let her know he and Karen were having a wonderful time and they would be staying on an additional seven days. She couldn't bring herself to tell her father about Greg. The two men had never seen eye to eye on anything.

Danielle and Drew were having dinner, when his beeper went off. He went outside to take the call. Dani's cell phone rang. When she saw Jeff's name, she picked it up.

"Hey Jeff, what's up?" she asked, picking up her water glass and taking a small sip. She put the glass down.

"Gabe just phoned. He's taking Liz to the hospital. Her water broke and the babies are moving a wee bit faster than expected. He said from the looks of things, those two babies are not going to wait for us to get there. Alissa and I are on our way now. We'll see you at Parkdale."

Danielle waited impatiently tapping her fingers on the table. She sprang to her feet when Drew walked up.

"We have to go," they chorused. They looked at each other bewildered. He waved for her to speak first.

"Liz's in labor," she said excitedly. Gabe is taking her to the hospital right now. I'm meeting Jeff there."

"That's great, but I have to leave also. There's a glitch in the program I wrote for a client and I have to go out and fix it. It could take minutes or hours. I'm not sure which."

"That's not a problem. I'll call a cab." Drew waited with her a few minutes, before he finally had to leave. Pulling her into his arms his lips brushed her lightly. "I'll call you."

She watched him get into his car and drive away, unaware that she was being watched. Danielle was startled when Greg caught her wrist.

"Don't sneak up on me like that," Danielle said glaring at him. "Why are you following me?" She asked, trying to jerk her wrist away from his grasp.

"I'm checking your pulse. If your lips weren't moving so much I'd swear you were a corpse." He released her hand smiling. "It's not even a little fast. No sparks I guess."

"Go away," she hissed, between clinched teeth. "I don't have time for your little games right now. I'm waiting for a taxi."

She walked around him, so she could peer down the street. Then she nervously began to pace back and forth. Looking down at the time, she began pacing again.

"Why bother?" He stepped in front of her and she maneuvered around him. "I'd be happy to give you a lift home."

"Thank you, but I don't think so. I have a better idea. Why don't you stop stalking me and popping up everywhere I go?"

"I guess I'm a glutton for punishment. I rather enjoy

listening to your verbal abuse. It's very amusing considering I know how you really feel about me."

"And how do I really feel. Angry? Disgusted? You're wasting your time tonight. If you want a bed partner you'd better go find Debra. I'm not going home. Liz is in labor and I'm going to Parkdale Hospital."

"Why didn't you say so? Come on. I'll drive you." Danielle opened her mouth to protest when he held up his hand to silence her. "Don't argue. We are wasting time. I'm not leaving you out here alone to wait for a cab."

He caught her arm and led her to his car. Unlocking the door, he pushed her inside. He went back around to his side and got in. Putting the car in gear, he drove to the hospital.

They found Jeff, Alissa, and Liz's parents in the maternity waiting room. Everyone seemed a bit surprised to see Danielle walk in with Greg, but no one said anything.

"Any news yet?" Danielle asked, taking the vacant seat next to Alissa. "I hear the waiting is the hardest part."

"Not quite the hardest part, I'll wager," said Jeff, pacing back and forth. He looked down at his watch and sat down.

"Dani and I are going to the cafeteria to get something to drink," said Alissa, coming to her feet. "Does anyone want anything?"

Confused, Danielle followed her cousin's wife out the door. They got on the elevator and went downstairs.

"Okay, Alissa," said Danielle, taking a seat at a vacant table. "You got me away from everyone because you obviously have something to say. What is it?"

"What's going on with you and Greg? I thought you had a date with Drew tonight. How did you end up with Greg?"

"It's not what you think. I did have a date with Drew. He had an emergency and had to leave the restaurant. We were going our separate ways when Jeff phoned me about Liz. I was waiting for a taxi and Greg offered to drive me here."

"I know this is none of my business, but I am your friend Danielle. I don't want to see you hurt again. If Lexi turns out to be Greg's daughter, you've got some tough choices to make. He's going to want you to be the mother of his child. Can you handle being a mother to her? Greg and Becky will be tied to each other the rest of their lives because of Lexi. She will always be a part of your life because she's Lexi's mother. Can you deal with that? Lexi will be a constant reminder of their betrayal."

"I'm not sure I can do it," she confessed, folding her hands in her lap. "I love Lexi with all my heart. She's a terrific little girl, but when I think about Rebecca and Greg, it infuriates me. If she is his daughter, I don't know what I will do. Alissa, Greg wants a family. I don't know if I can give him one. I may never be able to give him children. The doctors were not very optimistic that I could even get pregnant."

"Have you and Greg talked about this? Honey, you can't avoid the subject forever. When those results come in, good or bad you will have to face them. If you are going to keep seeing him, you need to tell him about your condition. He loves you."

"I'll think about it." Danielle got to her feet. "We'd better get back upstairs before they come looking for us."

About an hour later, Gabe came into the room beaming. His eyes were misty with tears of joy. "It's a boy and a girl. Babies and Mommy are all doing fine."

"Congratulations, Dad," smiled Danielle, through her tears hugging Gabe. "When can we see them?" she asked excitedly.

"They are cleaning them up as we speak. We knew

it was twins, but we didn't know it was a boy and a girl. Liz says she's done. She tried to get the doctor to tie her tubes." They all laughed. "I told him if he touched her tubes, he wouldn't get paid."

"I'm sure that made him put down his scalpel real quick," laughed Jeff slapping his brother-in-law on the back. "Congratulations, Dad."

"Congratulations," said Greg holding out his hand to Gabe. Gabe took his outstretched hand with a big grin on his face.

"Thanks everyone. I'm going back to sit with Liz. I'll let you know when you can come in."

They walked down to the nursery, but only got to see the babies for a moment, before the nursery closed the curtains.

The twins were little tiny pink creatures with a thatch of black hair on top of their heads. No question of where that hair came from.

Danielle tried to get Greg to leave, but he wouldn't budge. He insisted on waiting to drive her home.

Putting on a happy face, she knocked softly and entered Liz's room. Smiling at each other in silent communication, they embraced.

"I'm so happy for you." They held hands. "You are going to make a wonderful mother. Gabe, we'll have to work on." They both laughed at the private joke they shared. Gabe was not the most patient person either of them had ever met. They both knew children would change him.

Danielle was silent on the drive home. Liz's words kept ringing in her ears. *Someday I'll be here for you. It will happen. You have to believe.*

It was only wishful thinking on her friend's part and they both knew it. Dr. West told her the possibility of her getting pregnant was slim to none. The chance of her carrying a baby to term was even slimmer. Her endometriosis was a severe case.

If only she and Greg had married four years ago, when they first became engaged. They would have a child by now, maybe two. She wiped at her silent tears.

She couldn't help feeling a little envious of Liz and Gabe. Danielle had always wanted children of her own, a husband and three, maybe four children. She wanted to adopt the fourth child.

She tried to push all thoughts of family and happily ever after to the back of her mind. She knew happily every after only happened in fairy tales and her life was far from a fairy tale.

Greg followed her inside the house watching her closely. He knew there was something weighing on her mind by the sad expression on her face and he knew what it was. It tore at his heart to see her hurting this way. She was trying to put up a brave front for him, but was not succeeding.

"Don't think about it." She looked up at him in surprise. "I was thinking the same thing you were. It should have been us in the delivery room tonight. Given a chance, it could still happen. We can have the family we've always wanted."

"Looks like you started without me," she whispered, turning away from him. "Can you please go? I'd really like to be alone tonight."

Tears spilled down her cheeks and she took a step closer to him. He didn't realize how much those words hurt. It would never be them, in a delivery room, but she couldn't bring herself to tell him. She didn't want his sympathy or his pity. What she needed was for him to hold her. She needed to feel loved. Tonight she needed Greg.

"I'm not leaving you like this." His hand reached out and caressed her cheek. "The paternity test results came back." Her head shot up to look at him in surprise. "Lexi is not my daughter. I knew it all along. I wouldn't dream of starting without you. You are the only woman I want to be the mother of my children. Give us a chance to make that happen. Let me stay with you tonight."

He pulled her into the circle of his arms and held her closely. Leaning back slightly, she stared up into his handsome face.

"Make love to me." She touched her finger to his lips to keep him from saying anything. "Please don't say anything. I don't want to be alone tonight. Make love to me. Let me make love to you. I need you, all of you. I don't want to think about tomorrow. We have now. Let's make the most of it."

She felt his body stiffen in response and he looked down into her upturned beautiful face. Her eyes still glistened with tears as she pulled his head down to hers. Their lips touched lightly at first, then the kiss deepened into a heated exchange.

Her lips never leaving his, she shrugged off her jacket and dropped it to the floor. Unzipping the matching pants, she wiggled out of them.

Danielle was left standing before him, clad only in her bra and panties. Greg unbuttoned his shirt and let it join the pile of clothes on the floor.

He swung her up in his arms and carried her to the bedroom. He placed her in the middle of the big queen size bed. Turning down the bedside lamp, it cast a soft warm glow in the room.

She admiringly watched him remove the rest of his clothes. His sleek brown torso begged for her touch. Mesmerized she watched him unzip and step out of his black trousers. The snug fitting briefs he wore hugged his firm hips like a second skin. Kneeling on the bed, she beckoned him closer with the crook of her finger.

Smiling, Greg moved closer. Leaning forward, she hooked her fingers on either side of his underwear and pulled it downward, until it pooled at his feet. Her hands ran up and down his strong hard powerful thighs.

He kneeled on the bed in front of her and Danielle touched his chest tentatively. Her hands explored his hair-roughened flesh with relish. Greg closed his eyes when her lips lightly touched his chest and then moaned when she took his nipple into her mouth. She licked and nipped the other nipple while her hands traveled down his flat stomach to his stiff rod. Steady fingers closed around him and Greg trembled.

Danielle pushed him onto his back and straddled him. Leaning over him, she touched her mouth to his. She nipped at his lips lightly at first. Then slowly covered his mouth hungrily. Her fingers toyed with his pert nipples before traveling back down to his stiff erection.

Ever so slowly her lips followed her hands. Greg lurched forward and gasped when her mouth touched him for the first time. Boldly she took him into her mouth and watched his body tense and then relax, under her ministrations.

When he could stand it no more, Greg pulled her down on top of him. His dark brown eyes devoured her as she unsnapped her teddy, pulled it over her head and tossed it to the floor. She took the condom from Greg's hand. Her hand moved over him in a silken caress as she put the condom on for him.

On bended knees, she raised herself up over him and with a slowness that stopped Greg's breath. He let out a loud gasp as she lowered herself. Danielle moaned and closed her eyes to savor the moment as she impaled herself.

It had been so long. The pleasure was so intense she threw back her head and gasped aloud. In the same slow steady rhythm, she moved up and down on him. Not able to stand any more of the exquisite torture, Greg took control and sped up the pace. He gripped her hips and drove into her with a fierceness that startled and pleased her. He rolled them over and pinned her beneath him, so he could have better control of the situation.

She met him thrust for thrust. Danielle screamed, as she was pushed higher and higher into a vortex of pleasure. Brilliant bright lights flashed before her eyes as she reached out and touched a small piece of heaven. Her descent back to earth was slow and peaceful.

Danielle looked up to see Greg smiling down at her. He moved inside her and she knew it wasn't over yet. He may have taken her to paradise, but he had yet to go there. This time they would go together.

Greg had held himself back to make sure she was satisfied. The flood of emotions began to spark anew when he started to move inside her again. He was taking her again to that faraway place where everything was magical.

She was disappointed when he withdrew from her, until his mouth covered her breast and then descended downward. She twisted and squirmed as he applied his expert fingers and mouth to her quivering body.

Danielle thought surely she would die from the pleasure of his touch. Her body was reaching that pinnacle again, when he slid back up her and entered her in one smooth stroke. Danielle moaned in pure bliss when her body again, exploded into a million pieces. This time Greg found his own release and collapsed on top of her quivering body. Exhausted and spent, they slept.

A few hours later Greg entering her from behind awakened her. She sighed in contentment and moved against his thrusting body. Danielle was in dreamland when he maneuvered her onto her stomach and came into her again. He squeezed her breast and nipped at her neck.

His hard sleek member moved in and out her wet

chamber smoothly. Her mind may have been half asleep, but her body was awake, aroused, and responding.

Greg was definitely trying to make up for lost time and she didn't mind one bit. This time when they both fell asleep, they slept the rest of the night.

Danielle was the first one awake the next morning. She stared at Greg's sleeping form with a mixture of regret and longing.

What they shared last night was pure magic. Her entire body was still tingling from the aftermath. Easing out of bed, she grabbed underwear, shorts and T-shirt and slipped out of the room. She took a long shower in the spare bathroom down the hall before dressing.

Chapter 9

Sitting down at the kitchen table, she began to reflect on the events leading up to the previous night. She knew going to bed with Greg was inevitable. The sexual attraction between them was so strong she couldn't fight it. The question was where would they go from here.

It was just good sex—correction, great sex—but you couldn't build a future on a physical relationship. Even now, with a clear head, she wanted to hop back into bed with him and forget about tomorrow.

Maybe they could have a strictly physical relationship, until they both found someone else in whom they were interested. Men did it all the time, so why couldn't she? Being male, Greg would probably jump at the chance to sleep with her with no commitment. She would make the suggestion to him when he woke up.

That settled, she put on a pot of coffee and started breakfast. She smiled at the closed door, when she heard the shower running. Picking up the clothes off the floor, she laid his things on the couch and put hers in a hall closet.

Minutes later Greg emerged wearing only his

trousers. He slipped his white shirt on and buttoned it down the front.

"Breakfast smells wonderful. I guess I really worked up an appetite. I'm starving," Greg said sitting down across from her.

They conversed lightly throughout the meal. It was only after Danielle washed the dishes that she finally decided to broach the subject of their sex life. Wringing her hands nervously, she followed him into the living room.

"Greg, I've been thinking. I have a solution to our little problem. Since we are so great in bed together, I suggest we get together when we need to release some sexual tension. We can lead separate lives and we can date other people." There, she'd said it and now there was no going back.

Greg stared at her in shock and disbelief. He never would have guessed those words would come out of Danielle's mouth. She wanted an open relationship.

"Let me get this straight. You want to have sex with me, but you don't want to be seen in public with me," voiced Greg between clenched teeth. He was furious. "Just so I'm clear on what you are suggesting. You want to screw me while you flit around from guy to guy until you find one who satisfies you more, and then I'm history. Is that what you are suggesting? You want to have an affair with me, but not a relationship?" he asked unbelievably.

She tried to remain calm in the face of his anger. Okay, so maybe it did sound a little lame. "I don't mind if we date sometimes, but I don't want to be committed to you. I thought you would like the idea. You can still see whomever you want and so can I," she added reasonably. "Most men would jump at the chance for the kind of relationship I'm offering you. It's no strings and no commitments."

"I'm not most men! If I had made the same suggestion

to you yesterday, you would have slapped my face for it. Now I understand completely. You take me to your bed, to see what you've been missing and suddenly you decide, you like it there. You want to stay there, but only on your terms. So it's Danielle's way or no way, again. Is that it?" He grabbed her wrist and yanked her to him. Angry brown eyes clashed with wide gray ones. "Let me tell you something Miss Roberts. If all I wanted was a lover, there are plenty of women out there who are a hell of a lot more experienced at pleasing a man than you are or that you will ever hope to be. Debra comes to mind," he added coldly. Her face paled and then turned red in embarrassment. "I don't want Debra or other women. I want you Danielle. I want more than quick, easy, uninvolved sex. That's not enough for me, and it's not enough for you. I don't just want your luscious body, lady. I want your heart and your soul. I want the complete package. If what you are looking for is sex, then go buy it. You have the money, honey, so why don't you go hire yourself a male hooker? You want a boy toy you can control. I'm not interested."

"You are more than interested. You may want a relationship, but I deserve a man I can trust. I don't trust you," she fired back.

"And that's supposed to be a news flash. It's not just me. You don't trust any man. The only man you ever trusted was your father and look how that turned out. Jack Masters walks on water. Jack Masters can do no wrong. He withheld your paternity from you for twenty years and you forgave him. I slept with someone else while we weren't even together and you can't get past it. You can't forget it."

"How can I forget it? You could have had a daughter from that union. You slept with another man's wife. You weren't even responsible enough to use protection. You went from my bed to hers and then back to mine in the space of what, five days? You never even told me about it. You were going to keep it a secret from me forever."

"There was nothing to tell. We weren't together. It was technically none of your business. For the record, I did use protection! I would never take a chance like that. I wouldn't put myself or you at risk." He closed his eyes and took a deep breath.

"So just how many times were you unfaithful that you didn't take a chance? Was Becky even the first?" she raged. "Get out! I don't ever want to see you again."

"Always the drama queen. When you get an itch, call me and I might consider taking care of it for you or I might not!" He snatched up his jacket and stormed out, slamming the door behind him.

Closing her eyes, she plopped down onto the sofa and punched the pillow. She hadn't meant to insult him or hurt his feelings. She thought it had been a great solution to their dilemma. It seemed like a good idea at the time. Now, she wasn't so sure.

Maybe she didn't think everything through suffi-ciently. The only thing on her mind was self-preservation. She didn't want to be hurt by him again. It was a dumb idea anyway.

Danielle lay back on the couch and hugged the overstuffed pillow to her chest, wishing it was the man she loved instead. This time, she had blown it. In the back of her mind, she knew Greg wouldn't go for the idea. He reacted the way she was hoping he would.

Using his key, Greg unlocked the door and went inside Mark's house. Jogging up the stairs, he went straight to Mark's bedroom. Mark was asleep in bed, but he was not alone. There was a shapely brunette stretched out next to him on the massive waterbed. He should have known his friend would not be alone.

Greg was about to back out the door, when Mark bolted up. The startled woman next to him let out a squeal and pulled the covers up to her chin.

"Greg, there is a thing in this day and time called the telephone," said a sleepy Mark rubbing his eyes. "What are you doing here at 9 o'clock in the morning?"

"I'm sorry to barge in like this, but I really need to talk to you. You are not going to believe what happened."

"Okay," said Mark pulling on his pants. Can you at least wait downstairs? I'll be there in a few minutes."

Greg was pacing back and forth when Mark came into the room. He was wearing a paisley silk robe.

"So what couldn't wait until after lunch? What's going on with you and Danielle, now?" asked Mark sitting down on the sofa.

"You are not going to believe this. Little Miss Morals and Principles suggested to me we have an open sexual relationship. She wants to sleep with me, but date other people."

"You're kidding." Mark laughed. "I would kill for a relationship like that. Finally a woman who thinks like I do. Maybe I should call Danielle," he teased.

"You are not even funny," snapped Greg glaring at his best friend. "This is not the kind of relationship I want. I want to marry this woman. She is everything to me. Something is wrong. This is not the Danielle I knew. There has to be a reason for her to suggest this and I intend to find out what it is. You and I both know how Danielle views your life. I'm telling you man, something is very wrong."

"Maybe this is her way of getting back at you because of what happened with Rebecca. Did I miss something? The kid is not yours, so why is she still ticked off? You know how high maintenance she is. Why are you putting yourself through this crap again?"

"Because I love her. Something doesn't feel right.

I think there's more to it than Rebecca. Last night was incredible and this morning she wakes up and does a complete 180-degree turn. I don't know what to think, but I do know I am not letting Danielle slip through my fingers again. This may be our last chance and I am not going to let her throw it away."

"Then play it her way for now. A woman like Danielle will not be content for very long with this kind of relationship. Don't all women want husbands, kids, and happily ever after. Play her game and see what happens. When you finally get the upper hand, turn the tables on her. You know she loves you. Use it to your advantage. All's fair in love and war and all that jazz. At least that's what I've been told."

"This isn't a game. This is our life," Greg said coming to his feet. "I will not lose her again," he vowed.

"Then play to win," Mark said. "Throw away the condoms. Use whatever means necessary to get her back. It wouldn't be the first time someone married because they were pregnant. Think about it man, if Danielle gets pregnant, she would marry you in a heartbeat. It would solve all your problems."

"That's exactly what got me in this mess. I would say by far, this is the dumbest suggestion you've made. Let me solve one problem at a time, not create new ones," Greg remarked. "I don't even know why I bother talking to you about this. What do you know about love or relationships? You run for your life after the second date. Your advice always stinks," said Greg on his way out the door.

"And yet you keep coming back." Mark laughed as the door closed behind his best friend.

Danielle was on her way out the door, when the phone rang. Dropping her purse and briefcase on the small table, she picked it up.

"Hi, honey how are you?" said the smiling voice of her father. "Did we miss anything exciting while we were gone? We just got back a little while ago."

"I'm fine. I missed you guys. How was your trip? How was the reunion?" Danielle asked sitting down in the Queen Anne chair. She did not want to get into what happened while they were away. She would have to tell them about it soon enough, if someone else didn't beat her to the punch.

"We had a wonderful time. We might even go back next year. How about a late lunch today and you can bring me up to date on everything? Listen I have to run, but I'll see you in the office. Tell Katy I will be in around 10 o'clock."

Greg picked up the phone to call Danielle. He slammed it back down in frustration. Picking up his jacket, he walked out the door. He had to see her. He wasn't sure what he was going to say, but he needed to see her. They couldn't leave things this way.

Damn you, Danielle. Have it your way. The sexual revolution has just begun. I will show you no mercy.

He drove to the Masters Tower to agree to her terms. He parked his car and took the elevator up to the twentieth floor.

Greg was determined to make sure she regretted her decision for an open relationship. He would flaunt Debra Nelson and whomever else he had to in front of her to make her face her true feelings. He remembered the saying "all's fair in love and war."

"Hi," said Greg, smiling at the receptionist. "Is Danielle Roberts in? Please tell her Greg Thomas is here."

Greg knew that Danielle was usually the first person to arrive at the office. Today was no exception.

Lost in her own little world, she read over several new contracts and jotted down notes. Her first appointment wasn't due in for another hour. So, leaning back in her chair, she closed her eyes. Greg's smiling face immediately came to her. No matter what she did, she couldn't seem to forget him. He was always there in the back of her mind and always in her heart.

She picked up the phone to call him, and then hung it up again. No. This was for the best. A purely physical relationship with him would only bring her heartache. She was now glad that he had declined her offer.

I must have been crazy or desperate to even suggest such a thing! Stop it Roberts! Forget about him! No man is worth putting yourself through that kind of hell again!

"Yes?" Danielle said, pushing the intercom button. She put the folder in her drawer and took out her next case.

"Danielle, Greg Thomas is here to see you. Do you want me to send him in?" asked Valerie with a smile in her voice.

Danielle's heart stopped and she dropped the pen she was holding in surprise. She stared at the intercom speechless. "Give me a few minutes," voiced Dani, recovering her voice and her composure.

She paced a few seconds before walking to the door. Taking a deep breath, she opened it and waved an impeccably dressed Greg inside.

He looked smashing in a dark gray business suit. His brown eyes were cold and emotionless as they met hers.

"Please have a seat. I didn't expect to see you again," said Danielle, nervously sitting down behind her desk. She folded her hands in her lap to still their trembling.

In truth, the desk gave her strength. It made her feel stronger and gave her enough courage to handle whatever it was he had to say to her. She felt invincible.

"I've been thinking about what you said." Puzzled, she watched him open his briefcase and take out his PDA. "You may want to jot these dates down." He called out several dates and she marked them on her calendar. "These are the dates I have free in the evenings. You may want to check those dates with your datebook to see if they coincide with your plans. If you get an itch on any other day, I suggest you either wait for me or get someone else to scratch it," he stated rather crudely before turning off his PDA and putting it back in his briefcase.

She blushed furiously at his cutting words. "I've changed my mind. I don't think this is such a good idea after all," she hedged. Slamming her book shut, she glared at him.

"Now that I've had more time to think about, I think it's a great idea. I can have my cake and eat it too. No pun intended."

Her face turned beet red and she came nervously to her feet. He followed suit and came around the desk to block her exit.

"This was an extremely bad idea. In fact, it's one of the worst I've had. I can't go through with this," she whispered not meeting his penetrating stare.

"Sure you can. After all, I am willing to play it your way, Danielle. What more do you want?" His questioning eyes met her nervous gray gaze. Greg caught her wrist and slowly drew her to him. Catching her hand, he placed it on the front of his crotch and held it there. "What's wrong, Dani? Isn't this what you want with no strings attached?" She tried unsuccessfully to pull her hand away. The heat from him burned through his trousers to her hand. She froze when she felt him jerk beneath her trembling fingers. "So tell me Princess, how does it feel to want something so bad? I've agreed to your terms. Now I have a few of my own. The nights we set aside for our little trysts are strictly ours. You will be there waiting for me at my home or yours in something sexy and inviting. No T-shirts allowed. You are never to say no, unless it's the wrong time of the month. It's over when one of us meets someone else they want to sleep with. During our 'relationship' we only have sex with each other. I must warn you. I have an insatiable appetite where you're concerned. I will take you whenever and wherever I choose and I promise you'll enjoy it. Take it or leave it."

She stared at him for several seconds. Her mind was telling her to say no, but somehow she couldn't form the words. She was physically drawn to him.

"No," she whispered shaking her head. Danielle looked down at her hand, not realizing he had removed his and she was caressing him on her own. Looking up into his somber face, she wrenched her hand away guiltily.

"Yes," he replied, lowering his head to hers. His lips grazed her cheek and his hand raised to catch her hair. He applied just enough pressure to force her head to tilt upward. He saw the indecision in her eyes as she looked up at him.

"Maybe." She whispered as she drowned in his eyes. Danielle unconsciously wet her dry lips with the tip of her tongue.

"Definitely." Their lips met and clung. The bargain was sealed. Danielle swayed into him and put her arms around his neck. Her lips parted under the pressure of his and his tongue entered her mouth. Their bodies melded into one as she stepped closer into the circle of his arms and molded her body to his. His tongue did a thorough exploration of her mouth, while his hands did the same with her body. Her nipples hardened under his caressing hands. "We'd better stop

while we still can. I didn't lock the door behind me."
His hands slid down her waist and he took a step back
from her.

"Ahem!" The discreet cough behind them startled her.

Danielle pulled away guiltily and looked up to see
her father standing in the doorway. "Dad!" She turned
red in mortification as she extracted herself from Greg
and walked the short distance to her father's open
arms. He hugged her enthusiastically, before kissing
her flushed cheeks.

"I knocked, but I guess you were to busy to hear me,"
her father coughed. He was more embarrassed than she
was. "Are you going to introduce me to your, friend?"
Jack took a step forward and held out his hand. "I'm
Jack Masters, Danielle's father." Greg turned to face
them, and she felt her father stiffen beside her. He
looked from Danielle to Greg in confusion and his
raised hand fell. "Hello, Greg. What brings you back to
town?"

"Unfinished business." Greg's eyes strayed to
Danielle and she flushed under his heated gaze.

"So it would seem," Jack retorted as his eyes shot
daggers at the man who dared to hurt his little girl.
"With Danielle or with Rebecca?"

Danielle lowered her head to her hand. She knew
there was a lecture in there somewhere and she would
hear it later. She watched the two men nervously.
There was no love lost between the two of them. An
uneasy silence followed as they stared at each other
and then at her.

"I've got to run," said Greg, ignoring her father's
question. "Danielle, I'll see you soon. Jack, it was inevitable that we would cross paths. I guess it might
as well be sooner than later. I'm back, so deal with it."

"I'll call you," Dani said earnestly while Jack
watched her suspiciously. She breathed a sigh of relief

as Greg left the room. She braced herself as she faced her father.

Jack was still eyeing her thoughtfully. "So Greg Thomas is back in town with a bang. I can't wait to see how he gets out of this one. I had hoped you would have the good sense to stay away from him," scolded Jack taking the vacant seat across from her desk. "Dani, don't get caught in the middle of this mess."

"Dad, please don't start. I don't want to hear any lectures. I can see someone has already filled you in on all the juicy details, so I won't have to. I don't want to talk about Greg. What you saw was no indication we are back together." His eyebrows went up in question. "It was purely physical. We are attracted to each other. That's all," said Danielle not too convincingly.

"Who are you trying to convince? Me or yourself? I have eyes, Danielle. I saw the way you were looking at him. You were practically making out with him in your office. You still love him."

"I'm not denying it, but I will not let him back into my life, at least not on a permanent basis."

"I don't think I want to hear this." He held up his hand to silence her. "You are setting yourself up to be hurt, again."

"Maybe I am, but it's my decision. At some point in time, you are going to have to let me live my own life. I choose to see Greg. He's my choice. He doesn't have to be yours. What time are you free for lunch?" Danielle asked changing the subject.

"One o'clock works for me. I'll meet you at the elevator." Jack came to his feet. He started to say something, but then thought better of it.

The rest of the morning was less eventful. Drew called and they made plans for dinner. Danielle was going to grill hamburgers and Drew was bringing the movie.

She met Jack promptly at 1 o'clock at the elevators.

They walked in the downtown tunnel to one of their favorite Mexican food restaurants.

Over lunch, Danielle tried to steer the conversation away from Greg, but Jack kept bringing it back. She did not want to discuss Greg with her father.

"How do you feel about Lexi being Greg's child? A custody fight could get ugly and I don't want to see you get caught in the middle of it."

"He received the results back. She's not his daughter. I guess now that narrows the field down to Jason and Richard."

"So he got lucky. The man cheated on you. If he did it once, he will do it again. You can't trust him."

"Dad, stop. I know how you feel about Greg. You've made no secret of it. You can save the lecture. Greg and I are not back together despite what you saw earlier. I've met someone. His name is Drew. He's a friend of Gabe's. He's a really nice guy."

"You're playing a dangerous game, kiddo. Be careful. You and Greg have too much baggage right now for you to add another person to the mix. Drew is going to get hurt. You are going to get hurt. It's inevitable if you keep up this fiasco. This game you are playing is a train wreck waiting to happen. I see it coming and I refuse to watch it happen."

After work, she dropped by to see her stepmother. Mrs. Mason, the housekeeper told Danielle that Karen was upstairs unpacking.

Danielle jogged up the stairs in search of her stepmother. She knocked on the door and was told to enter.

Karen dropped the armful of clothes she was holding and met Danielle in the middle of the room with a warm hug. "Danielle, I'm so glad to see you. How are you holding up? I can't believe what happened at the party," she said without preamble. "Your father was torn between murdering Greg and John."

"I see good news travels fast." She dropped down to the king-size bed. "I bet Dad couldn't wait to call you and share all the juicy details from today with you."

"Yes, he called me. He's worried about you and so am I. I'm so sorry about you and Greg. I really like him. I was happy to hear he was back in town. I thought it was a new beginning for the two of you. You guys are so perfect for each other."

"I also thought we had a chance," confessed Danielle sadly. "I guess we were both wrong. Let's not talk about Greg. Did you have a wonderful time on your trip?"

"It was glorious. My parents are both fine and they send their love. Sit there." Karen walked over to the closet. "Wait until you see what I bought for you."

Danielle's mouth dropped open when Karen pulled out a large suitcase. She rolled it over by the bed and opened it.

Danielle was overwhelmed. There was an assortment of business suits, dresses, pantsuits, and handbags. They were all designer fashions from some of the best shops in London. Heaven knows Lady Beatrice could afford it. Karen's parents were one of the oldest and wealthiest families in England.

"Are you sure you're okay? This can't be easy for you. I'm here if you need me. I'd like to help if I can."

"I know and thank you for caring. I'll be fine. Anyway, there is a new man in my life. His name is Drew Murray. Believe it or not, he's another friend of Gabe's." Karen rolled her eyes heavenward. "You can relax. I actually like this one. He's a nice guy. He is self-employed and has his own computer consulting company. We've gone out a couple of times."

"And what about Greg? Where does he fit into the picture? Honey, I know you still love him."

"We will probably date occasionally, but that's as far as it will ever go. Greg and I have no future. I know we can't go back to the way it use to be."

"Danielle, stop," said Karen, catching her hand and leading her to sit on the bed. "Is this smart? Wouldn't a clean break be easier?"

"It probably would be, but I'm not sure if I want him in or out of my life. Sorry to cut this visit short, but I have dinner plans. I'm grilling burgers for Drew." Danielle hugged her again. "Thank you again for the clothes. They will brighten my wardrobe considerably, according to Dad. He has already given me a standing invitation to bring Drew for dinner so you guys can check him out."

Chapter 10

Danielle was putting the last two burgers on the grill when the phone rang. She wiped her hands on a towel.

"Hello," she said picking up the cordless phone. Leaning over, she turned down the burner on the gas grill and closed the lid.

"Danielle, it's Doris Thomas," said the warm friendly voice. "It's been a long time. How are you?"

"Fine, Mrs. Thomas. How are you? Did you get the flowers I sent to the hospital?" Danielle smiled into the receiver in surprise.

"Yes and they were beautiful. Thank you. I'm doing fine, I'm not letting a little thing like a stroke stop me," said the friendly voice. "Since you and Greg are seeing each other again, I thought it would be nice if you came to his surprise birthday party. It's next Saturday night?"

"Mrs. Thomas, it's nice of you to invite me, but Greg and I are not back together." Guilt stabbed at her heart and she gripped the phone. She couldn't tell his mother the truth about their relationship.

"You will be," she stated confidently. "You and Greg love each other so much. It's only a matter of time before you two work things out. So how about it? Travis and Anita would love to see you. And you can see my new granddaughter," she added persuasively. "All of Greg's old friends will be here. Bobby Shedd and his wife are flying in from Atlanta. Everyone would love to see you."

Danielle gripped the phone tightly not knowing what to say. She liked the older woman and would love to see her again, but to spend an evening in the same room with Debra and some of Greg's other ex-girlfriends was putting herself to the test.

She hadn't seen any of the Thomases, or the friends she and Greg had, since Travis' wedding two years ago. Travis and Anita had a two-month-old baby girl, Brianne.

Greg had told her what an adorable, even-tempered baby she was. She was sure she didn't want to spend an evening trading barbs with Marie and Leo, her two favorite Thomases.

"What time should I be there and do I need to bring anything?" She found herself asking against her better judgment.

"If you can be here by 7 o'clock to help me get everything ready I would really appreciate it. Travis is going to keep Greg busy for most of the day, so we can get things set up."

"I'll see you then." Danielle stared at the telephone in her hand. *Why am I doing this? I don't want to give Greg the wrong impression.*

Greg was reading over a divorce decree when visions of Dani half-clothed kept flashing in his mind. His body jerked in remembrance of her mouth on him.

He got up from his desk and paced the room. Staring out the window, he couldn't appreciate the spectacular view today. He only had one thing on his mind.

Okay, Thomas, forget her for five minutes. You have work to do. Sit back down and concentrate.

He sat down at his desk and picked up the file again. He laid the papers on the desk and took out the contents.

It's no use. I have to see her. I have to touch her, to taste her.

He lay down the papers and closed the folder. He picked up the phone, and dialed Dani's office to make sure she was in before he put his plan into motion. Slipping the condom in his wallet, Greg pulled on his suit jacket and left the office.

Get ready Roberts, because here I come. You are about to be swept off your feet into a whirlwind of pure bliss. I only hope you are ready for this. I'm giving you what you asked for Dani, a no frills sexual encounter.

When he got to her office, Valerie picked up the phone to buzz Dani. He stopped her, by putting his finger to his lips.

"Don't buzz her. I want to surprise her," smiled Greg. "You might want to hold all her calls until further notice."

Danielle was reading over a contract, when a sharp rap on the door startled her. Before she could respond, Greg strode in smiling. He locked the door behind him and advanced on her with a wicked gleam in his eyes.

She looked at him a bit puzzled and rounded the desk to meet him. Dani melted in his arms as their lips met and clung. His hungry mouth explored, teased, and devoured hers. His tongue plunged into the sweet haven of her mouth while his hands moved over her body in a hungry caress. Coming up for air at last, his mouth left hers.

"You taste like an apple," he smiled, nibbling her bottom lip. "Mmm, I love apples. They are the forbidden fruit."

"I had an apple as my afternoon snack. This is a nice surprise. What are you doing here?" she asked caressing his razor-stubbled cheek.

"This." He lifted her off her feet and carried her to the desk, where he deposited her on top of it. "You see, Roberts, I've had this fantasy about you and a polished oak desk for a long time." Smiling, she watched him push the intercom button. "Valerie, definately hold all Ms. Roberts' calls for the next hour."

"What's gotten into you? You've never been a spur of the moment sort of guy. I like it," said Danielle kissing him full on the lips.

"You've gotten into me. You are in my blood, lady. In a few minutes, I'll be in you," whispered the seductive deep voice.

He pulled the red silk blouse from the waistband of her skirt and slipped it over her head, carelessly tossing it aside. She kicked off her pumps and helped him out of his jacket. Sure hands pushed her black skirt up to her waist.

Danielle leaned back and watched him slide the panties and panty hose down her long shapely legs. Pulling him closer, she unsnapped and unzipped his pants. Laying the pants on a nearby chair, he came back and kneeled down between her parted thighs.

"Whatever you do, babe, don't scream," warned Greg before his mouth covered her hot pulsating mound. She lurched forward and then bit her hand to keep from crying out in pleasure.

He expertly brought her body to the boiling point, only to pull away before she spilled over. She wiggled and squirmed under the heated tongue-lashing he was administering to her quaking body.

Danielle was about to protest when his mouth left

her body. The protest died on her parted lips when she heard the distinct tear of plastic. In one smooth thrust he was inside her and sent her careening over the edge. Clasping her legs around his waist, she clung to him as he pounded into her unmercifully. Withdrawing again, he lifted her off the desk and turned her around facing away from him. She braced her hands on the desk and let out a loud gasp as he entered her.

He cupped her breast, and squeezed as he drove into her. Danielle was again spinning in that same familiar vortex of pleasure. When her body exploded, she went limp against him. Finding his own release, Greg tensed and then relaxed against her. Slowly they both sank back to reality.

"So tell me, Mr. Thomas, do you have any more wild fantasies you care to try out?" In answer he nibbled her ear, before turning her around to face him. Then, his mouth covered hers in an incredibly tender kiss.

They dressed in silence. Danielle watched him dispose of the condom, without comment. Greg had told her he would take care of the birth control problem.

"I'm not going to tell you, sweetheart. I'll show you when the time comes. Well I guess you passed the test," said Greg in a distant voice slipping on his jacket.

"What test?" she asked not sure she wanted to hear the answer. She tensed waiting for his reply.

"The anytime, any place test. You were so hot and ready for me. It's hard to believe you were celibate for the past two years. I guess you have a lot of lost time to make up for. I'll see you next week, for our next appointment," he stated coldly, closing the door behind him.

Danielle flinched as if he had slapped her. Her body was still trembling from the passion they shared, and it had only been a test.

She was so furious she threw her date book at the closed door. Now she knew firsthand what it felt like to be used. He had treated her like a wanton and it was all her own fault. She had made her bed, so now she had to lay in it.

So what am I going to do now? I started this train wreck, so I might as well stay on and enjoy the ride. Tomorrow night is his party and I'm not sure I can face him.

Danielle sat down at her desk. Leaning back in the overstuffed chair she closed her eyes and unconsciously rubbed her temples.

I could always take the coward's way out and cancel. Or I could go there and make Greg uncomfortable? She smiled at that idea. He deserved it after the way he treated me just now. I can't wait to see the expression on Greg's face when everyone yells surprise and he sees me there. I can tempt, tease, and tantalize and go home alone. It would serve him right.

"Danielle," said Valerie buzzing the intercom. "David Saxon is here to see you. He's a few minutes early."

"Give me five minutes and show him in." She came quickly to her feet and fumbled through her purse for her perfume. She lightly sprayed into the air. Turning on the small hand-held fan, she circled the room with it to circulate the perfume smell.

She squirted the breath freshener into her mouth and swallowed before giving the room the once over. Satisfied, she opened the door.

"Hello, I'm Danielle Roberts, please come in." She watched the tall elegantly dressed gentleman come to his feet and walk toward her. She extended her hand to him and he caught it.

The rest of the afternoon was less eventful. On her way home from work, she stopped off at the liquor store to get a bottle of red wine, to go with the spaghetti she was having for dinner. Tonight was the one night she had to herself and she was going to make the most of it.

After cooking, she took a long, relaxing, hot bubble bath. It helped to ease her tired muscles and relax her. She hadn't been relaxed since Greg came back to town.

Not tonight Roberts. No men allowed. So don't think about him. Think about anything other than him.

She dressed in a two-piece shorts sleep set and padded out to the kitchen. Popping a plate of spaghetti into the microwave, she put a piece of garlic bread in the toaster oven. She poured a liberal amount of red wine into a wineglass and waited for the timers to go off.

Carrying the plate and the glass of wine to the living room, she sat them down on the coffee table. She picked up the remote and switched on the television. She was halfway through dinner and the movie when the phone rang.

No calls tonight. I just want one quiet peaceful night alone. I need tonight people. Leave a message and I will get back to you tomorrow.

She waited for the machine to click on, before going over to turn the ringer off. Beep. "Danielle, it's Greg. I'm sorry for what I said this afternoon. It was thoughtless and insensitive. I agreed to play by yours rules, so I shouldn't take my anger out on you. Call me when you get home. Please let me know if you'd like to have dinner tomorrow night."

She caught herself as her hand was poised to pick up the receiver. Dropping her hand, she backed away from the phone.

He probably thought no one remembered his birthday. How could she forget? Greg was turning thirty-five. Danielle only hoped Doris could pull off the surprise without him getting suspicious.

Greg was a suspicious person by nature anyway. He questioned everything. He believed no one did anything without a reason. It would be hard to pull one over on him.

Greg stared at the phone in his hand. He had no intentions of spending his birthday alone. He wanted to spend it with Dani. If that fell through, he would call Mark for a boys' night out.

This was the first year his mother actually forgot his birthday. His whole family forgot. He was disappointed because his mother always made a big deal out of birthdays.

Danielle arrived at the Thomas home promptly at 7:00 P.M. She took a deep steadying breath before she got out of her car. She locked her car door, dropped her keys in her purse, and slid the strap onto her shoulder. She nervously clutched the gift in her left arm and raised her right hand to ring the doorbell.

When the door opened, she stared briefly into the smiling brown eyes of Doris Thomas. The tall dark woman held out her open arms to Danielle and she walked into them. They embraced each other warmly.

"Let me look at you," said Doris beaming from ear to ear. "You are a sight for sore eyes. You look beautiful. I'm so glad you could make it."

She pushed Danielle at arms length so she could take a good look at her. Dani was dressed in a Rayon two-piece dark purple pantsuit. The jacket was short sleeved and slightly low cut, with a pinched waist that stopped just past her rear. Her hair was loose and bounced on her thin shoulders in a mass of curls.

Greg's mother was clad in a black jumpsuit, with a red and black belt at the waist. Her once-long hair was now cut in a short sophisticated style. She had lost a

considerable amount of weight and looked stunning
for sixty.

"Thank you, and thank you for inviting me. You look
pretty incredible yourself. You have lost a lot of weight."

"You know me. I'm always on somebody's diet.
Come on in." She pulled Danielle into the house and
closed the door.

"I thought I heard voices," said Anita approaching
them carrying a small wiggling bundle. She hugged
Danielle and placed the baby in her arms. "Meet your
Aunt Dani, sweetie."

Danielle's heart constricted when baby Brianne
smiled at her and caught her finger. She was indeed a
beautiful child. A mop of black curly hair covered her
head and her dark eyes sparkled like jewels. She was
dressed in a red and white sundress.

"That's it, Travis," said the aggravated voice. "We
have been to almost every store in the mall. I am tired
and I am ready to go home. I can't even believe I let
you talk me into stopping here."

"One more stop," said Paul. "I want to get a bottle
of wine. I'm making dinner tomorrow night for a very
special lady."

"They are all special," was Greg's sarcastic reply. "I
must be nuts for letting you two waste my whole day
and part of the night. Let's get the wine and go home.
I might have plans tonight."

"Damn I knew I forget something," said Paul apolo-
getically. "I forget to tell you Danielle called and said
she was busy tonight."

"You forgot," Greg seethed. "That's just great.
Thanks for nothing little brother. You better hope you
never need a kidney or something."

* * *

"Sorry to run out on you guys, but I'm dropping Bri off at my parents. I'll be back to help out as soon as I can," said Anita. Picking up the diaper bag, she reached for the baby and Danielle placed a kiss on her forehead, before placing her in her mother's arms.

They were just putting the finishing touches on the house, when the guests started to arrive. Mrs. Thomas greeted them while Danielle chatted with Anita's brother John, who was roped into being the D.J.

Danielle was pouring herself a glass of punch when she heard the approaching footsteps. She whirled around and froze.

"Well, if it isn't the little uptown girl," said Leo walking over to Danielle. "I knew it was only a matter of time before you graced us with your presence, Princess Danielle."

"Hello, Leo. I heard you were home. Is this another short visit or do you intend to stay for a while this time?" smiled Danielle sweetly.

"Oh, I don't know. I thought maybe I'd visit Highland Park, or is it Garland now? Who knows where I might stumble into next. I'd keep my doors and windows locked if I were you, Princess. I've been in prison a long time, and with my appetite I might just gobble you up."

Danielle knew a threat when she heard one. She shivered at the coldness and hatred in his black eyes. He leered at her and then walked away. Dani rubbed at the chill bumps on her arms.

"Are you okay?" asked Anita coming further into the room. "Looks like I got back just in time. What did he say to you?"

"Leo was being Leo. It's not important," said Danielle changing the subject. "Would you like some punch?" Her hand shook as she picked up the ladle.

"You are shaking like a leaf." She took the ladle

from Danielle and placed it in the punch bowl. "Now tell me what Leo said."

Danielle repeated the conversation to her word for word. Anita was fuming when she finished.

"Anita let it go please. Leo is harmless. This is Greg's birthday party. I won't ruin it by causing trouble between him and his brother."

"I'll drop it for now. But I won't let it go and neither should you. Leo was pretty bad before he went to prison, but now he's worse. He's not harmless, Danielle. I'm afraid to be alone in the same house with him. Sometimes, I catch him watching me, and he just smiles. He gives me the creeps. Travis had a talk with him, and of course Leo said I was imagining things. I know he's only been here two months, but he hasn't lifted a finger to do anything. Mom washes his clothes, puts them away, cooks his meals, washes dishes, and even makes up his damn bed. He stays out all hours of the night and then sleeps most of the day. If Greg knew, he'd have a fit."

"If Greg knew what?" Marie asked looking from Anita to Danielle. "Who invited you? How did you get here, I didn't see a horse-drawn carriage out front?"

"I can't believe you missed it. I parked it right next to your broom," Danielle shot back rising to her taunt.

"Ladies, play nice. Mom invited her," supplied Anita. "You know she thinks of Danielle as one of the family," she smiled sweetly.

"Here comes my guest now," smiled Marie waving Debra over to where they were standing. "I'm glad you made it, girlfriend. I was getting worried."

"I got tied up in traffic," said Debra, glaring at Danielle. She smoothed down her tight minidress and adjusted the bodice.

"I'm sure you're used to being tied up," mumbled Danielle under her breath. Anita stifled a giggle and elbowed her lightly.

"Please excuse us, ladies. We need some fresh air,"

said Anita, catching Danielle by the arm and steering her away. Danielle and Anita left the two witches of Oak Cliff staring after them. They went out to the patio and sat down. "I have no idea why Marie invited her. She's not important. Travis and Greg should be here soon. We specifically told Travis to have Greg here at eight o'clock."

They both looked up when the sliding glass door opened. Mark Carter, Greg's best friend, came over and kissed both their cheeks.

"It's good to see you again, Danielle," smiled Mark. "Anita, Aunt Doris is looking for you. I'll keep Danielle entertained while you're gone. We haven't chatted in, what, almost two years? We have a lot of catching up to do."

"That's what I'm afraid of," said Anita coming to her feet. "Give her a break, Mark. No passes and no lectures tonight, please. Go easy on her."

Mark took her vacated seat without comment. He waited until Anita went back inside before turning to look at her. "So Danielle, what exactly are you doing here?" asked the tall, dark and handsome playboy. Mark was always impeccably dressed in black and straight to the point.

"I'm here for the party," she answered sweetly folding her hands in her lap. Her eyes met his. "Aren't you?"

"I think you know what I mean. Make up your mind, sweetheart. Either you want Greg in your life or you don't, but stop playing these stupid little head games with him," he warned. "You are making a big mistake."

"I don't particularly care what you think, Mark. This is my life. I get to choose how I want to live it. You have no say. You're Greg's confidant, not mine."

"You are some piece of work. You are by far the original drama queen. If all you want is an experienced lover, I'd be happy to volunteer my services."

"Thank you, but I think I'll pass," Danielle snapped

blushing under his stare. "I'm a little more discriminating than you are."

"Are you? You almost made love with me two years ago. I can definitely see why Greg keeps coming back for more," he taunted.

"Am I ever going to live that incident down, or are you going to throw it in my face every possible chance you get?" she snapped. "Keep your voice down. What if someone hears you?"

"There is no one out here, but the two of us," he stated looking around the empty backyard. "You know if you wanted to end things permanently with Greg, all you have to do is tell him what almost happened on our date."

Danielle sat frozen. Her eyes clashed with his and she saw the amusement in his dark eyes. "You are enjoying this aren't you? Well I am not playing your game. You and I both know I only turned to you to hurt Greg. Nothing happened between us. We both had too much to drink, but came to our senses before anything happened. You are a first-class jerk and will always be one." With that parting comment, Danielle shot to her feet and stormed back into the house. She was so shaken up by Mark's words that she had to get out of there. Danielle couldn't stay now. She found Mrs. Thomas in the kitchen.

What if Mark told Greg what almost happened between them? Then it really would be over for them, for all of them. Greg wouldn't understand. She didn't understand how it happened either.

"I'm sorry, Mrs. Thomas, but I can't stay." She headed for the door, before anyone could stop her. As she opened it, she came face to face with Greg. He stared at her in confusion.

Chapter 11

"Surprise!" Everyone yelled in unison. They all laughed at the shocked expression on Greg's face. He was truly surprised.

Danielle tried to move past him, but he caught her hand to prevent her departure. Her startled gray eyes met his pleading gaze. She tried to look away, but couldn't break eye contact.

"Please stay," Greg whispered for her ears only. Danielle nodded and closed the door behind them.

"It's good to see you," Travis said smiling at her. Travis embraced her warmly and she returned the hug.

"It's good to see you too, Travis. I saw Brianne. She is so adorable. I'm so happy for you and Anita."

"She is pretty cute isn't she? I'm a little biased, but isn't she the most beautiful baby you've ever seen?"

"I second that," smiled Paul moving forward and hugging Danielle. "It's good seeing you again, Danielle."

Danielle remained at Greg's side for most of the evening. Debra tried unsuccessfully to keep him away from her, but he kept coming back.

Her otherwise pleasant evening turned into a nightmare when Mark's date showed up. Danielle turned white and almost dropped the cup she was bringing to her lips.

Nurse Rolonda Sanders from St. John's Hospital smiled up at Mark. He kissed her lightly before pulling her over to meet Greg and Danielle.

Greg was getting her a glass of punch, when Mark and Rolonda walked up. Mark introduced them and Danielle remained cool. Rolonda stared at her puzzled.

She asked Danielle if they had met before. Danielle denied it smoothly and almost lost her composure when Rolonda asked her if she had any children.

Rolonda informed her she was an ER nurse. In the end she told Danielle she would eventually remember where she had seen her.

She caught Mark watching her curiously. He knew something was amiss, but didn't know what. He watched Dani's expression, when he informed her he would let her know when Rolonda remembered her. Danielle wished he would just mind his own business for a change, but then that wouldn't be Mark.

She panicked and slipped out to the kitchen. Turning on the cold water, she splashed some onto her face and blotted it dry with a paper towel. She took a deep breath before turning around. She let out a startled squeal when she saw Leo blocking her path.

"Just the piece I was looking for. Oh pardon me. I mean person. So elegant. So beautiful, and so untouchable. Never a hair out of place. Are you like that in bed? Does Greg ever mess up your hair? I bet you are a wildcat in bed." Danielle stared at him in anger and disgust. "How do you know Mark's date? The expression on your face was priceless when you saw her. Come to think of it, that's not the first time I've seen you and Mark so close. You got pretty upset with him earlier out back. Is there something Greg should know? He was gone two long years. A lot can happen in that time."

"I don't know what you're talking about," Danielle lied looking for an escape, but not finding one without brushing up against him. "Greg will be looking for me. I have to go."

He advanced on her, blocking her between the sink and his body without touching her. When he reached out to touch her face, Danielle turned her head away. Leo only smiled and grabbed her chin with the same hand.

"Now let's start again, shall we? How do you know the babe with the good doctor? Are you sleeping with Mark? Is he as good as they say?" Danielle tried to jerk her face from his grasp, but he tightened his hold, causing her to wince in pain. "I'd hate to bruise such a beautiful delicate work of art."

"Then let go. I don't know Mark's date. I've never met her. Even if I did know her it's none of your business. Let go of me," she said tense and shaking.

"Brave words from someone who's trembling like a little school girl. What's the matter, never been this close to a real man before?"

"If you were a real man you wouldn't be trying to intimidate me." Danielle shoved at him and he laughed.

"We could have some fun if you would just relax a little. Are you always this uptight, Princess? Do you ever let your hair down and have fun?"

"You're not my type, Leo. Yes, I know how to relax and have fun, but you see I'm not attracted to the criminal element."

"Leo!" Mark hissed barreling into the room. Leo released her, held up his hands and took a step back. "Have you lost your mind? If I had been Greg, I would kill you for touching her." His eyes strayed to Danielle. "Are you okay?" She nodded and slipped past Leo to stand behind Mark.

"We were just talking. Why are you so protective

toward Greg's girlfriend? Is there something we should all know? Now I see how it is. Are you doing her, too? I wonder what good old Greg would say if he knew his fancy little piece was sleeping with his best friend."

"He'd say you are full of it. Your imagination knows no bounds. I guess it gave you something to do while you were in lock up. Get out of here or I will tell Greg what you were doing in here. He won't be as lenient as I am."

"Is she any good, Doc?"

Danielle turned red in embarrassment and stayed shielded behind Mark so Leo couldn't see her face.

"I guess she would have to be to make you betray your best friend," Leo added before turning to walk away.

"I wouldn't know," he retorted. "Why don't you ask your brother that question? But I'm sure you won't like the answer he gives you. Stay away from Danielle. Do I make myself clear?"

Leo glared from Mark to Danielle still shielded behind him. He caught a glimpse of her crimson face and something flashed in his dark beady eyes.

"I'm right," he smirked winking at Danielle. "Princess, you are one busy woman. You must have all sorts of hidden talents to keep both Greg and Mark happy. Maybe you like threesomes. I always figured you for the type who would just lay there," he sneered. "From Mark's expression, I guess I was wrong. How about it, Doc? Is she any good?"

Mark punched him and he went reeling back into the table. He charged Mark and was knocked back into the table a second time.

"Don't try me, Leo! I want you out of here right now! I don't know what kind of grudge you have against Danielle and I don't really give a damn, but this is Greg's birthday party and I am not going to let you ruin it the way you ruin everything else. There's the door. Use it."

"Who do you think you are? This is my mother's house. You can't order me around. You leave and take that tramp with you."

"Greg bought this house for your mother. You are not only disrespecting Danielle, but you are disrespecting your mother by forcing yourself on your brother's girlfriend. Leave while you can or face the consequences."

"I won't forget this. You will both pay for this. Nobody treats Leo Thomas like this and gets away with it!" he yelled slapping his hand to his chest. "No woman should ever come between brothers or friends. This is your fault," he raged at Danielle. "Princess, you will regret the day you were ever born. You will pay dearly for this. That's a promise. You made a serious mistake and I won't forget it, Doc. You'd better watch your back."

"I always do," stated Mark following Leo to the door. "Cowards attack from the back. I want to see you coming. Be a man and come straight at me." Silence filled the room and the door slammed behind Leo.

Danielle was shaking when he left. Mark pulled out a chair for her and pushed her gently into it. She hugged her arms to still her quaking.

"Don't let him get to you Danielle. He's all talk. He knows if he tries anything with you, Greg will kill him. He just needs some time to cool off. You stay here. I'll go find Greg." Her eyes flew to the back door with apprehension. "You're safe. He won't come back. I promise. Sit down and try to take it easy until I get back. I'll only be gone a few seconds."

Danielle was not reassured. She was terrified. Leo was out of control and he now blamed her for being thrown out of his mother's home. What if he came after her? She was lost in thought when a hand touched her shoulder.

Startled, Danielle jumped to her feet. Staring up at Greg with fear in her eyes, she flew into his open arms. He hugged her to him protectively.

"It's all right," he soothed, brushing her hair with his hands. "I'm here, babe. Nothing is going to happen to you. I promise. Leo will not come after you. I'll talk to him." His arms tightened around her and he kissed the top of her head. Pulling her down onto his lap, he held her until she stopped trembling. "You're coming home with me tonight. No arguing." Danielle nodded and buried her head into the curve of his neck.

After two glasses of wine, she was calm enough to rejoin the party. She and Greg left the kitchen hand in hand.

Danielle breathed a sigh of relief when they left. She and Greg spent the next half hour chatting with old friends of Greg's. She was more than ready to leave by the time the party was over.

After everyone had left, she and Greg said their goodnights. Dani followed him back to his house. This was not exactly the way she wanted to see his new home.

When they arrived, he gave her the grand tour starting with the large cozy den. The room was two steps down off the hall entrance. The brick fireplace made it homey and comfortable. There was a cherry wood coffee table in front of the blue overstuffed couch. In one corner was a pair of matching easy chairs. There was also a stereo, a big screen television, DVD player, and a built-in bar in the other corner.

The kitchen was all white. It didn't look as though he had even been in it before. Everything was incredible. Unlike her house, there were no glasses in the sink. The formal dining room was also spotless. He had a large carved wood table, with eight chairs and nothing else. He also had a small kitchen table in the small breakfast nook off the kitchen. It had a bowl of apples and oranges on top, and a newspaper.

There was a full bathroom downstairs and a spare bedroom, which he had converted into an office. Inside were a desk, computer, and printer and fax machine. There were two file cabinets and a small table in the corner.

His workout room was conveniently across the hall from his workroom. There, he had a home gym, stair stepper, life cycle, and free weights.

There were three additional bedrooms upstairs, two guest rooms and the master bedroom. His room was the only one with furniture. The black queen-size waterbed filled the massive room. A matching dresser and chest of drawers took up a good portion of the room.

Danielle opened the sliding glass door off the balcony and stepped outside. Below his bedroom window was a huge swimming pool.

Greg walked up behind her and put his arms around her waist. She leaned back against him and breathed in his fragrance.

"I'm glad you came tonight." He planted soft kisses on her neck. "You being there means a lot to me."

"Me, too. I love your home. It's beautiful. Not only that, but it's so you. You have done a remarkable job with this place."

"Thank you. I like it, too. I knew the first time I walked inside I was home. This place says 'me.'"

She turned around in his arms and pulled his head down to hers. Dani's lips parted under his. He swung her up into his arms and carried her to bed.

Mark's words kept ringing in his head. Forget the condoms. Get her pregnant and she'll marry you.

Greg knew he couldn't do that to her. Their relationship was already on shaky ground. Bringing a baby into their lives would only complicate things further.

They made love for what seemed like hours. Exhausted, they lay spent and content in each other's arms.

"Can we talk?" asked Danielle absently running her fingers through the hair on his chest. "I feel we have so much unresolved."

"What's on your mind? Talk to me. The lines of communication are open. What do you want to know?" he asked looking down at her.

"Why did you sleep with Becky?" Danielle didn't pull any punches. She went straight for the jugular. "Were you drunk or did you know what you were doing?"

Greg took a deep breath and closed his eyes. He knew Danielle wouldn't accept anything less than the truth and she deserved nothing less.

"No, I wasn't drunk. I knew what I was doing. I took John's fiancée—now his wife—to bed to get back at him and to get back at you. I know how stupid it sounds, but it's the truth. It happened the night of the Christmas party at your parents' house. As I recall, we weren't on the best of terms that night. I was witness to a fight between John and Becky. She left furious at him. I came to her defense and John accused me of sleeping with his fiancé. It escalated from there. Jack reprimanded us like children and I lost it. Then . . ."

"You and I had a fight about my father. I gave you back your ring and told you the wedding was off and you stormed out of the house." His arms tightened around her.

"I ran into Becky by pure accident at a night club. We had a few drinks and one thing led to another. When I woke up the next morning, regret does not even come close to what I was feeling. I felt like a total idiot for using her. She was as upset as I was. We parted and never saw each other again."

"I went to your condo that night to apologize. I was wrong to do what I did. I knew you were with someone else when you didn't come home. You never knew I was there. I must have left before you came home the next morning. I knew it was partially my fault. I pushed you away. I pushed you into the arms of another woman. I can accept that. I just find it hard to think about the woman whose arms I pushed you into."

They chatted into the wee hours of the morning.

The next day, Greg dropped by his mother's house without calling. He wanted to catch Leo off guard. He knew his mother would be at church and he didn't want her to witness a confrontation between him and his brother.

He heard loud music when he stopped the car. Shaking his head, he used his key and went inside. He found his younger brother sprawled on the couch with the stereo blasting and the television on. He was drinking a beer with his lunch.

Greg walked into the living room without saying a word. Leo didn't even notice him. He turned off the stereo and his brother jumped to his feet. They stared at each other for several seconds, neither saying a word.

"I didn't do anything to her," he said defensively backing away. "They are both lying. Mark is the one making time with your girlfriend."

Greg kept approaching saying nothing as his brother backed away. Grabbing Leo, Greg slammed him against the wall. "I will say this one time and one time only," hissed Greg through clenched teeth. "Stay away from Danielle. Don't go near her again or I will forget we're brothers. That's simple enough even for you to understand." Releasing him, he shoved him away and stormed out of the house. He had to get away from him for both their sakes.

The days and weeks that followed were a mixture of pain and pleasure. The pain was because she knew without a doubt she would always love Greg and she could never give him the family he desperately wanted. The pleasure was each night spent in his arms.

Although he was never out of her heart when she had let her guard down. He had somehow eased his way back into her life. She saw less and less of Drew and more and more of Greg.

She also spent a lot of time with Liz and the babies. At their christening, she and Gabe's brother, Antonio, were godparents.

The service was beautiful and the babies were little angels. Greg went with her to the christening and the reception.

Things got a little tense for Danielle when Drew showed up. She smiled nervously as Drew walked over to them, but then relaxed when he and Greg shook hands. He told Dani he had no hard feelings because he had known from the start Greg had her heart.

Even Jack and Karen were happy to see her and Greg back together. Well, maybe not Jack. Karen was thrilled for them. They joined her parents for dinner a couple of times at her stepmother's invitation.

There were several close calls, and quite a few arguments, but Jack and Greg got through the evening without any bloodshed. For Danielle's and Karen's sake, they made an effort to get along. Jack shocked everyone by extending an open invitation to Greg to his Country Club to play golf.

Chapter 12

"It was nice of you to invite us to lunch," said Rolonda sitting down on the sofa. "You are a wonderful cook Greg. I hate that Danielle couldn't join us."

"He's no Chef Tell. He can only cook one meal and that was it." Mark laughed slapping Greg on the back.

"Thank you, Rolonda, but I'm afraid Mark is right for once. This is the extent of my culinary skills, the Danielle Roberts special."

Rolonda frowned.

"What's wrong?" Greg asked meeting her troubled expression. "Every time I mention Dani's name you get this odd look on your face. Are you remembering something?"

"For some reason, her name and her face seem familiar to me. It's almost like we met before your party. I forget names, but not faces."

They watched her come to her feet and walk over to the picture on the mantle above the fireplace. She picked it up and studied it intently.

It was a portrait of them taken about four years ago. The only difference in Dani then and now was that Danielle's long curly hair was now shoulder length.

Rolonda turned to face Greg and Mark with a troubled

look on her face. She replaced the picture and walked back to the sofa and sat down.

"Now I remember her. I'm not sure I should say anything," she answered looking from Greg to Mark. "If this is her secret, then she should be the one to tell it, not me. I think you should ask her."

"Rolonda, for God's sake don't keep us in suspense," said Mark impatiently. "What secret is Danielle keeping from Greg? Quit stalling. Spill it or walk home."

"You're so gallant, Mark. I probably shouldn't be the one to tell this. If she wanted you to know, she would have told you."

Mark pulled her aside and whispered something in her ear. His words were followed by a playful nip to her neck.

Greg saw the surrender in her eyes.

"About a year and a half ago when I was working ER at St. John's, Danielle came into the emergency room. She was experiencing severe pain in her pelvic area." She paused and looked over at Greg. "She had a severe case of endometriosis. The doctor performed a laparoscopy on her. Although the surgery was a success, the chances of her getting pregnant are slim. She was crushed when the doctor told her she may never become pregnant."

Her words hit Greg like a physical blow. Danielle had endometriosis. He was very familiar with the term. His sister Marie had the same thing. She ended up having a hysterectomy before she was thirty.

Danielle may have trouble getting pregnant, if she could get pregnant at all. His plans for a family with her were not realistic. What if she couldn't give him a child? Could he handle it? His dream always included children. What if that was not possible? Would he still feel the same way about her? Would he still want to marry her? Family meant everything to Greg, and Rolonda's confession had shaken him to the core.

"Greg," said Mark sitting down beside his best friend. "I'm so sorry. I had no idea," said Mark putting his hand on Greg's shoulder. Greg looked up at him with anger and tears in his eyes. "Rolonda, can you leave us alone for a few minutes?" Mark waited for her to leave the room. "This must have been devastating for her. Greg, this isn't about you. It's about her. This explains why she didn't want a relationship with you. She didn't want you getting too close and finding out her secret."

"Why didn't she tell me?" Greg asked in a tortured voice. "Why didn't she feel she could confide in me? This affects both of us. It affects our future. She never said a word. I thought all the secrets were out in the open. Danielle was keeping the biggest one of all."

"Give her a chance to explain. Don't just assume the worst. Talk to her and listen to what she has to say. We're going to take off. Call me later," said Mark pausing in the doorway. "Anytime you need to talk, I'm always here."

Greg lay back on the sofa and closed his eyes. It suddenly all made sense to him. It explained her not wanting a serious relationship.

This is the reason you were trying to push me away. You didn't think I could handle the truth. Well, I can handle it. I can handle anything you throw at me as long as we are together.

He also remembered the way Dani had reacted at the hospital, after Liz had given birth. This secret was the reason for her sadness.

It was the perfect time to tell him when they got back to her house, instead they had made love. Correction, she had made love to him feverishly and desperately. She had used him to erase all her unpleasant memories.

* * *

Danielle missed Greg so much she couldn't wait to tell him her news. She still couldn't believe it herself. Her father dropped a bombshell on her when he told her she had a twin sister. She drove to his house and jumped out of her car, running to the front door.

After ringing the doorbell twice, she used her key and went inside. There she found Greg sitting on the sofa with his eyes closed.

"Greg, are you okay?" asked Danielle sitting down next to him. "I rang the doorbell, but I guess you were so deep in thought you didn't hear it. Was that Mark I saw leaving? I hope he didn't leave on my account."

"No, I'm not fine. Mark and Rolonda came by for lunch. She wanted to see you again. She thought seeing you might jog her memory." He watched her for a reaction and wasn't disappointed when he got one. Dani turned away from him. "She remembers you, Danielle."

He knows and he can't handle it. He knows I may never be able to give him children. He doesn't want me anymore. I can feel the distance between us.

He walked over to the bar and poured a shot of something and drank it. Dani walked over to him not sure he heard her correctly. She took the shot glass out of his hand and set it down on the bar.

"Isn't it a little early to be drinking?" she asked quietly. She didn't know what else to say to him.

"Rolonda was working in the emergency room the night you came in. She told me what happened. Why couldn't you tell me?"

Danielle flinched at the calmness in his voice. She fought back the tears that threatened to fall as she stared at the man she loved. She slowly breathed in and out, trying to remain calm. Her heart constricted as her eyes met the sadness in his.

This was not supposed to happen. I never wanted you to find out. I can't give you the family you want.

We have no future. I'm scared and I'm not willing to put myself through the mental anguish and disappointment of trying to conceive a child. I don't want you to end up resenting me later.

Since Greg had reentered her life, she had done a lot of reading about in vitro fertilization and other experimental procedures, and she decided she wasn't mentally strong enough to go through any of them—especially because there were no guarantees that any of them would even work for her. She had been told even if she got pregnant, the chance of her actually carrying a baby to term were slim to none.

Danielle didn't want Greg to resent her years later if nothing worked and they still had no children. She was embarrassed to tell him she was a failure at being a woman. Her chances of conceiving without help were slim to none. And odds were not much better with help because of all the scar tissue and damage to her uterus.

"My doctor and several specialists told me I might not be able to conceive." She stopped talking as her voice began to crack. Clearing her throat again she continued: "I was shattered at the prospect of never being able to have children. It was no secret how much I have always wanted a big family. So just imagine how I felt when they told me there was little hope for me to have children. At first, I was devastated. Then I became depressed and withdrawn. I refused to believe it. I couldn't believe it. I tried to ignore it and put it all behind me. I tried to pretend it didn't matter to me since you were gone. I decided if I didn't seriously date anyone then it wouldn't matter because I would never fall in love again or get married. Then, I wouldn't have to face the fact I would never be a mother. It was working, too. I had put it completely out of my mind until you came back into my life. You reminded me of what I could never have. You wanted a family and I knew that was the one thing I couldn't give you, so I tried to push you away. I didn't want you to resent me later for not being able to give you the family we both wanted. I tried so hard to fight my feelings for you and keep you at arms' length. I told myself if I stayed away from you, I wouldn't have to face the possibility of a childless marriage. You would never find out about my problem. It's hard to explain, but it made me feel less of a woman because I couldn't conceive a child." She took a deep breath and tried unsuccessfully to stop the flow of tears.

"Why couldn't you tell me this months ago?" he asked in a choked voice. He walked over to her and led her back to the sofa. "Why couldn't you tell me the truth, Dani?" He raised her face with his finger so he could look into her eyes. "You continue to underestimate me. I wanted you. I didn't need a breeder. I can't say I wouldn't have been disappointed if we couldn't have children, but I want you more. There are always other alternative methods of having children. We could have tried some of them. I would not have let you go because you couldn't give me a child. I would never have turned my back on you. And for you to believe I could tells me you have no faith in me or my feelings for you," said the hurt voice.

"I know, but I wasn't thinking rationally at the time. I was only thinking about myself. I know it was selfish of me, but I was afraid of being a failure in your eyes. I was so sure none of the other methods of conceiving would work for me. I wasn't willing to take the chance. I should have believed in your love for me. I was scared Greg. I didn't want this to be a problem for us later in life. I thought I was doing what was right for both of us. I wanted to spare us both more heartache."

"But you didn't. You only caused more. You have put me through the ringer!" He took another deep breath and looked heavenward to calm all the conflicting emotions he was feeling.

"The pain and the uncertainties stop today for both of us. I want you to forget about me and get on with your life. Find a woman who will make you happy and who can give you the family you want. You deserve more than I can give you. I'm sorry, but it has to be this way."

He sat in stunned disbelief as Danielle got up and walked out the door. Greg blinked several times to make sure he hadn't dreamed the whole thing, but the smell of her perfume lingered in the room.

She was throwing away love because there was a chance she couldn't have a baby. She was a coward. Danielle saw the easy way out and took it. The bottom line is she doesn't think I'm worth the trouble. We're not worth the trouble. Then so be it.

Danielle was a nervous wreck as she drove to her parents' house. She didn't know where else to go. Through tears of misery, she had poured her heart out to Jack and Karen.

Jack held her until her tears finally ceased. He and Karen then tried to make her see that her life was not over because she couldn't have children. Jack scolded her and informed her she was acting like a selfish spoiled child.

Karen especially understood after having a hysterectomy at a young age. They went on to encourage her to make an appointment with a specialist and talk to several fertility specialists.

Danielle declined. There was no way she was going to put herself through anymore poking and prodding only to be told the same thing her doctors had already told her.

"Jack, can you leave us alone for a few minutes?

Danielle and I need to have a mother–daughter talk." Karen waited for the doors to close behind him. "Jack and I had given up hope of having children when your mother showed up on our doorstep with you and your brother. When she asked us to take both of you, I looked at it as a gift from God. He was not just giving us one child, but two. I had a son and a daughter. You were ten years old and Michael was four when you came to live with us. I remember what a big adjustment it was for all of us. You tried to put on a brave front, but I saw your fear and I understood it because I was afraid as well. I was afraid I would say or do something wrong. I didn't know the first thing about combing your hair or anything, but I learned. I learned everything I needed to learn to help you and Michael adjust. I know you weren't thrilled with having me as a substitute for your mother."

"You were, are a great mother," said Danielle, catching her hand. "I know you love me and I love you. This is different."

"No sweetheart. It's not different. You may not be the child of my loins, but you are the child of my heart. I will always love you and genetics has nothing to do with it. Having a child does not define you as a person. If you have to adopt, or whatever route you choose, you will love your child just the same as if you bore her. In that moment of realization, you will understand the depths of my feelings for you."

"I'm scared. I don't know if I'm as strong as you are. You and Dad have gone through so much to be together. You gave up everything for him. Your parents disowned you. They wouldn't speak to you for ten years."

"Danielle, I would do it all over again to be with your father. Anything worth having is worth fighting for. Don't give up on having the family you want. It is a very real possibility. Without your dreams, what would you have to look forward to? There are so many options open to you. You can adopt. You and Greg can hire a surrogate. Try the in vitro first. If it fails, then move on to the next option, but don't give up. I didn't raise a quitter. I raised a fighter."

It took her a while, but Danielle was finally coming to grips with the fact the she would never have children of her own. Maybe one day she too could adopt a child.

She picked up the phone several times to call Greg, but each time she chickened out and hung up. She couldn't bring herself to call him. In the past month he hadn't called her once. It was really over this time. He took her advice and got on with his life.

Danielle couldn't blame him for being angry. She had done everything possible to push him away, and now she had finally succeeded.

She talked to Drew periodically just to say hello. When she told him she and Greg were not seeing each other anymore, he invited her to a cocktail party.

Danielle was hesitant at first, but he talked her into it. He told her she couldn't bury her head in the sand forever. It was time to get out of the house and have some fun.

Greg was sitting at his desk staring out the window. He hadn't spoken to Danielle since the day she walked out of his house.

It pained him to know she thought so little of him. She believed he wouldn't want her if she couldn't bear his children.

He had to admit the idea did bother him, but not enough to walk away from her. He loved her unconditionally.

He talked it over with Mark and there were a lot of options open for them to become parents. He did his own research on endometriosis and in vitro fertilization. Danielle was giving up without a fight. He never knew her to be a coward.

Staring at the phone for several seconds, he picked it up. He didn't know what he was going to say to her, but he dialed her office.

A brief knock sounded on the door, before it swung inward. Jacob Markowitz, senior partner walked in. Greg hung up the phone.

"Sorry to interrupt, but I'm in court the rest of the week. I'm having a little get together at my house this Saturday," he said without preamble. "Can you make it?"

"I think my calendar's clear for this weekend." His calendar was spotless now that he and Danielle were on the outs again. "Formal or informal, and what time should I be there?"

"Around 8 o'clock would be great. Informal. Don't bring anything but a date," said Jacob, closing the door behind him.

"Great," said Greg sarcastically. "Just call me 'Dateless in Dallas.' If I weren't so ticked off at Danielle, I'd call her. Where am I going to find a date on this short notice?" He snapped his fingers in answer to that problem.

Jennifer Johnson, Elijah Jacobs' new assistant, had been giving him the come on since the day she started two weeks ago. She was pretty enough and she had a dynamite body.

Greg wasn't one to dip the pen in the company ink pool, but he was in a bind and needed a quick date. Against his better judgment, he asked Jennifer to the party.

He picked her up around 7 o'clock and they arrived at Jacob's house around 8:00 P.M. There were already several cars there.

Jennifer looked great in a red silk low-cut dress. Her hair was cut short in a chic style and Greg concluded she would look terrific in anything. Her long, slim legs were encased in off black hose to match her smooth dark skin tone. She wore just enough make-up and blush to make her look like an Ebony model.

Jacob met them at the door, smiling. "Come in. Everyone's here except for Drew and his guest."

"Who's Drew?" asked Greg stepping inside. "Is he a new employee? The name sounds familiar, but I'm not sure why."

"Drew is the man doing the complete overhaul on our computer system. Since he is going to be around for a while, I thought he should get to know us. He's also coming up with some new programs for us. Jennifer has already met him. They are going to be working pretty closely over the next few months."

Chapter 13

Drew arrived at Danielle's door promptly at 7:00 P.M. with a bouquet of flowers. She smiled, stepped back, and waved him inside.

"You look terrific," said Drew eyeing her appreciatively. He twirled her around and whistled. "Who is this sex goddess and what have you done with Danielle?"

Danielle was wearing a royal blue Rayon minidress. The dress hugged every curve of her body, leaving very little to the imagination. She wore matching pumps, and her hair was a mass of loose curls that rested on her almost bare shoulders.

"I don't know if I should feel complimented or insulted by that statement," she smiled back. "You look very handsome yourself."

"Thank you, my lady. Danielle you are always beautiful, but you have to admit, this dress is out of character for you. What gives?"

"I thought I could use a change. If you don't like the dress," she smiled, turning to walk away, "I could go upstairs and change."

"Don't you dare change! We'd better get going,"

said Drew holding the door open for her. "I'm glad you decided to come."

"Me too. It seems like all I've been doing lately is moping around and feeling sorry for myself. Thank you for asking me."

"Hey. That's what friends are for. You need to get out and meet people. Mr. Right is not going to come knocking on your door." They both laughed. "At least that's what my mother used to tell my sisters." He helped her into the sports car. "Just for tonight, can you forget about Greg Thomas and have fun?"

"With such stimulating company, I don't think that will be a problem," she teased. "You're good for my ego. I might have to keep you around."

They talked the entire ride across town and arrived at the house a little after 8 P.M. Drew helped Danielle out of the car and escorted her to the door. He rang the doorbell and they waited. They were greeted at the door by their smiling host and his wife.

"Hi, please come in," said the smiling brunette. "I'm Josephine Markowitz, and this is my husband Jacob. Welcome to our house."

Danielle stared at them both in surprise. As the implication of who they were hit her, her mouth dropped open.

No! It couldn't be! Markowitz was not an uncommon name! Fate wasn't this unkind. Or was it? Please don't let this be Greg's company!

"Drew, glad you could make it," said Jacob extending his hand. The two men shook hands as Danielle and Drew stepped inside.

"This beautiful lady with me is Danielle Roberts," said Drew smiling down at her. He frowned at her nervousness.

"Hello," responded Danielle taking both Jacob and Josephine's hands. "It's a pleasure to meet both of you."

Jacob waved them toward the bar and Danielle's worst fears were confirmed. Her eyes immediately went to the man facing away from them.

Greg was in deep conversation with a striking lady in a red dress. He threw his head back and laughed at something she said. Danielle would recognize his profile and his laugh anywhere.

As if sensing someone watching him, Greg turned around and his eyes locked with hers. Danielle froze momentarily, before she looked away. Stunned, she let Drew lead her on wooden legs over to the bar.

"Just relax," he whispered in her ear. "I'm sorry. I had no idea he would be here. Why does this town suddenly seem so small? It can't be coincidence that he turns up everywhere we go. What is he doing here of all places?"

"Greg is the new partner in the firm," she whispered back slowing her steps. "You've been there how long and haven't met him yet?"

"He is Thomas of Markowitz, Lebowitz, Shapiro, and Thomas?" Drew asked.

Danielle nodded.

"Small world," Drew remarked. "Too small. Come on. Let's go over and say hello and get it over with."

"I'd rather not, and say we did." Danielle balked and refused to take another step in their direction. "I don't want to do this."

"It's either now or after a few drinks. Who knows what you'll say then? Don't be a coward, Danielle. Face your fears. Lean on me if you need to."

They stopped beside Greg and the gorgeous female who was with him. After giving Danielle the once over, he made the introductions.

"Danielle Roberts, meet Jennifer Johnson." He held out his hand to Drew. "Drew, I'm sorry I don't recall your last name."

"Drew Murray," he responded taking Greg's outstretched hand. "Jennifer, it's good seeing you again."

"You too." She smiled, flirting with Drew. "Greg, Drew is installing the new computer system we bought. He's actually the owner and designer of the software."

Greg made no comment as his eyes met Danielle's. There was an uneasy silence as Greg and Dani stared at each other. Neither was sure what to say to the other one. Danielle realized it was up to her to clear the air.

"Drew, Jennifer, do you mind if I steal Greg away for a minute?" Danielle asked twisting her hands nervously. Confused Jennifer stared at them and then at Drew, who shrugged.

"I'll entertain Jennifer until you get back," said Drew, leading Jennifer over to the bar. "What would you like to drink? If I weren't driving, I'd have a double anything."

Greg followed Danielle out to the patio without saying a word. When he turned to face her, his hungry eyes devoured her. Danielle flushed hotly under his gaze.

"What are you are doing here?" he asked taking a sip of his champagne and turning away from her before she saw the longing in his dark eyes.

"If I had known it was your firm Drew was contracting with, I wouldn't have come. If this is uncomfortable for you, I can leave. I don't want to cause any problems for you."

"It's not my party," he said sarcastically. "You don't have to leave because of me. I'm a big boy, Danielle. I can handle it if you can." She stared at his proud back. Reaching out her hand to touch him, she realized what she was about to do and let her hand drop to her side. "So you are back dating Drew?" he asked casually.

"No, we are not dating. Drew and I are friends. Am I not allowed to have friends? Greg, please look at me," she said softly. He turned around to face her. "I know it's not possible for us to be friends, but does it have to come to this? Can't we at least be civil to one another after everything we've meant to each other?"

"I am being as civil as I can be under the circumstances. You thought so little of me to keep something so important from me. You thought I wouldn't want you because you can't breed," he said viciously. "I don't know you at all and you definitely don't know me to think such a thing. This is the reason you pushed me away? This is the reason you can't commit to me? So be it, Danielle. Have it your way. You always do. But you are right about one thing, there is no way we could ever be friends. Too much has happened for that. We can't be lovers and we can't be friends. So tell me, Danielle, where does that leave us?" he asked staring intently at her.

"I'm not sure," she responded quietly meeting his questioning dark gaze. "Greg, I'm sorry. I misjudged you. I know how much a family means to you. I was trying to save us both from pain."

"No, Danielle, you took the coward's way out. You ran. Instead of running to me, you ran in the opposite direction. It's obvious you don't think I'm worth taking a chance on. You don't think we are worth the risk. If you want to wallow in self-pity that's your choice to make, I choose to get on with my life. If you want to come along for the ride, fine. If not, I bid you adieu."

"I'm sorry," she whispered wiping the tears from her cheeks. "What do you want me to say? I'm scared. The thought of not being able to give you what you want terrifies me. I don't know where this leaves us."

"That makes two of us. Let me know when you figure it out. We are at a standstill, Danielle. We can't go backwards and we can't move forward. The ball is in your court, but don't expect me to wait around twiddling my thumbs while you try and boost your courage," Greg said walking away. He stopped and turned back to face her. "On second thought, don't bother. It wouldn't make a difference. You have no trust or faith in me. It's kind of hard to build a relationship on nothing."

"Greg, we need to talk. There's something I have to tell you. Can I come by your place tomorrow?"

"No. Speak now or forever hold your peace. Tell me now or forget it." When she remained silent, he turned to walk away.

"My endometriosis didn't just happen overnight. I've had it for years and I never told you. It's gotten worse over the years." Her eyes met his and he made no comment. Danielle took a deep breath and closed her eyes. "I knew there was always the possibility I might have problems getting pregnant, but I never told you. I was afraid and I didn't want to lose you. I kept thinking if I didn't think about it, maybe it would go away, maybe the problem would correct itself and you never had to know. I should have told you. I should have trusted you to be able to handle the truth. Can you handle it? What if I am never able to give you children? Would you still want me for your wife? What if you had to settle for it being the two of us the rest of our lives? What if there were no sons or daughters to carry on the Thomas line? Would you feel the same way about me?"

Greg stared at her speechless. He couldn't believe she would ask him such questions. Her insecurities knew no bounds. He turned away from her and then turned back to face her without saying a word.

Greg was fighting a losing battle with his emotions. He was so angry he wanted to hit something. His pain was so intense he wanted to lash out.

She looked up and her eyes met his. The pain and anger in his eyes made her flinch and take a step back from him.

"I'm done," he sighed. "I can't do this anymore. There is nothing I can say or do to convince you of how I feel. Baby or no baby, I love you, but it's not enough is it. You can't believe I would still want you. Do you think so little of yourself? Is your total self-worth based on whether or not you can conceive a child? Where is the confident woman I fell in love with?" He threw up his hands in frustration and left her standing outside.

Through her tears, she watched him go back inside. He whispered something to Jennifer and they left the room.

Danielle watched with a heavy heart. She took a few moments to pull herself together before walking back inside. Drew was instantly at her side.

"Do you want to leave?" asked Drew, putting his arm around her shoulder and pulling her to him.

She shook her head no. She was not going to keep running away whenever she saw Greg. It was time to stop running.

"Ignore him and let's mingle. You're a lawyer, Danielle. Where's that poker face?"

Danielle laughed and then got her emotions in check. "How's this?" she asked smiling. The smile didn't quite reach her eyes. "Hey, I'm doing the best I can under the circumstances."

Greg led Jennifer out one of the side doors. He needed a few minutes to clear his head after talking to Dani.

"Drew's date is very beautiful. Have you known her a long time?" Jennifer asked casually. "Old fling?"

"Jennifer, you're about as subtle as a freight train," he smiled down at her. "Yes, I know her. I know her very well."

"Care to elaborate on the topic, Counselor?" She raised her face to his and she waited for his answer.

"Not really," he hedged. "Can we forget about Danielle and have a good time?" His eyes followed Dani and Drew around the room.

"Easier said than done if you can't take your eyes off her." Her statement had its desired effect.

"How's this?" He turned to face her giving her his undivided attention. "Would you like to dance?" He held out his hand to her.

"I'd love to dance." She took his outstretched hand. "As long as we don't have to dance next to Danielle and Drew."

Greg was packing for his trip to Atlanta when Mark dropped by. He let his friend in and led him to the den.

"Hey, I didn't expect you. I was packing for my trip." He noted the weird expression on Mark's face. "Okay what's up? You have that look."

"Have you talked to Danielle, lately? Allow me to play devil's advocate for a few minutes," said Mark sitting down.

Greg rolled his eyes at his best friend. He knew from the way the conversation started, he was not going to like what he had to say.

"Mark, if you're here to give me relationship advice, don't," he warned. "You don't know the first thing about relationships, and I've moved on. There's nothing to talk about."

"Sure you have." Mark turned the laptop to face Greg. "I suppose that's why you're researching in vitro fertilization."

Greg closed the laptop with a snap and glared at the smirk on Mark's face. What could he say? He couldn't deny the truth. He was caught red-handed.

"Fine," said Greg, sitting down. "You might as well

give me your two cents. I'm sure that's about all it's worth. So what's your take on all this?"

"Put yourself in Danielle's position. What would you do if the tables were turned? What if you had the problem and not her? I have a story to tell you and I want you to really think about everything I'm saying."

Greg listened as Mark shared with him a story about a friend. His friend was diagnosed with a low sperm count. Seeing this as a slur against his masculinity, he began sleeping around to prove himself. He was afraid of commitment because he didn't want anyone to know his secret. He didn't want to face the fact he may never be a father. He buried himself in his work and in countless women to keep his mind off his real problem. He finally shared his secret with a friend.

Greg stared at Mark in shock. It only took him a few seconds to realize Mark was talking about himself. He had no idea what to say to his friend. He could see Mark's pain as he shared his secret.

"I'm sorry," said Greg, past the lump in his throat. "I had no idea. I don't know what else to say. Not being able to father a child does not make you any less of a man." Mark made no reply. "I can even understand how you would feel. Every man wants a son to carry on the family name. It has to be a blow to the ego if it isn't possible."

"You can relate to a male's sense of loss, but not a woman's? Greg, it's the same thing. Whether it's Danielle or me, the end result is the same. The feelings of pain and the sense of loss are the same. She's afraid and I understand her fear. You should understand it as well. This is not just about her. It's about you, too. Can you honestly say you won't be disappointed if she can't give you children? This is me talking to you. I know how much you want kids."

"I never said I wouldn't be disappointed. I would

be lying if I said that, but it's not the end of the world. It shouldn't be the end of our relationship."

"Maybe not for you, but it is a blow for her. What if it were only the two of you? What if you weren't able to conceive or adopt or anything? Could you settle for that? Would you settle for that? Do you love her enough to be satisfied with it being just the two of you? If not, this is your out. You can take it and not look back. Is that what this is really all about?"

"I love Danielle and nothing would ever change the way I feel. I would never resent her if we couldn't have children, and yes, I could be satisfied if it were only the two of us. It would be hard, but I could deal with it."

"You don't sound very convincing," said Mark, meeting his wary expression. "If you can't make me believe you, how do you hope to convince the woman you love? Think about what I said." Mark came to his feet and headed for the door. "And for the record, there's nothing wrong with my sperm count." Smiling his friend closed the door behind him.

Greg couldn't help but laugh and shake his head. Mark had made his point in the only way he knew how. He brought the situation home to Greg.

A few days later, he was on a plane headed for Atlanta. The firm was taking on a huge racial discrimination lawsuit. It was a white-owned company being sued by a number of its black employees for unfair paying practices. To prove they were not prejudiced, they wanted Greg to handle the case.

He hated cases like this. In the end no one really won, and he would end up being the bad guy for defending white corporate America against his own race.

A death in one of the families forced the judge to postpone the trial. The earliest he could put it back on the court docket was two months.

Greg flew back to Dallas the next day. He had other

cases to work on until this one came to trial. With nothing but time on his hands, he called Jennifer and invited her to dinner. Tired of restaurant food, he planned a nice quiet romantic meal at home for them.

Danielle went in for her six-month check-up. Dr. West told her to get dressed and meet her in her office. She eased off the table with a sense of foreboding. Danielle knew without being told something was wrong. She sensed the endometriosis was back. Her last period was painful and heavy, and she feared the cause. Her fingers trembled as she buttoned the last button on her red silk blouse. She put on a brave front as she left the room and walked down the short hallway to Dr. West's office.

"Have a seat Danielle," she said looking over the chart. Closing it at last, she met Danielle's questioning eyes.

"The endometriosis is back," Danielle blurted out. "How bad is it this time?" She braced herself for the bad news.

"I only felt one mass," she said softly, "but in your case, we know this is only the beginning. It always starts with one. Danielle, if you have any plans for having a family, I would advise you to start right now. We are looking at a small window of time before we possibly have to do a complete or partial hysterectomy."

Danielle's heart fell at her words. The words small window of time kept ringing in her ears. She was running out of time.

"Are you saying if I get pregnant now, there's a chance for me to carry the baby to term? What about the endometriosis? Will it harm the baby?"

"I'm not saying anything is one hundred percent. It won't harm the fetus, but you may have a hard time conceiving, if you conceive at all. The question I need answered, is it worth the risk to you? It's now or never Danielle. Each time your endometriosis comes back it's worse. Think about it and get back with me. I know how much you want children. If there is no one in your life, we can also go the in vitro route with a sperm donor."

"There is someone," she whispered past the lump in her throat, "but I'm not sure this is the right time or right decision for us. Our lives are complicated enough without bringing a baby into the world together. I'll have to get back with you." Danielle got to her feet and left the office. She was in a daze as she paid the bill and left the office.

She sat in her car replaying her conversation with Dr. West. Her time was running out. If she wanted a baby, she had to have one now or never.

Danielle wanted a baby. She wanted Greg's baby. This is what she had always wanted. The family she desperately wanted was slipping away from her.

I can't let that happen. I can still have it all. I'll ask Greg to marry me. If he turns me down, I'll ask him to be a sperm donor. What am I thinking? I can't ask him something so personal. Yes, I can. I don't have much of a choice. Time is not on my side.

For the next few hours, she pondered whether or not she should go over to his house. Around 7:00 P.M. she picked up her car keys and left the house. She knew what she wanted and she was determined to get it this time.

Chapter 14

She stood outside the house ringing her hands nervously. Greg's car was parked in the driveway, so she knew he was home. Danielle rang the doorbell.

I have no idea what I'm going to say. I hope I don't make a fool out of myself. I want this so badly. I only hope he wants it, too.

She shifted nervously from one foot to the other as she waited for him to answer the door. After a few minutes, she stared down at the key in her hand. She was torn between letting herself in and waiting patiently for him to open the door.

Unlocking the door, she stepped inside and closed the door behind her. She stopped when she saw the two wine glasses on the coffee table. She felt something painful squeeze at her heart as she took in the hor'derves and wine on the table. Danielle was turning to leave when she heard Greg's voice.

"I'm coming! I'm coming!" Greg yelled vaulting down the stairs. He came to an abrupt stop when he saw her. Continuing down the staircase at a slower pace, he stopped at the bottom.

"Hello Greg," she said nervously clasping her hands together. "I rang the doorbell, but there was no answer."

"What are you doing here?" he asked bluntly. "I didn't think there was anything left for us to say to each other."

"Greg, who was at the door?" Jennifer asked jogging down the stairs. She too stopped when she saw Danielle. "Hello, Danielle."

"Hello, Jennifer," she responded, past the lump in her throat. She couldn't help but notice the other woman's rumpled shirt. It was obvious she had interrupted something.

"Jen, can you go warm up dinner? I'll be right there," Greg said, pulling Jennifer to him and kissing her on the lips.

"Sure," she said, looking from one to the other in confusion. "It'll just take a minute."

"That's all the time I need." Turning, he watched the other woman leave the room. "Now, back to my original question. What are you doing here? I hope you have a good reason for barging in uninvited. I am about to enjoy a romantic dinner with Jennifer. After dinner, I plan to have an even more enjoyable night," he added hurtfully. Danielle's heart cracked into tiny pieces at his confession. "Now, you have two choices. You can either leave or you can stay and join us. I've never tried it before, but it might be fun," he winked. Danielle stared at him in disbelief. She could not believe he had actually said, what she thought she heard him say. "So how about it Danielle?"

"You really are a pig," she said in disgust. "You are sounding more and more like that perverted friend of yours every day. The way you fall asleep afterwards, I doubt you could take us both on."

"Care to give it a try?" he asked advancing on her. He stopped when he had her body pinned to the door. Reaching out a hand, he touched her flushed face with the back of his hand. "I think maybe Mark has the right idea about women. Love them and leave them before they leave you. In case you haven't figured it out, our little sexual agreement is null and void. You see, sweetheart, I've found someone else I want to sleep with more than you." She flinched at his harsh words and jerked away from his touch. "Unlike you, Jennifer is full of surprises and she has no hang-ups."

Danielle unsuccessfully tried to blink away the tears pooling in her eyes. She stared up at Greg sadly and a single tear slipped down her pale cheek followed by another.

Touched more than he wanted to admit by her tears, Greg moved away from her. He turned his back on her so she wouldn't see how her pain affected him.

"I'm sorry I interrupted your evening," she whispered past the lump in her throat. "I promise you, it won't happen again." Danielle took the key off her chain, and threw it at Greg, who caught it in his hand.

She opened the door and rushed out of the house. Unlocking her car door, she got in and leaned her head on the steering wheel.

Picking up the car phone, she dialed Liz's number. When the answering machine picked up, she hit disconnect.

She needed to talk to someone. Danielle dialed Drew's number. She waited patiently for the machine to finish.

"Drew, it's Danielle. Please call me when you get this message. You told me if I ever needed a friend to call. I need one now."

"Dinner was terrific," said Jennifer leaning back on the couch closing her eyes. "Your culinary talents surprised me."

"I'm glad you liked it," said Greg pulling Jennifer into his arms. "I'm sorry about the interruption earlier."

"Did you and Danielle get everything resolved? She seemed pretty upset when she saw me here."

"What can I say? Danielle is an excitable woman. Everything upsets her delicate sensibilities. There was nothing to resolve. It's over between us. It has been for a while now." His hand caressed her cheek. "I don't want to talk about Danielle. There are other things I would rather be doing," he whispered nibbling at her earlobe.

"Really. I can't imagine what," laughed Jennifer staring up into his twinkling eyes. "Tell me. No. Show me."

"This," said Greg kissing her full on the lips. "And this," he said nibbling at her neck and throat. She pulled his head up to hers and her mouth met his in a hungry kiss.

He swung her up into his arms and carried her up the stairs. Slowly, he let her body slide down his until her feet touched the carpeted floor.

With infinite care, he unbuttoned her blouse and pushed it from her shoulders. He felt her tremble when his hands cupped her small breasts.

She unbuttoned his shirt and it joined her blouse on the floor. Soon all their clothes were in a pile by the bed.

He heard her indrawn breath as his naked body covered hers. Greg stared down into the face of the woman he was about to make love to, not really seeing her. His mouth covered hers hungrily and she responded to his every kiss and caress.

"God how I want you, Dani," he whispered into her throat. The woman beneath him froze and then shoved him off of her.

The passion fog cleared and Greg stared up at the ceiling. It only took him a moment to realize his slip of the tongue.

He looked over at Jennifer, but couldn't say anything while he watched her get dressed. He knew he had hurt her and wished he could take it back.

"I don't know why I'm not surprised," said Jennifer quietly. "You still love her. It's not over, Greg, when you take someone to bed and call them by your ex-fiancé's name. Until you decide who you want, don't bother calling me again."

"I'm sorry, Jennifer," said Greg, closing his eyes. "I didn't mean to hurt you. I guess maybe I do need some time alone to sort out my feelings."

"There's nothing to sort out. You are still in love with Danielle. You want to be with her, so what's stopping you other than your own foolish pride. Goodbye Greg."

He lay there for a few minutes after she was gone before getting up. He needed to talk to someone. He showered and then called Mark. After spilling his guts to his best friend, he held the phone and waited for Mark's response.

"I still can't believe you asked straight-laced Dani if she wanted to have a threesome. It's pretty scary, Thomas. You are beginning to sound more and more like me every day and that's not a compliment," said his friend seriously.

"I made her cry," confessed Greg, closing his eyes. "It really got to me. I can't stand to see Dani cry."

"It was supposed to get to you. Dani's high strung. She'd cry over a broken fingernail," reasoned Mark.

"Now who's exaggerating? She's not unstable. I wanted to hurt her the way she hurt me."

"Well I'd say you succeeded, and to top it all off, you called Jennifer the wrong name. It sounds like you had a fun evening. Never call a woman someone else in the throes of passion. It could be detrimental to one's health or other body parts. So what are you going to do now? Why did Danielle come to see you? I thought she broke up with you again, or did you break up with her? I can't keep it straight."

"Very funny. I have no idea why she was here.

Frankly I don't care. I'm just thankful I didn't follow your advice and get her pregnant. Can you imagine what the situation would be like now, if she were pregnant? What I don't need is more problems with her. Maybe it is best for us to stay away from each other."

"I think you're wrong. Tomorrow morning, go see her. She made the first move my friend. Now the ball is in your court. At least find out what she wanted. What can it hurt?"

Danielle was sitting in front of the television with a bowl of popcorn, when the doorbell rang. She ignored it and turned up the volume on the television.

"Danielle! Danielle, are you in there?" Drew yelled, banging on the door. Coming to her feet, she went quickly to the door. "I came as soon I got your message. What's wrong?" he asked taking in her puffy eyes and tear stained face. "Come here." He held out his arms and she went gladly into them.

Through hiccups and tears, she finally told him the whole story. Drew sat silently and listened to her sad tale. He held her and stroked her hair as she talked.

"I didn't even get a chance to tell him what I wanted," she sniffed wiping her eyes with the tissue.

"Danielle, I may be overstepping the bounds of friendship, but what exactly were you going to say to him? Were you going to propose marriage or just ask him to be a sperm donor?"

"You make it sound so cold and calculating," she snapped getting to her feet. "I don't know what I was going to say. It's kind of a moot point since I didn't get to say anything." She turned back around to face Drew. An idea began to formulate in her head. "What's your blood type?"

"Don't even think about it," he said seriously holding up his hands to ward her off. "If you have my child, you can consider me part of the package. Honey, we are friends. Neither one of us expects or wants more than that. I can't be your donor."

"I'm sorry for putting you on the spot. I don't know why I said that. I guess desperation makes for strange bedfellows. Drew, if it comes down to the wire for me and there is no other option in sight, would you reconsider it?"

"If there are no other options," he said meeting her teary gaze, "then yes, I will consider it. I think you are going to make a terrific mother someday." He got to his feet and enfolded her in his arms.

"I don't want to be alone tonight." She looked up at him. "Can you stay?"

His eyebrows rose in question.

She hit his arm playfully as he winked at her. "I am not propositioning you. The guest room is already made up."

"Sure," he laughed, kissing her forehead. "I'll stay, but you're definitely going to have to change the channel. I am not watching Lifetime. Do you have Sci-Fi?"

"Sci-Fi. Are you a closet Trekkie? Oh come on. Don't you want to get in touch with your feminine side?" she teased poking him in the ribs.

"I'm as in touch as I want to be. I have no feminine side. I'll trade you an hour of Lifetime for an hour of the basketball game. I think the Mav's are playing tonight." He led her back over to the couch.

They watched television into the wee hours of the morning. Around 2:00 A.M. she led him to the guest room and said goodnight.

Danielle got very little sleep. She tossed and turned the remainder of the night. Her biological clock was ticking loudly in her head.

She was awakened the next morning by the smell of

frying bacon. She got up, brushed her teeth, dressed and went downstairs to join Drew in the kitchen.

"Morning," smiled Drew dishing eggs onto a plate. "Sit down and I'll get you a plate. I hope you don't mind me making myself at home."

"Of course I don't mind." She took a plate from the table and ladled on it, eggs, bacon, and waffles. "You didn't have to do this, but I'm glad you did. It looks delicious." She said a brief prayer and lifted the fork to her mouth. "Mmm, this is good." She savored the taste of the waffle with fresh strawberries and whipped cream. You have hidden talents, Mr. Murray."

They chatted easily over breakfast. After breakfast, Danielle cleaned up the kitchen while Drew went upstairs to change from his shorts and t-shirt back into his jeans.

Danielle was loading the dishes in the dishwasher when the doorbell rang. Drying her hands on the towel, she made her way to the door.

Opening the door, she froze when she saw Greg standing there. Brushing past her, he walked into the house.

Danielle took a deep calming breath and then closed the door. She knew if Drew came down at just the right moment, Greg would misinterpret him being there.

"What do you want?" she asked tightly turning around to face him. "Please make it quick. I have to leave for an appointment in a few minutes." The lie came easily, but she wanted him to leave before Drew came down the stairs. She didn't want a confrontation this early in the morning.

"Are you okay?" he asked. Her beautiful face was pale and her eyes were red from crying. "I'm sorry about what I said to you last night. I shouldn't have said what I did. You didn't deserve that."

"No. I didn't," whispered Danielle hugging her arms

to herself protectively. She stared up at him. "I hope your evening was everything you hoped it would be."

"Actually, it ended rather abruptly. Danielle, Jennifer isn't the woman I want. I came by because . . ." Greg's words trailed off as his eyes moved up the stairs.

Danielle swallowed the lump in her throat as she followed Greg's eyes up the staircase. He turned accusing eyes toward her and she flinched at the pain in his dark eyes.

"Danielle, I'd better get going," Drew said coming down the stairs buttoning his shirt. His steps slowed when he saw Greg. "Sorry, bad timing." He looked from Danielle to Greg.

"Your timing is perfect, Drew." She turned her eyes back to Greg. "You made it perfectly clear to me it was over between us. You moved on, so why shouldn't I?" She knew what he was thinking and she let him. "How long am I supposed to hold onto hope, Greg? How long was I expected to wait for you?"

"I never asked you to wait, but at least you could have had the decency to wait more than an hour. Forget I came by," fumed the angry voice. "Forget everything! You wanted me out of your life! Consider me gone!" After giving her one last accusatory glare, he stormed out of the room, slamming the door behind him.

Danielle flinched and fought back the tears. She had no idea why she said what she said to him. Her anger and quick temper got the best of her again.

"Why did you do that?" Drew asked in confusion. "Hello, anybody in there." He knocked lightly on her head with his knuckles.

"I don't know why I did it!" She paced the room crossing her arms over her chest. "Sometimes my mouth and head overrule my heart. I'm great at sabotaging my life. I have to think. I have to come up with a plan."

"You just blew your plan to hell and back. You'll be lucky if he ever talks to you again. I'm out of here. I am not going to let you drag me in the middle of this mess. You need to go talk to him. You need him!"

"Drew!" Danielle let out an exasperated growl as he slammed the door behind him. She dropped down to the couch and closed her eyes. "Now what am I going to do. They are both furious at me. I'll give them both a chance to calm down and then talk to both of them."

Greg was on a plane bound for New York a week later. He was negotiating a lawsuit for one of his clients. His two-day trip turned into a week stay. The negotiations dragged on for days.

He received several messages on his cell phone from Danielle. His secretary also forwarded a few messages to him as well.

He didn't return any of her calls. By his way of thinking, there was nothing left to say. He dated a lot of women since their break-up, but had not made love to any of them. He was still holding out hope for them patching things up. Danielle ended things when she slept with Drew.

Greg was ecstatic when both parties finally came to an agreement. He was on a plane bound for home the same night.

He was exhausted when his plane landed at the airport. Taking the shuttle to his car, he decided on impulse to drop by Danielle's house.

Chapter 15

Dialing his office, Tara informed her Greg was out of town again and he wouldn't be back for a few weeks. Dani wasn't sure whether to believe her or not anymore. She left several messages on his cell phone asking him to call her.

Danielle showered and got ready for bed. The ringing doorbell startled her. Padding out to the living room in her fuzzy slippers, she peered out the peephole. She nervously pulled open the door.

Greg was leaning against the doorframe with his ankles crossed. His jacket was slung casually on his shoulders. He looked tired and not to pleased to see her.

His dark suit was slightly rumpled and his white shirt was unbuttoned at the top two buttons. His tie hung loosely around his neck. Straightening up, he walked past her into the room. Danielle closed the door behind him.

"I came to answer your phone calls in person. I just got in a little while ago and came straight here. I've been away for five days and you've left me seven messages. Why? What is so important? What can I help you with? Was Drew unavailable?" he asked sarcastically shrugging his shoulders. "Out of curiosity, do you have the same agreement with him you had with me?"

His barb stung, but she had to brush it off. Ignoring his sarcasm, she nervously followed him over to the couch. She sat down next to him and turned to face him.

"No, Drew and I don't have the same agreement. We're just friends. When you came by and found him here, it wasn't what it looked like. I led you to believe there was something going on between us and there wasn't. Drew and I are not lovers and never have been."

Holding up his hands to silence her, Greg came slowly to his feet. He couldn't and wouldn't do this anymore. It was time to get on with his life. He and Danielle were finished. Taking a deep breath, he turned away from her.

"As far as I'm concerned, you can do what you wish with Drew or whomever. It's none of my business. My being here tonight is pointless. We are pointless. I don't even know why I came. I'm tired and I'm going home. Have a nice life."

"Greg, please listen to me. I know it's been a vicious cycle. I hurt you and you hurt me and so on and so on." Danielle blocked his exit. "It stops now."

"Why, because you say so? Oh, I get it. It's Dani's way again. Whatever Danielle wants, Danielle gets. Not this time, sweetheart. Been there, done that. I'm not catering to your wants and needs anymore. I don't know what kind of game you are playing this time, but I'm not interested. Maybe you can get Drew to play by your rules?"

"I want to have a baby and I want you to be the father." Her words came out in a rush as she tried to stop him from leaving.

Greg had started out the door, but Danielle's words stopped him in his tracks. He turned around to face her with a look of surprise on his face. His eyes held her glued to the spot. He blinked not sure he heard her correctly.

"Okay. Now you have my undivided attention. What are you trying to pull now? Why would you want to have my child? You don't even want me in your life."

"That's not exactly true either," she said softly lowering her head. "If you will have a seat, I will explain everything."

Still mystified, he walked over and sat down on the sofa. She followed him at a much slower place. She had to get her thoughts together. She didn't want to come off insulting him or putting her foot in her mouth as she often did with Greg.

Over the next half hour, she told him about her endometriosis returning. She explained to him what the doctor told her about her condition. Her time was running out and if she ever hoped to get pregnant, it had to been soon.

Greg listened without comment as she poured out her heart to him. Her words were like a knife in his heart. Danielle didn't want him. She wanted his baby. She didn't want him in her life.

It wasn't so much as what she said, but the way she said it. There was no mention of them raising this child together. There was no mention of marriage and happily ever after for them.

"What you want is a sperm donor," he voiced crudely. "Does it even matter to you who the father is as long as you get what you want? What happened to Drew? Did he turn you down?" Her face flushed and she broke eye contact with him. Greg came angrily to his feet. "I take your reaction to mean you did in fact ask him first. Why doesn't that surprise me? He turned you down and you immediately thought of me. Should I feel honored being donor Number Two?"

"That's not what happened," she defended, getting

to her feet and facing him. "The night I came to your place to ask you, you were busy entertaining Jennifer. As I remember, you took great pleasure in rubbing my face in your affair with her."

"So you called up good old Drew to do the job? So you slept with him and didn't get pregnant. So now it's my turn. No thanks."

"I have never slept with him. He's a friend. Drew was my second choice. You were my first. He turned me down."

"Smart man." Greg threw his arms in the air in defeat. "He knows when he's being used. I bet he ran for his life."

"No, he said he'd consider it if you turned me down. Are you turning me down?" Her eyes met his and she held her breath as she waited for his answer.

"So, Drew's the back-up. I guess you had to make sure all your bases were covered. Is this to be clinical or the old fashioned way? Is that why he turned you down?"

"This is not about you or Drew!" she yelled losing the battle with her emotions. "This is my last chance to have a baby! I want a child, Greg! I want to be a mother!"

"What about me, Danielle? What about this baby? Everything is always about you! This child deserves to have a mother and a father! You are being selfish and thoughtless. What about my feelings?"

"I will give you visitation rights. I won't even ask you to pay child support! I can support us! I'm asking you to do this for me. Please think about it."

"No way! You are out of your mind if you think for one minute I would impregnate you and walk away from my child! You don't know me at all and I certainly don't know you!" Greg slammed out of the house in a rage.

Danielle dropped back down to the sofa with her

head in her hands. Leaning back on the couch, she closed her eyes and prayed for a miracle.

Greg is furious and will probably never speak to me again. She knew she wouldn't have tried to cut him out of his child's life. She wanted him to be a part of the baby's life. Danielle wasn't sure what role she wanted him to play, but she knew she wanted him there.

I've really done it this time. I hurt him and I insulted him. I alienated the man I love and may have lost him for good.

Greg paced back and forth in front of the door. He was tempted to walk away and not look back, but the haunted expression in Danielle's eyes wouldn't let him. He knew pain when he saw it. He knew longing. She wanted a baby—his baby. She was desperate and she set aside her pride to ask him to father her child.

His hand shook as he reached out and touched the knob. He turned it slowly. He wasn't sure what he was going to do or say to Danielle, but he couldn't leave things like this. The thought of her having Drew or anyone else's baby was worse than walking on hot coals. He couldn't let it happen. He had to do something.

He opened the door and walked back inside. Her eyes flew open and met his. She was as surprised as he was that he came back.

"There is only one way I will agree to do this. If you want to have my baby, it's a package deal. Marry me," he said softly.

Danielle couldn't speak past the lump in her throat. She stared transfixed at the man she loved. This was what she wanted more than anything. It wasn't the circumstances she wanted, but it was her dream.

"Greg, you don't have to marry me. I'm more than willing to share the baby with you. I'll agree to any demands you make within reason of course."

Her heart was in her throat as he walked toward her.

Sitting down on the couch next to her, Greg ran his hand over his hair. He turned to face her.

"You've heard my answer. My terms are simple. Marry me or there's no deal." She broke eye contact with him. "I know it's not what you wanted, but those are my conditions. After we are married, we do whatever it takes for you to get pregnant. If you don't agree, I walk out that door and never come back. I'm sure you can talk Drew or someone else into whatever arrangement you had in mind. You either marry me or say goodbye to me. Those are your options."

"Don't be such a romantic," replied Dani sarcastically folding her arms over her chest. "No bended knee proposal. Instead you blackmail me."

She hated being backed into a corner and lashed out at him. He knew she would agree to his terms to get what she wanted.

"I am not blackmailing you. You have a choice. I gave you an option. It's up to you whether you take it. I tried to give you romance and you threw it in my face," he said defensively. He picked up the romance novel off the table and flung it across the room. "That's part of your problem. You read that garbage and expect life to imitate fiction. I am not a knight in shining armor and you are not a fairy princess. There is no happily ever after. You need to wake up from the fantasy world you are living in and join the real world. Life and happiness is what we make of it."

"I am not living in a fantasy world. I know fact from fiction. You're right about one thing, you are definitely not a knight in shining armor and I am not a damsel in distress."

"You could have fooled me. You seem pretty distressed. You're willing to marry me to get the baby you desperately want."

She folded her arms across her chest and said nothing. His words though painful to hear, were true. She was willing to marry him to have his child. So why couldn't she admit to him she still loved him? Why couldn't she tell him this is what she has always wanted? Anger and pride wouldn't let her. She didn't want to open herself up to be hurt again by him.

"This time we do things my way. You have exactly two weeks to plan a wedding. In case you had any notions of this not being a real marriage, you can forget it. This will be a real marriage, Danielle, in every sense of the word. There will be no divorce, so you think long and hard before you accept my proposal."

"Is that what you call it? I don't remember hearing a proposal. I remember you trying to manipulate me. I . . ."

The hard pressure of his mouth cut off any further protests. He enfolded her in his arms and she parted her lips and kissed him back with all the pent up passion she had been holding inside. All thoughts and questions about him and Jennifer were wiped from her mind as his mouth covered hers.

The time for those questions would come later. For now, she had everything she wanted right here in front of her.

After Greg left, Danielle took a shower and got ready for bed. She dropped down to bed and turned on the television. Picking up the phone, she dialed a number and waited.

"Hi," said Danielle turning off the television. "I hate to call you so late, but I have a problem. Do you have minute to talk?"

"You sound upset," said Liz picking up on her vibes. "What's wrong? Did something happen with you and Greg?"

"Oh yeah. I asked him to be my donor for a baby.

He agreed, on the condition I marry him. So we're getting married in two weeks."

"Okay, so is this good or bad? You knew he would turn down your request. Maybe subconsciously this is what you wanted all along?"

"I love Greg. You know that, but we still have so many unresolved issues and now we are bringing a baby into the middle of them."

"Then fix them. You need to work this out before you get married. Honey, communication is the key in every relationship. You love Greg and he loves you. This is a chance for you guys to finally get everything you want. Bridge the gap between you and take a chance. A baby needs a mother and a father."

When Greg got home, he phoned Mark with the news. Stunned and finally at a loss for words, Mark offered his congratulations.

"How are you dealing with this? Last night you were glad Danielle wasn't pregnant and now you're telling me you're marrying her to have a child. What's up with that?"

"Danielle's endometriosis has returned. If she intends to have a baby, it's now or never. Eventually, she will have to have a hysterectomy."

"When is the wedding? You are having a big Master's celebration, I assume?" he teased. "Oh boy, I can't wait, caviar and champagne."

"In two weeks," replied Greg ignoring his friend's sarcasm. "It will be whatever she can pull together in the next week or so. We don't have a lot of time to waste. The truth of the matter is she wanted to have my baby without benefit of a wedding ring. I forced the issue and she agreed."

"Well at least you two are finally getting married. I told you if you got her pregnant, she would marry you. So now she has to marry you to get pregnant. What sounds wrong with what I just said? I'm throwing the bachelor party. Leave all the details to me. I'll let you know when and where."

"Just keep it somewhat low-key. I don't plan on spending the night before my wedding in jail. Danielle would kill me."

"At least not until after the honeymoon." Mark laughed. "Hey, if you can't trust your best friend to plan your bachelor party, who can you trust?"

"My point exactly," said Greg, disconnecting the call. He knew whatever Mark was planning would be loud, raunchy, and something of which his fiancé would definitely not approve.

He dialed his mother's number and waited anxiously for her to answer. He knew she would be thrilled at the news. She didn't need to know all the details.

"Mom, hi. It's me. Guess what?" He carried the portable phone over to the sofa and sat down. "Danielle and I are getting married."

"Oh Greg, that's wonderful," beamed his mother excitedly. "When's the wedding? Where is the wedding being held?"

"We're getting married in two weeks. I'm not sure of the location yet. Danielle is making all the arrangements. I'll let you know the plans as soon as I know them."

"Honey, I am so happy for you both. I know how much the two of you love each other. This time, don't let anything come between you."

The next two weeks were total chaos for Danielle. Between work and planning for a wedding, she was exhausted.

Danielle called Drew and told him her news. He was happy for her and wished her and Greg all the best.

After finally breaking down and confessing to her father and Karen about why they were marrying so quickly, Karen took over most of the wedding preparations.

This gave Danielle time to catch her breath. She was already stressed enough wondering if she would be able to conceive a child.

After several big fights, Greg finally relented to having the wedding at Jack and Karen's home. He wasn't happy about it, but Danielle refused to get married anywhere else. She had jumped at the offer as soon as her father made it.

The bridal shower was held at the Masters Club, a week prior to the wedding. Liz had paid for two male strippers to entertain them, while Karen paid them not to strip. It was a small group of family and friends. They had a wonderful time. She had more sexy nighties than she would wear in a lifetime.

Three days before the wedding, she went officially on vacation. Greg came by to pick her up for the blood test and they had lunch together.

Greg changed right before her eyes. He was polite, but nothing more. He kissed her cheek when he left her each day, but he didn't push for anything more.

She tried to seduce him to make love to her, but he pulled away. She tried to get him to spend the night and again he refused and left.

Greg told her he was not about to risk getting her pregnant before the ceremony and having her dump him. Danielle was hurt that he thought she was that devious and conniving.

Chapter 16

Dani was awakened from a deep sleep by a noise. She crawled quietly out of bed and tip-toed into the living room. When she saw a darkly clad figure climbing into the window, she put her hand over her mouth.

Slipping back into her room, she locked the door, and picked up the phone to dial 911. She panicked when the phone went dead in her trembling hand. The door to her bedroom was kicked open, and she screamed.

Jumping off the bed, she ran to the dresser and picked up a pair of scissors. The intruder only smiled at her in amusement. A blue ski mask covered his face, but Danielle sensed something familiar about him. He advanced on her and she held up the scissors in front of her.

"Don't come any closer," she threatened in a shaky voice. "I will use these if I have to. Get out of my house."

"Sure you will, Princess," laughed the familiar voice. "But I can hurt you more." The man took out a small pistol from his sweater and leveled it at her. "Drop it," said the muffled voice.

Gasping, Danielle dropped the scissors. Her intruder grabbed her by the hair and threw her on the bed. Danielle stared up at him with fear written all over her beautiful face.

"Please don't hurt me. I'm pregnant. Please don't hurt my baby," she lied. Something flashed in his eyes and he took out a piece of rope and tied her hands. "What are you going to do to me? I'm begging you, please don't hurt my baby."

Dani struggled and fought him with everything she was worth. She bucked and kicked out at him as he attempted to place a piece of wide tape over her mouth.

When she bit his hand, he drew back to slap her. Catching himself in midswing, he pushed her on the bed. He taped her mouth shut. When he finished he stood back and looked at her with hatred in his black eyes.

"So the little ice princess is pregnant. Who's the father? Greg or Mark? Or do you even know?"

Danielle's head shot up in surprise. She knew why the voice sounded so familiar. A chill went down her spine when she realized whom the intruder was. Leo.

Leo continued, "I warned you to watch out for me. I told you, you never know who might crawl through your window. It was quite easy to. Maybe you should invest some of that money you have in a security system or burglar bars that actually work." Dani threw muffled curses at him. "I like you better this way. You have a nice house, Princess. Not exactly a castle, but it's you: soft, sensual, and inviting. So you and big brother are tying the knot tomorrow. I wonder what would happen if I raped you. Knowing Greg, he would never touch my leftovers. He would never look at you the same way again. He'd despise both of us. It would be worth it to see the look on his face."

Danielle watched in horror as Leo took off his ski mask and tossed it on the bed. Her look turned to one of pure terror when he pulled the sweater over his head and dropped it on the floor. He laid the gun on the nightstand next to the bed and advanced on her. "I'm going to show you what a real man can do, Princess. I have been in prison a long time. Tonight, I'm going to make up for lost time." Danielle inched away from him to the other side of the bed. Leo grabbed her and pushed her onto her back. "Careful, sweetheart. We don't want any harm to come to my little niece or nephew." Her eyes shot daggers at him as hot tears coursed down her face. "I'm not going to hurt you, unless you make me. I could tell you real stories of pain. Do know what they do to new inmates in prison? I won't bore you with all the sordid details. I'm sure you've seen movies. Sometimes I would even imagine it was you. You know it's your fault, I was sent to prison. You were monopolizing Greg's time when he should have been planning a winning defense for me. You put me there."

Think Dani. You have to delay him. Greg will be here in a few minutes. Greg will save you. He has to.

Thinking fast, Dani doubled over in pain. She then rolled over onto her side in a protective ball. She felt Leo's eyes on her and moaned. She noted the panic in his eyes. He ripped the tape off her mouth and stared at her.

"Leo, help me! I think I'm losing my baby! Please help me!" cried Dani closing her eyes. "I can't lose this baby!" she wailed.

"You are ruining all the plans I have for you. I have waited a long time for this. I have dreamed about this moment. Nothing ever goes right for me! " He untied her hands in frustration and moved away from her.

"Please call an ambulance. For God's sake this is your brother's unborn child we're talking about! You have to help me. Please!" Inside she was thanking God for all those years of drama classes.

"Can't a guy have a little fun? I was only trying to

scare you! Greg is going to kill me!" Leo scrambled off the bed and ran out of the room and out the front door.

Dani sighed in relief when she heard the front door slam. Taking another deep breath, she got to her feet. She picked up the gun, she went into the living room, and locked the front door.

She was still sitting on the couch shaking, when she heard a noise outside the door. Her hand was shaking as she held the gun aimed at the door. Her heart was pounding as the knob turned slowly.

"I can't believe you are cutting out on us," laughed Mark slapping Greg on the back. "You are so whipped. This is your last night as a bachelor and you want to spend it with Danielle. You are going to spend the rest of your life with her."

"Mark, I don't expect you to understand true love. Incidentally, I can't wait until you meet Miss Right. I am going to give you the same hell you've put me through."

"I wouldn't hold my breath," voiced Travis. "Mark may be a chick magnet, but he also knows how to run them off left and right."

"Thanks, Travis," smirked Mark. "You're whipped, too. You now have two females who have you wrapped around their little fingers."

"And proud of it. At least I have someone to grow old with. You chase everyone away who tries to get close to you."

"Okay, kids. Time out," whistled Greg signaling with his hands. "You two can continue this without me. I expect all of you at the Masters Estates no later than 4 o'clock. Goodnight." He whistled a merry tune on his way to his car. Easing inside, he started the engine. Reaching for the cell phone, he started to hit

Danielle's number on his speed dial. Instead, he hung up the phone smiling.

I won't wake her. I'll just ease into bed with her and surprise her. This is our last night of sinfully delicious sex. Tomorrow we will go to bed as man and wife.

Greg was still smiling as he pulled into Danielle's driveway. Getting out of the car, he walked up to the front door. He tried to be quiet as he slipped his key in the lock and turned the knob. He opened the door and stepped inside.

Danielle fired the gun when the door opened. A scream was ripped from her throat when she saw Greg propelled backward by the force of the bullet. She dropped the gun and ran to where he lay unmoving.

"Greg!" Her heart stopped the moment she saw him fall. She fell to her knees beside him. His shirt was blood soaked and he wasn't moving. After checking for a pulse, she grabbed her cell phone and dialed 911. "This is Danielle Masters at 7207 Mill Creek," she said. "I shot my fiancé. I thought he was an intruder and I shot him. There's blood and he's not moving."

"Ms. Masters, an ambulance is on its way," said the calm voice. "I need you to stay calm. Is the victim conscious?"

"No, he's just lying there. I think he may have hit his head when he fell. There's blood all over his shirt."

Greg's moan caught Danielle's attention. Disconnecting the phone and dropping it on the sofa, she rushed to him. Greg tried to sit up, but Danielle's hand stopped him.

"Don't move. Honey, you have to stay still. The ambulance is on its way. I'm so sorry." Her words were jumbled and rushed as she leaned over him.

It took him a few seconds to remember what happened. After the bachelor party, he came by to surprise her. Danielle shot him. His side aching attested to the pain from the bullet wound.

Seeing the fear in her eyes, he wanted to calm her nerves. He pulled her head down to his and kissed her.

"If you wanted to cancel the wedding, all you had to do was say so," teased Greg brushing the tears from her face.

"That's not funny. You scared me to death. I could have killed you," she scolded. "What are you doing here? You're supposed to be at your bachelor party." He tried to rise, again. "Don't you dare move another muscle! The ambulance is on the way."

"God, my head hurts almost as bad as my side. I'm here because I wanted to surprise you. I guess I'm the one who got the surprise."

The sounds of sirens in the background grabbed their attention. The next hour was the longest hour of Danielle's life.

Greg was examined and ready for transport to the hospital. The paramedic told them the bullet was lodged in his side.

Danielle wanted to ride with him in the ambulance, but the police wanted to question her. She asked them to follow them to the hospital and she would answer all their questions.

At the hospital, Danielle waited in the emergency room while Greg was rushed to the operating room. She was on pins and needles while she waited. She used the phone in the waiting room to call Travis. Danielle told him about Leo breaking into her house and how she mistook Greg for Leo and shot him. Travis said he would break the news to his mother before heading to the hospital.

When the police arrived to question her, she had no idea what she was going to tell them. She was torn between telling them the truth about Leo and hurting Greg and his mother. She didn't know if he was bluffing or if he would have raped her had she not faked a miscarriage.

Danielle didn't want to risk Doris Thomas having another heart attack from this news. She didn't have a chance to tell Greg the truth about what happened. She didn't want him to hear this from anyone but her.

She gave her statement to the police. As volatile as Leo was, she was afraid not to tell the truth. With a heavy heart, the told them the full story.

They left and she sat with her head in her hands. Her fear of Leo coming back and raping her caused her to shoot Greg. Greg was in surgery now because of Leo.

What if he didn't make it? What if I killed him? I'll never forgive myself if he doesn't make it. I'll never forgive Leo. He'll pay for this if it's the last thing I do.

She was sitting in a chair in the waiting room with her hands clasped and her eyes closed. She was praying for a miracle. A hand touched her shoulder and her eyes flew open.

Travis sat down next to her and held his arms open. She flew into them and he held her as she cried.

"When you're ready to talk, I'm ready to listen," he said softly caressing her back. "Take your time. This time, I don't want the abbreviated version. I want to know why Leo was at your house."

"I'd like to know the same thing," stated Mark towering over them. "When Greg left the party tonight, he was on cloud nine about getting married today. What happened between then and now?" Mark sat down in the chair across from Danielle and Travis.

Danielle retold the tale, not leaving anything out. Both Mark and Travis were in shock when she finished. They both stared at her speechless.

"Leo tried to rape you," Travis fumed getting to his feet. "Greg is going to kill him. The police better find him before Greg does. I don't understand this. What possessed him to go after you?"

"He blames me for his going to prison. He said

Greg was too busy with me to defend him properly. Leo also wanted to hurt Greg. Before he ran out he said he was only trying to scare me. He said he wasn't going to hurt me. I don't know if I necessarily believe that. He was so angry and bitter. When I heard the knob turn on the door, I thought he had come back to finish the job. I panicked and I shot Greg by mistake. I thought he was Leo."

"I guess we should have taken his threat against you more seriously," said Mark, getting to his feet. "Greg and I had no idea he would come after you."

"Now what are you talking about?" Travis asked turning to face Mark. "Could one of you shed some light on this for me? I seem to be in the dark."

"Leo cornered me in the kitchen at Greg's birthday party." Danielle folded her hands in her lap and took a deep breath before continuing. "He made some lewd suggestions and told me to keep my windows and doors locked. Mark walked in, and he and Leo got into a fight. Leo threatened Mark and I before he left."

"Does Greg know about this?" Travis asked baffled. Danielle nodded. "How much more can this family take? He's like a ticking time bomb. Who knows what he's going to do next? This is going to kill Mom."

"Then don't tell her," said Danielle softly. "I will only press charges for assault and breaking and entering. I don't want to be the cause of a setback in your mother's recovery. She's doing so well."

"That's an excuse, Danielle. And Greg?" asked Mark, "Are you going to sugarcoat the truth for him as well? I think enough lies have been told. The truth always has a way of coming out."

"I will tell him the truth as gently as possible, but I'm not telling him this morning. I want to make sure he's out of the woods first." Danielle put her head in her hands. "This is supposed to be our wedding day." Her tears started again. "This was supposed to be our wedding day and my fiancé is in the emergency room with a bullet in him. I shot him!"

"Ssh," said Mark putting his arms around her. "He's going to be fine. Dry your tears. You don't want Greg to see you like this. We all know this was an accident. We know you love Greg and he loves you."

"Can you go back and observe the surgery? It would make me feel much better." She pulled herself out of his arms and wiped her face. Danielle knew she had to be strong for Greg's sake.

"Sure thing. I'll be back as soon as it's over. Be strong." She watched him go through the double doors.

Chapter 17

Greg drifted in and out of consciousness. Everything was fuzzy and hazy as he tried to focus. He turned his head and took in the white room and the nurse checking his pulse.

He had a flash of being shot. That explained why he was in the hospital. He had no idea how, why, or who shot him.

He was so tired. His eyes were heavy and he could barely keep them open. Giving up the fight, his lids fluttered closed and he fell asleep again.

When he woke again it was light outside. Danielle was asleep in the chair beside the bed. Travis and Mark were both asleep on the couch.

His throat was so dry and he tried to clear it. Three pairs of eyes were immediately open, alert, and focused on him.

"Welcome back," whispered Danielle getting to her feet. She planted a soft kiss on his forehead and caressed his face.

"Thanks," he croaked catching her hand and kissing it. "What happened to me and why am I here?"

"Good to have you back, friend." Mark came forward and clasped Greg's hand. "You gave us a scare."

"Some people will do anything for attention," Travis chided as he leaned over and hugged his big brother. "How do you feel?"

They were both trying to sidetrack him to keep him from asking questions about the shooting. None of them were ready to tell him the truth yet.

Travis and Mark both stayed for about half an hour and left. They needed to make phone calls and go home and change.

This left Danielle and Greg alone to talk. She knew she couldn't avoid the topic of the shooting forever. Greg kept going back to it and she knew she had no choice.

As gently as she possibly could, she told Greg about Leo breaking into her house. Greg stared at her, too torn up to speak.

His brother not only broke into Danielle's house, but he attacked her. What else did he do to her? He didn't want to think about it, but he needed to know.

Greg knew Leo didn't like her, but he never imagined he would do anything like this. He didn't just go after any woman. He went after his brother's fiancé the night before the wedding and held her at gunpoint. Greg's mind began to wonder.

Did Leo rape her? Would he? No he couldn't do something that horrible. Leo was a lot of things, but I don't want to believe he is a rapist. Is Danielle protecting him?

The very idea of Leo putting his hands on Dani infuriated Greg. He had to know if his brother sexually assaulted her.

Greg closed his eyes and visions of Leo and Danielle haunted him. He sat up in bed and winced in pain. His pain was a reminder of all that happened that day.

Turning to face Danielle, Greg asked in a tortured voice, "Did he rape you?" He held his breath waiting for her response.

"No," she whispered past the lump in her throat. "I swear to you, he didn't rape me." She wiped the tears from her cheeks.

"But he meant to?" Greg persisted. "What stopped him? If he hates us both enough to do this, then words alone wouldn't have stopped him from carrying out his ultimate goal. He wanted to hurt you, to hurt me. Why did he stop?"

"I lied and told him I was pregnant." She took a deep breath. "I then told him I was losing the baby. He believed I was having a miscarriage. I begged him to call an ambulance and he ran out."

"And he left you? You could have been dying for all he knew and he ran out and left you? He deserves to rot in jail for what he did to you."

"Greg, Leo said he wasn't going to hurt me," she sniffed. "He said he only wanted to scare me."

Greg snorted in disbelief. If Leo went through all that trouble to get to her, it wasn't just a scare tactic and they both knew it.

"Danielle, you shot me thinking I was Leo coming back to hurt you. Clearly, you didn't believe him. You were terrified."

She dropped her head to her chest and took a deep breath. She couldn't deny what he was saying. She hadn't believed Leo any more than Greg believed his story.

"No, I didn't believe him. I truly believed he was going to rape me. He was so angry. He blamed me for his being sent to prison."

"That's garbage. That's not a reason. It's a convenient excuse for him to act like an animal." Greg shook his head sadly. "Why didn't you press sexual assault charges against him?" He caught her hand and pulled her to him. She sat down on the edge of the bed careful not to bump him. He laced her fingers through his.

"You and your mother have been through enough

because of Leo. I didn't want to risk her having a set-back and I didn't want to hurt you."

Greg told her to go down to the police station and press sexual assault charges. They both knew Leo would not get off lightly this time. He only got out of prison three months ago and now he would be headed back. With the charges of breaking and entering, sexual assault, and the gun, he would do some serious jail this time around.

Danielle was home changing when Mark called to tell her the police picked up Leo. She felt both relief, and sorrow for Greg's family.

When she thought about how close she came to losing Greg, she trembled. Greg was and had always been the man she wanted to spend the rest of her life with.

Her parents came by to see how she was doing. She visited with them for a short time before going back to the hospital. She wanted to be there when Greg woke up.

Greg had trouble sleeping and turned to Mark, who was sitting in a chair beside the hospital bed. "I can't believe any of this is happening. Leo went after Danielle. I let it happen. I knew he hated her. I thought his threat against her was all talk. I didn't take it seriously."

"None of us did. I heard it, too. I blew him off as well. Do you think he's using again?" Mark asked shifting in his chair.

"I don't know. Watch your back, Mark. Danielle wasn't the only one he threatened that night. He may come after you as well."

"Then you won't need to worry about a trial. If he comes after me, I won't see him as your brother. He will be the enemy and I will take him out. You need to relax and not worry about this. The police picked him up already. There's no way he can make bail without you. You are not to blame for what that worthless brother of yours did. He is twisted, Greg. He always has been. You need to concentrate on you and on getting well. Let the boys in blue handle Leo. I hear you're being discharged tomorrow."

"Yes, and I can't wait. Danielle's picking me up at noon. She's already moved most of her stuff into the house. I can't believe this happened the night before our wedding."

"Have you guys rescheduled yet?" Mark's beeper went off. "Hold that thought. I need to call the nurses' station." Mark picked up the phone and dialed. "This is Dr. Sanders." He paused and listened. "I'll be right there." He hung up the phone. "I'll drop by when I'm off duty."

Greg watched his friend leave the room. He knew Mark well enough to know if Leo went after him, his brother would lose. Mark was a doctor, but he grew up in the streets. He knew them as well as, if not better than, Leo.

"Tell me it isn't so," cried Doris Thomas coming into the room. "Tell me Cain didn't shoot Abel." Approaching the bed, she embraced her oldest son and kissed him. "Tell me Leo didn't do this to you." Her troubled brown eyes held his captive.

"Mom, Leo didn't shoot me," said Greg softly taking her hand in his, "but he was indirectly responsible. Have a seat."

Telling his mother the truth about her youngest son was one of the hardest things Greg ever did in his life. He would never forget the look on her face.

The pain was etched so deep in her eyes as she cried silent tears. Her hand gripped his tightly as she tried in vain to control her emotions.

Her pain was his pain. Greg wanted to wipe the floor with his brother for putting their mother through so much grief. She didn't deserve this. His mother was the kindest most unselfish person he knew. She deserved better.

Doris Thomas worked and struggled her whole life to give her children a better life than the one she had. She made sacrifice after sacrifice for her family. She devoted her life to her children and this is the thanks she gets.

Greg was determined to make sure this was the last time Leo hurt their mother. She deserved some peace and he was going to try and give it to her. He would not let her blame herself for Leo's mistakes. Leo was an adult capable of making his own decisions. He committed the crimes and he would do the time again.

Danielle went by Greg's house to pick up pajamas, a robe, and slippers. She prepared the downstairs guest bedroom for him. She didn't think he would be up to taking the stairs to get to his bedroom.

She arrived at the hospital around 11:30 A.M. to help Greg pack his things. They checked out at noon and she drove him home, where she made him go straight to bed. Once she had him settled in, she went to the kitchen to prepare a light lunch.

Greg was drifting off to sleep when she came in with the tray of homemade chicken soup, crackers, and juice. He eased into a sitting position and she set the tray across his lap.

"I thought you might be hungry. Is there anything else I can get for you?" She sat gingerly on the bed next to him.

"You can sit down and relax. Honey, this is not your fault," he said reading her mind. "It was an accident. I know you would never hurt me. There is no reason for you to feel guilty. You thought you were defending yourself."

"I almost killed you. I could have lost you. Greg, when I saw you fall, my life flashed before my eyes, and I couldn't imagine my life without you in it."

He moved the tray aside and pulled her into his arms. They held on for dear life, each realizing how close they came to losing the other.

"You are not going to lose me." He framed her face in his hands. "We have been through too much to let go now. I am in this for the long haul. We need to reset a wedding date. The sooner, the better."

After lunch, Greg took a pain pill and went to sleep. Danielle left and went home to pack some clothes. Until Greg was back on his feet, she was moving in to take care of him.

Greg was still asleep when she returned to his house. Danielle unpacked her things in one of the upstairs guest rooms and put them away. She would stay and take care of him until he was back on his feet.

She took out chicken and vegetables. Dinner would consist of baked chicken and steamed vegetables. She turned on the oven, while the chicken was defrosting in the microwave. When the timer sounded, she retrieved the dish from its resting place. Danielle seasoned the meat and covered the casserole dish before placing it in the oven.

Leaving the kitchen, she went to check on Greg. She found him still sleeping. Without making a sound, she kicked off her shoes and eased into bed beside him.

She stared at the peaceful figure lying next to her. Greg looked so peaceful in sleep. She resisted the urge to reach out and stroke his rough cheek. He now had three days' growth of beard covering his handsome face.

You have no idea how much I love you, how much I've always loved you. I almost lost you, but never again. For better or worse, I'm here and I'm staying. I'll just rest my eyes for a few minutes.

"Wake up, sleeping beauty," whispered Greg caressing her soft cheek. "Something smells wonderful."

"Hi. I didn't mean to fall asleep. I only shut my eyes for a minute. I didn't realize how exhausted I was." Yawning, Danielle sat up. She brushed the hair back from her face and smiled at Greg.

"After dinner, why don't you go home and get some rest? You look exhausted. I promise I will be fine for the night. I'm not an invalid. If I need anything, I will call you."

"Not a chance, Thomas. I'm staying. Whether or not you are too pigheaded to admit it, you need me as much as I need you. I'm not going anywhere. I'm supposed to be on my honeymoon, so I have the next two weeks free, and so do you."

They spent time laughing, talking, and getting to know each other again. Getting out the board games was a big mistake. Both Danielle and Greg were competitive to the bitter end.

Greg was reluctant at first to let Danielle take care of him. He never had to depend on anyone before and it unnerved him. Once he got over the initial problem, he enjoyed it. He loved having her around pampering him.

Danielle was quick to tell him not to get used to it. Once he was on the road to recovery, she was moving back into her house until they were married.

Greg's comeback was to go down to the Justice of the Peace and make it legal. He said they didn't think they needed a big wedding to be man and wife.

But Danielle had already bought a beautiful wedding gown and she had every intention of wearing it. She threatened him with a butter knife to keep the wedding on.

By the end of the first week with Danielle shadowing him, Greg was going stir crazy. He was used to an intense workout in his gym and running every morning. He had to settle for walking for the next four weeks, at least.

Danielle went with him the first couple of times to make sure he didn't overdo it. Then she realized Greg needed some time alone and gave it to him.

They sat down with their PDAs to set a date for their wedding. Danielle wanted two weeks from now. Greg couldn't do it. He was scheduled to be in Atlanta for a big trial.

The case he was working on was a difficult one and it required him to work a lot of long hours. They had no idea how long it would take.

Danielle was disappointed as she closed her PDA and said they could wait until he got back. Greg hated the idea and again tried to persuade her to go to the Justice of the Peace.

After their two weeks of solitude, they both went back to work. Greg worked from home preparing for his case.

Danielle didn't move out. She decided to stay until he left for his trip. She wasn't sure when she would see him again and wanted to make the most of the time they had.

She prepared a special meal for their last night together. Danielle went all out to set the mood. The table was set with fine china and crystal wine glasses. She added candles and soft music in the background.

"Wow," Greg said walking into the formal dining room. "Everything looks wonderful. Are you by any chance trying to seduce me?"

"That's depends," she smiled stepping into his open arms, "on you. What would you like for dessert?" Her mouth touched his lightly. "I bought strawberry cheesecake and a bottle of whipped cream."

"Mmm," he moaned seductively. "Sounds delicious. How about we skip dinner and go right to dessert? Is the whipped cream for the cheesecake or for after dessert?"

"You can have it any way you want it." She pulled

his mouth down to hers and kissed him hungrily. The kiss left him no doubt what she wanted.

Greg moaned again as his hands moved over her body in a gentle massage. He broke off the kiss and took a step back from her. His breathing was harsh and labored.

It was more than a month since they made love and he was having a hard time controlling himself. He didn't want to rush tonight. He wanted everything to be perfect for both of them.

"We'd better stop now or we won't get to dinner." His eyes spoke volumes as he took a seat at the table.

They talked through dinner discussing the cases they were working on. Greg talked about his reluctance to handle the case he was going to Atlanta to defend. He wasn't overly enthusiastic about defending corporate America in a racial discrimination case. He knew the only reason they chose him was because of race.

Danielle listened and reminded him everyone deserved their day in court. He had to separate himself emotionally from the case. He was a lawyer first.

Greg clicked on the remote to the stereo and the soulful voice of John Legend filled the air. "May I have this dance, Ms. Roberts?" Smiling up at him, she caught his outstretched hand and let him pull her to her feet. They both felt the spark as their hands touched.

When his arms closed around her, she almost moaned aloud at the sensations that shot through her tingling body. They moved seductively against each other.

"I want you," whispered the husky emotion-filled voice against her neck. "I've never wanted any woman as much as I want you right now." He raised her face to his. He saw his own need reflected in her gray eyes.

"I want you, too," she whispered against his mouth. "It's been much too long. Make love to me."

His mouth covered hers in a hungry kiss. Danielle responded with a passion of her own. Her lips parted beneath his. His tongue plunged into her mouth seeking and finding the hidden treasure he was looking for. Breaking the kiss, he caught her hand and led her up the stairs to the master bedroom.

Between hungry kisses, clothes flew everywhere as they quickly undressed each other. Greg pressed Danielle down against the cool, crisp, white cotton sheets. His body followed hers as she pulled him down on top of her.

Rolling to his side, he took her with him. His hand moved up her ribcage and still further up to cup and caress her breast. Danielle arched against his hand. He toyed with her nipple until it hardened. Greg's lips trailed a path down the side of her neck to her breast.

She gasped as he tongue snaked out and licked her nipple. He sucked her breast into his hot mouth and she held his head to her throbbing breast. He kissed and licked his way to the other breast and administered the same tongue-lashing. As his hand glided down her stomach, she quivered in anticipation. His hand followed the same path down to the juncture of her thighs. She opened for him like the petals of a flower.

Her eyes closed in pleasure when he gently slipped one finger inside her wet folds. Her legs parted to give him greater access. He stroked her until she was withering beneath him.

Danielle's body was on fire as he increased the pressure of his caressing fingers. She felt tightness in her loins as liquid fire spread through her body. The pressure continued to build until she exploded into a million pieces.

"That's only the beginning," promised Greg as he kissed his way down her stomach. He brought his fingers to his lips to taste the essence of her.

He moved down her body and gently parted her legs even wider. The air left her lungs as his tongue traced her nether lips. His tongue delved inside and Danielle lurched beneath him.

Gasping for air, she surged against his magical mouth. With his experienced hands and mouth, he took her over the edge again and again. She was gasping, panting, and clawing at the sheets when he moved back up her body.

Greg knew she was more than ready for him. She was hot, wet, and slick. He quickly tore open a plastic condom wrapper.

Rising above her, he joined his body with her inch by delicious inch. Danielle's moan of pleasure egged him on. He slowly began to move in and out of her tight, yet receptive body.

Danielle clung to him and mimicked his movements as he took her higher and higher. They came together in an explosion so brilliant they were both momentarily rendered unconscious.

Several times during the night, they turned to each other and made love again and again. They were both insatiable in their hunger. Finally exhausted, they both fell into a deep, relaxed sleep in the wee hours of the morning.

Danielle had to blink the tears from her eyes when Greg rose to leave the next morning. They weren't sure when they would see each other again. The case could be a long one.

He held her close for several seconds, before kissing her deeply. Wiping the tears from her flushed cheeks, he kissed her again.

"Take care of yourself, Roberts. I have a lot of years invested in you. I love you. Don't ever doubt it." Dani smiled through her tears and nodded.

"I love you, too," she whispered past the lump in her throat. Giving him one last hug, she released him and sadly watched him leave.

Chapter 18

The days turned into weeks. They talked on the phone every night, but it wasn't the same. She wanted to see him, to feel his arms around her.

Her workload prevented her from making a weekend trip to Atlanta. She worked three straight Saturdays preparing for her case.

Danielle was getting ready to leave work for one day when Jack came bursting into her office. His face was flushed and he was excited about something. He told her Holbrook had a lead on Alfred Roberts, her stepfather. Jack felt sure Alfred was the key to finding the child he convinced his deceased wife to give up for adoption. He was leaving for Atlanta to question him.

Danielle readily jumped at the chance to go with him. She wanted to be there when and if they found her long-lost sister. They made arrangements to leave on Friday night. Her father made all the reservations for them to fly out. She was more than a little excited upon learning they were staying at the same hotel as Greg.

After checking in, she told her father she was exhausted and turning in for the night. Grabbing her overnight case, she bribed the desk clerk into letting her into Greg's room.

The waiter wheeled in the meal she ordered along with the non-alcoholic cider and wine glasses. She tipped him and he left.

She put the food containers on the table, and then took the crystal candleholders and candles, out of her suitcase.

Next, she applied lotion and perfume to her body. Smiling, she slipped the silk thigh-high deep purple nightgown over her head. She stepped gingerly into the matching purple panties. Taking the clip from her hair, she ran her fingers through the curly mass and gave her head a shake.

Laying down on the bed, she moved from side to side trying to find the best seductive pose. She had just positioned herself on her side horizontally across the bed, when she heard the key in the lock.

Pushing one thin spaghetti strap off her shoulder, she leaned her head on her elbow and casually draped one arm the length of her bare thigh. Wetting her lips, she smiled and waited.

When the door opened, Danielle froze, then let out a squeal and pulled the coverlet over her half naked body. Greg stepped in front of the bed to obstruct the vision in his bed from his business associates.

Danielle's face turned red in mortification. There stood three men, not including the one who was supposed to be there, staring at her in open admiration. Danielle slid deeper under the covers.

She heard Greg usher the men back out the door into the hallway. Dani barely heard him say something about a rain check before the door closed muffling his voice.

A few minutes later, she was still under the covers when Greg pulled the comforter from over her head. Smoothing down her hair, he sat down on the bed next to her. Smiling into her flushed face, his lips brushed hers.

"Surprise!" said Dani pulling his head back down to hers. His mouth met hers this time with a hunger and urgency that thrilled her to the tips of her red-painted toenails.

Her tongue met his in a mating ritual. Without losing the contact, Greg layed down next to her and pulled her into his arms.

"God, I've missed you," whispered Greg's hoarse voice before his mouth covered hers again. His strong hands pushed the strap of her nightgown off her shoulder, and he caressed her heated flesh with his hands. His mouth followed hands as he nibbled at her bare shoulder.

"I've missed you, too," confessed Dani unbuttoning his shirt and pushing it off his broad shoulders. Her lips touched his bare flesh and she felt him tremble under her gentle exploration of his hair-roughened chest. She lovingly bit his nipple and felt him quiver.

With steady hands, she unzipped and unhooked his pants. Pushing them down past his muscular thighs, pants and boxers pooled at his feet and he kicked them aside.

"Don't make me wait any longer. I want you. Right here. Right now. Take me," whispered Dani nibbling his ear.

"I can't believe you flew all this way to see me, but I'm so glad you did. I've been dreaming about this night for weeks."

Feeling a twinge of guilt at not correcting his assumption, Danielle pulled his head back down to hers. "We'll talk about it in the morning," she hedged nibbling at his lower lip. "Right now, I need you." Rolling onto her back, she lifted her hips for him to slide the panties down her shapely thighs. He dropped them on the floor on top of his things.

"Just a second," said Greg leaving her long enough to get a condom from his wallet. Positioning himself above her, he slowly eased into her slick wet canal. Danielle let out a gasp of sheer pleasure as he slipped in all the way. Their bodies fit perfectly together. He was the hand and her body was the glove as she wrapped herself around him and held on.

Ever so slowly, he moved in and out and Danielle thought she would go crazy from pure bliss. She met him stroke for stroke until her body jerked and then exploded into a million pieces. Finding his own release, Greg collapsed on top of her. Slowly lifting his body off her, he pulled her into the circle of his arms and they both drifted off to sleep.

The next morning, the door banging against the wall abruptly awakened them. Jack came barreling into the room followed by hotel security.

Danielle sat up quickly, pulling the comforter up to her chest. Greg stared from her to Jack in confusion.

"What is going on?" Greg asked angrily glaring down at her. Her face turned red and she slid further down into the comforter. "What are you doing here, Masters?"

"I'm here looking for my daughter who is supposed to be in her room sleeping. You told me you were going to bed early. Had I known whose bed you meant, I wouldn't have been worried sick about you," chastised Jack. "I have been ringing your room for the past hour. I finally called the front desk and then hotel security. When they unlocked your room and I found your bed hadn't been slept in, I panicked. You have never acted this irresponsibly before. It must be the company you're keeping."

"I'm sorry you were worried," she said quietly. "As you can see I'm fine. If you knew where I was and whom I was with, you shouldn't have barged in. A phone call would have sufficed. I wanted some time alone with Greg. I should have told you he was staying here."

"Get out of my room Masters and take him with you," fumed Greg pointing to the security guard. "Next time try knocking on the damn door!"

"Dad, please go. I'll be there as soon as I can." After one last glare at her and Greg, Jack walked out the open door.

"Sorry, Mr. Thomas, he demanded to be let in," apologized the confused security guard closing the door behind him.

She watched Greg climb out of bed and pull on his silk boxer shorts. He sat down on the bed and turned around to face her.

"Now I suppose you'd better tell me the real reason you're here. God, it was so stupid of me to assume you actually came here to be with me. When will I ever learn?" he mumbled. Dani bit her lip at the pain she saw in his troubled brown eyes. "Let me guess. Since Jack is here too, that must mean this has something to do with your family. Is your long-lost sister here in Atlanta?"

"No, she's not here. Jack's detective traced my stepfather to Atlanta. We went by yesterday to see him and he reluctantly told us where Janelle is. She's living in New York. Jack and I are flying there today. I didn't tell you this last night because I wanted the night to be special. I didn't want to fight with you. I know you're angry with me, but please try to understand. I need to find my sister."

Without saying a word, Greg came to his feet and left the room. A few minutes later, she heard the shower running. Danielle climbed out of bed and got dressed.

She was combing her hair when Greg walked back

into the room. He had a white towel draped around his waist. He ignored Danielle and he put on a pair of gray sweats and sneakers.

"Greg. Say something. Look at me," pleaded Dani. "Please try to understand why I'm doing this. I need you to understand. Finding my sister is important to me."

"What's there to say, Dani? I'm tired of competing with your family for your attention. Is that simple enough for you? You didn't think twice about hopping on a plane to look for your sister, but you didn't think for a minute about coming here to see me. Anything to do with the Masters family is priority and I'm just an afterthought. Well, I'm sick of it. When we get married, I will become the center of your life, not them. If we say 'I do,' it's for life. There's no turning back. Go to New York with Jack. I doubt if I could stop you anyway. I hope you find your sister, but when I come home, you are going to have to make a choice about who is more important to you, your family or me. It's not a choice. It's a fact. I'll see you when I get back to Dallas." With that Greg left the room.

Greg slammed the door behind him furiously. He had let her do it to him again. This time around, he thought things would be different, but he was wrong. Her family still came first and he was somewhere down the line. Where he wasn't sure.

He had been overjoyed when he had opened the door to find her lounging casually on his bed half-naked. At first, he had thought he was dreaming.

Closing his eyes, he tried to erase the vision of her in that bed covered in purple silk. It was no use, though. The image of her was forever branded in his mind.

Taking the elevator down to the ground floor, he jogged out of the building and down the street. Maybe if he became totally exhausted, he wouldn't think about her and it would dull the pain a little.

Danielle and Jack were back on the plane two hours later headed for New York. Jack tried to make conversation, but she was not in the mood for it. She was still thinking about what Greg said and the painful realization of the truth. Greg was right. She did put her family first and him second.

Over the years, she had chosen to be with her family over being with him on several important occasions. Dani wondered if it were possible to make it up to him. She had hurt him too many times to count. Was there any way for him to get past it?

She could still see the pain in his eyes when he discovered she had not come there to see him, but to find her sister. She also remembered his joy when he thought she had come there to see him. He had been thrilled to see her. Dani closed her eyes to try and erase the memory of his pain.

The meeting with Janelle turned out to be another disappointment. Janelle sent her 4-year old son, Tony, from the room as soon as she saw them. Her sister didn't believe them, when they told her Danielle was her sister and Jack her father. They went on to tell her how Alfred convinced the twins' mother it would be best to put one of the girls up for adoption. She didn't want to believe or accept what they were saying. Janelle threw them out of her apartment and told them never to contact her again.

When Danielle arrived home, her message light was blinking. Dropping down to the sofa, she kicked off her shoes and laid back.

"Beep. Dani, hi. It's Liz, call me when you get back.

Beep. Dani, it's Drew. Just calling to request a wedding invitation. I'll catch you later. Beep. Ms. Robert, it's Policewoman Susan Powers. Leo Thomas is going to trial in two weeks. We need you to be there to testify. You should be receiving a call from the district attorney's office in the next few days. Beep. Ms. Roberts, this is Alexis Jeffreys from the District Attorney's office. I'd like to set up a meeting with you some time next week. Please call me. Beep. Danielle, it's Randy. You married yet? If not call me. Beep. Click. Beep. Click. Beep. Dani, it's Mrs. Thomas. Call me. Beep. Dani, it's Greg, give me a call when you get home. Beep. Click."

Danielle ate a light dinner and watched television for a while. She took a shower around 9 o'clock and got ready for bed before returning any phone calls.

"Room 512 please." Lying back on her pillow, she clicked on the television and hit mute as she waited to be connected to Greg's hotel room. "Hi. It's me." There was silence on the other end of the line. "Are you there?"

"I'm here," said the tight voice. "I'm a little surprised you called. I know how low I rank on the totem pole."

Danielle winced at the barb. She knew he resented her family and there was nothing she could do about it, but she didn't want to fight with him tonight.

"I didn't call you to fight. I called to say I'm sorry I didn't tell you the truth about why I was in Atlanta. I really was going to tell you the morning my father beat me to the punch."

"I don't want to fight either," he said sighing heavily. "When did you get back? Did you find your sister?"

"We got back a couple of hours ago. We found her. It didn't exactly go the way I wanted it to, but I got to meet her. How is the case going?"

"The judge gave us two weeks to wrap things up.

You have about three weeks to plan our wedding. This is the last wedding attempt, Roberts. If this fails, we go straight to the JP."

"It won't. I never meant to hurt you, and I hated leaving the way I did." She twisted the phone cord around her finger.

"That's part of our problem. We never mean to hurt each other, but we always end up doing it anyway. Maybe we need to try a little harder to think about each other's feelings. I have to admit when I walked into the room and saw you lying there I was ecstatic. I thought, 'wow she did this just for me?' I was on cloud nine. The kicker was when Jack walked in and I knew you weren't there because of me. It was like a knife through my heart."

"I'm so sorry," she apologized again. "I would give anything to redo that evening. I wasn't thinking about why I was there. I was so happy we were staying at the same hotel. I wanted to see you, to surprise you. I missed you so much."

"If we are going to have any chance, we have to be open and honest with each other. I want us to do this the right way this time."

Danielle had dinner once a week with her parents. She also spent a lot of time with Liz and the twins. The babies were getting big so fast.

Danielle missed Greg, so to keep distracted she called her cousin Betsy. They went out to dinner and then took in a movie. With so much in common, it didn't take long for the two of them to form a close friendship. They liked the same music, movies, and books.

Thanksgiving came. The Masters had their usual family get-together. Thanksgiving dinner was at Jack's; Christmas dinner would be held at Lawrence's. Everyone was required to bring one home-cooked dish and a big appetite.

After dinner, everyone sat around in the den watching football and talking. All the family was there, except for John, Richard, and Rebecca. The family had a nice dinner without all the drama, which came alone with John. No one mentioned any of the missing three.

Danielle slipped out of the room and went out the back door to the gazebo. She breathed in the cool fresh air, hugged her arms around herself protectively, and sat down on the bench. Millions of stars twinkled down at her and lit up the sky. For late November, the weather was still fairly warm.

"Dani," called Liz, who followed her. "What are you doing out here? The party is inside. Okay, the noise is inside." Liz joined her on the iron bench.

"I miss Greg. I'm so tired of this long-distance relationship. I want him home with me. It's just so frustrating. For the past five years of my life I have been looking forward at one time or another to becoming Mrs. Greg Thomas. Sometimes I think it's a pipedream that's never going to come true."

"It will happen. Think positive. As soon as Greg returns, you two are finally going to get married. He loves you and you love him."

"I have tested his love for me so many times. I have pushed him away and pulled him to me so many times; he didn't know which way to respond. If it wasn't for the baby issue, I'm not sure we would be getting married. We can't seem to get it together."

"You guys will get it together. You both have your whole future to look forward to. I can't wait to hold my little godchild on my knee."

"I'm praying it will happen. He was furious and hurt when he found out why I was in Atlanta. I should have told him the truth. I didn't trust in his love for me. I was afraid to tell him there was a possibility that I may never be able to have children. Instead of being honest with him, I kept pushing him away. I even walked out of his life. I don't know if he will ever be able to forgive me for it."

"Honey, I think he already has forgiven you. We have all made mistakes. You are not perfect. I have to agree with him about family. You have always put Uncle Jack ahead of everyone. I understand part of it is the fact you found out he was your real father. You don't have to try and constantly please or appease him. He's going to love you know matter what. You need to come to terms with the fact that you are marrying Greg. He will be your family. He should be your first priority and Uncle Jack, Aunt Karen, and Janelle are all going to have to take a back seat to him. If you want this marriage to last, you better make him feel like he comes first in your life. You have to prove to him he is the most important person in your life. If you can't do this your marriage is doomed from the start. Saying you love someone is not enough. You have to show them."

"I have loved Greg for as long as I can remember. The problem is, I don't always know how to show him. I don't know what I'd do if I lost him again." Dani came to her feet restlessly. "What am I saying, I won't lose him? He feels sorry for me. He knows how much I want a baby. Greg wants a family as well. I just don't want this to be the driving force in our marriage. I want more. I want his love and his respect. How do I make up for all the heartache I've caused him?"

"That's something you are going to have to figure out for yourself. From where I'm standing, you'd better do it pretty quick. You can start by showing and not telling him you love him and go from there. Why don't you go give him a call? He's probably alone in that miserable hotel room on Thanksgiving thinking about you, missing you, and wishing he were here with you. So tell me Dani, why aren't you there with him? Why are you here and thinking about him?"

"OK. OK. I get your point. Thanks Liz for always knowing the right thing to say," said Dani hugging her best friend.

Mark was attending a medical convention in Mobile, so he flew to Atlanta to spend Thanksgiving with Greg. It saved them both from being alone for the holiday.

They had dinner at a nice family-owned restaurant. Greg had eaten there on several occasions since being in the city and the food was wonderful.

"Thanks for coming Mark," said Greg sipping his drink. "I really didn't want to spend Thanksgiving alone."

"Neither did I," admitted Mark raising his beer bottle. "A toast. To good friends. Have you talked to Danielle today?"

"No," said Greg taking another gulp of his beer. "I suppose they are having a big Masters get-together like they usually do. How I used to hate those things! I was always this close," said Greg separating two of his fingers about an inch apart, "from cutting John's throat with a butter knife. The more pain the better. I don't know how Dani can stand to be around him knowing how he feels about her. And don't get me started on Jack. No one will ever be good enough for his little girl."

"Are those his feelings or yours?" Mark held up his hand to silence his friend. "Forget I said that. I'm not having the 'I'm not good enough for Danielle Roberts Masters' conversation again. You miss her. Call her when we get back to the hotel."

"No." Greg shook his head. "I am not giving in this

time. Why do I have to always be the one who calls? Why can't she call me?"

"Pay the check Thomas and let's get out of here," voiced his friend throwing up his hands in exasperation. "You are not only whipped, but you are hopeless."

"I am not whipped," he snapped bringing the beer bottle to his lips. "There's a difference between being in love and being whipped."

"There is? I didn't know there was a difference. You are so whipped," Mark teased, taking a gulp of his beer. "Danielle has you wrapped around her . . ."

"Don't even say it, Doc," warned Greg frowning at his friend. "Let's get out of here." Greg finished his beer and sat the bottle on the table. Paying the check, they left the restaurant.

The ensuing argument continued until they were back at the hotel. Once there they got into a drinking contest and as usual, Mark won. Shaking his head, he helped his friend back up to his hotel room.

Taking Liz's advice, she took out her cell phone and dialed his hotel room. It rang several times before it was answered. She was disappointed when the receptionist informed her Greg was out for the evening. She hoped he was at least not spending Thanksgiving alone.

Greg called her the next day. He informed her Mark had flown down to Georgia to spend Thanksgiving with him.

Danielle flinched involuntarily. *Why didn't I think of that? I should have been with him, not Mark, who was probably trying to talk Greg out of marrying me.*

He also told her the judge gave them an extension on the case and he probably wouldn't be finished by Christmas. He was unsure of whether he was flying home or not at this point.

During the weeks leading up to Christmas Danielle was swamped at work. As a result she waited until the last minute to do her Christmas shopping. The malls and the outlet malls were like a three-ring circus.

She spent a lot of time with Betsy. They went to dinner, to movies, and had sleepovers. Her cousin Teresa would occasionally join them for a night out on the town.

She phoned Janelle on several occasions. Janelle's nanny, Mrs. Sanchez always answered and told her Janelle was out. When Danielle had asked how Janelle and Tony were, she grudgingly admitted the Corinthos, her ex-husband and his father were causing trouble for Janelle at her job. They had filed a petition for sole custody of Tony.

When Dani called Jack to tell him this, he flew off to New York to lend his support. When he got there he discovered that Janelle had disconnected her phone and moved without leaving a forwarding address.

Jack hired a New York private investigator to track her down. He discovered Janelle had been fired from her job at the hospital because of the Corinthos and that she and Tony were about to be evicted from their home when they fled. There was no sign of Janelle.

Danielle had been doing a lot of thinking and decided to fly to Georgia and spend Christmas with Greg. She had not yet informed her parents of this decision. She'd thought about waiting to call them once she got there to tell them. She was counting her traveler's checks when the doorbell rang.

She looked down at her watch and frowned. Whoever it was only had about ten minutes before she had to leave for the airport.

She peered out the peephole and saw Karen. She opened the door and stepped back for her to enter.

"Hi. This is a surprise. What are you doing here?" asked Danielle hugging her and leading her inside.

"I'm not sure. Call it mother's intuition or something. I just felt like you needed to see me." She immediately spotted the luggage by the door. "Going somewhere?" she asked with raised eyebrows. "Sneaking off like a thief in the night are you? Were we at least going to get a phone call on Christmas day?" she teased.

"I wasn't exactly sneaking. I was simply trying to avoid an argument with Dad about how families should be together on the holidays. As much as I love you guys, I love Greg, too. I'm spending Christmas in Georgia with him. He has to come first in my life and Dad will have to understand."

"Good for you. I'm glad to see you finally understand what marriage is all about. Leave your father to me. I hope you have a wonderful Christmas. Give Greg my love." She smiled.

"Thanks, Aunt Karen. I knew you would understand." Danielle hugged her. She loved her stepmother dearly.

"We'll miss you, but I do understand, and I'll make Jack understand. I think he needs a little reminder of what I gave up to be with him. I would do it all over again. Your father and you mean the world to me. Come on I'll walk you out," said Karen putting her arm around Danielle's shoulder. "Have a safe trip."

Chapter 19

Greg tried to not be disappointed Danielle hadn't taken his advice, as far as he knew, and hopped on a plane to spend Christmas with him. He could have just as easily gone home for Christmas, but he tested her and she failed, again.

He was having some serious doubts about their future. He wondered if she was marrying him strictly to get the child she so desperately wanted. She said she loved him, but actions spoke louder than words and she had yet to prove it to him.

Would a marriage between them be disastrous? Was it doomed from the start? Those were all questions he kept asking himself. Was love enough to get them through this? Greg wasn't so sure anymore.

He tapped his foot in impatience as he waited for the message on Mark's cell phone to finish. "Mark, it's Greg. I wanted to make sure you still needed me to pick you up at the airport at 9:00 P.M. Since you're not there, I'll take that to mean yes. I'll see you when you land. I'll meet you in the baggage claim area."

He hung up the phone and dropped down to the bed. He had several hours to kill before Mark's plane arrived. He'd give almost anything if it were Dani instead of Mark coming.

Dani slept all the way to Georgia. She only woke up when they asked everyone to put their seats in an upright position.

She collected her luggage before calling the hotel. She dialed the hotel excitedly and asked for Greg's room.

"Hi. How are you?" asked Dani smiling into the receiver. She was giddy with excitement and couldn't wait to see him.

"Lonely. Missing you. Feeling sorry for myself because I'm spending Christmas here in this place, when I should be home spending it with you," said the deep husky voice.

"Do you mean that?" she asked hopefully. "And what would you do if I were here with you?"

"I'd probably rip all your clothes off and make love to you on the floor. I doubt I could make it as far as the couch and the poor bed wouldn't stand a chance. I'd make love to you all night long and then wake you in the morning. It's been almost two months, Roberts. Abstinence is not exactly my strong suit. You'd either be begging me to stop or to continue. I'm not sure which it would be at this point. I'd better stop before I have to go take a cold shower and call you back."

"Forget the shower." She smiled. "I'm at the airport. Why don't you come and get me. I'll be waiting at American gate five."

The phone went dead in her hand and Dani laughed hanging up the telephone. She paced back and forth impatiently before going outside to wait.

Half an hour later, she was a bit startled when a sleek black Bonneville, came to a screeching halt beside her. Her face lit up when Greg vaulted out of the car. In seconds, they were in each other's arms.

Neither knew who moved first, nor did it matter. Lips met and clung, as did bodies. They were both grinning from ear to ear.

Greg pulled back slightly and held Danielle at arms length so he could look at her. Caressing her cheek, his lips crushed hers again. She melted in his arms and returned his kiss eagerly.

"I can't believe you're here. This is a wonderful surprise. We'd better get you out of the cold," said Greg opening the car door and helping her inside. He put the luggage in the trunk and then climbed in next to her. "Are you hungry?"

"I'm always hungry, but not just for food. I've missed you so much." Her hand slid into his. "I'm so glad I came."

"Me, too." Greg squeezed her hand. "I missed you, too. I can't wait to make you Mrs. Greg Thomas."

They ate at an elegant chic little Italian Bistro down the street from the hotel. Dani ordered chicken primavera and Greg ordered chicken Parmesan. They hardly tasted the food. Their eyes were too busy drinking in the sight of each other. Two months seemed like a lifetime away from each other.

"I still can't believe you're here. This is not a trick this time, is it? You are here because of me. Tell me I'm not dreaming."

"If you are, then we are both having the same dream. I'm here and I'm real." Her hand caressed his cheek. "I am here because I love you. I want to spend the holidays with you. Greg, you are my family. We are getting married soon, I hope."

"I bet dear old Dad is in a tizzy with his little girl away from home during the holidays." Danielle dropped her head guiltily, and didn't respond. "Let me guess," he said intuitively, "You didn't tell him." Her face flushed a beet red. "What did you do, leave him a note? Dear Dad, I'm spending the holidays with your worst nightmare. Merry Christmas, Danielle."

"No, I didn't leave him a note and believe me you are not his worst nightmare. You rank at second place. I told Karen. She's going to tell him. She caught . . . I mean she came by when I was leaving."

"You ran away from home," he teased. "You were sneaking off like a teenager for a weekend tryst with your lover and you got caught." Greg laughed in amusement.

Danielle joined in his merry laughter. It was good to hear him laugh again. She saw the happiness is his eyes, which mirrored her own.

"Okay, so it is pretty funny, but it's the thought that counts. I wanted to be here with you. My father will have to understand I'm not a little girl anymore."

"I guess it is the thought that counts." He caught her hand and brought it to his lips. "So can I look forward to spending Christmas with just you, or is Jack showing up and bringing the whole clan with him?"

"I promise you, he won't be putting in an appearance this time. I told Karen I wanted to spend Christmas with you and you alone."

"I just wish you had the guts to stand up to your father yourself. You shouldn't put Karen in the middle of your fight. You always let him treat you like a child."

"Thank you for your closing remarks, Counselor, because this conversation is over." She pulled her hand free. "I didn't come here for a lecture. Please don't spoil the time we have together. If you want to fight about my father, I can catch the next flight back to Dallas. I'm here Greg, with you. Let the rest go for now." Her eyes flashed angrily at him.

"OK. I'm sorry," said Greg quietly. "I don't want to fight with you either. I really am glad you're here. I've

missed you." His hand covered hers and gave it a light
squeeze. "Let's go back to the hotel. I'll prove it to
you, again and again," he whispered. At his leering
smile, Dani's anger melted away. He brought her hand
to his lips and then pulled her to her feet. "Come on.
I'm ready for dessert."

When they got back to the room, Greg showered
and slipped on a pair of silk pajama bottoms. He
pulled back the covers on the bed.

Her mouth watered as she stared at the bronze
Adonis standing before her. Her hands itched to reach
out and run themselves over the muscular chest. She
resisted the urge and grabbed her overnight bag.
Giving him one last look of longing, she went into the
bathroom.

After showering, Dani applied perfumed lotion to
her body from head to toe. Slipping the slinky red
satin thigh-high nightgown over her head, she surveyed herself in the mirror. Fluffing out her hair, she
closed the bathroom door behind her.

Entering the bedroom, she was taken aback by the
dimmed lights and soft jazz playing. Greg was already
in bed and the comforter was pushed to the foot of the
bed. His gaze met hers and his eyes devoured her.
Danielle shivered at the blatant hunger in his eyes.

Slowly, she walked toward him. She slipped into
bed beside him and he pulled her into his arms. Raising up on one elbow his hand caressed her flushed
cheek. His lips touched hers lightly and his caressing
hand traveled downward. Warm fingers circled her
breast, and her nipple hardened at his light touch. His
hot mouth slowly followed his hands. He slid the
straps of the gown down to her waist. She gasped
when he took her breast into his hot mouth. His

tongue gave her breast a tongue lashing that left her breathless and panting for more.

Her hand covered her head to hold him in place. She withered beneath wanting more, needing more. She was on fire. Her passion for him was burning out of control.

When his hand covered her mound, she sucked in a deep breath. Danielle tensed and then relaxed as one finger slipped inside her already wet passage. He stroked her until she was withering beneath his experienced hands.

"There is so much I want to do to you, but I can't wait," confessed Greg breathlessly against her throat. "It's been too long."

"Then don't wait. I want you, too. We've got the next three days for you to make it up to me," whispered Dani pulling him down on top of her.

Their bodies came together in a powerful thrust. Her gasp and his guttural groan filled the air as his body filled hers.

Greg willed his body to go slowly, but Danielle was having none of it. She moved feverishly beneath him making him speed up the tempo. They moved together until both of their bodies exploded into a million tiny particles. The fiery explosion left them both shaken at the intensity of their coming together.

Soaring back to earth, Greg smiled down into Dani's passion-glazed silver eyes. When he attempted to lift his body from hers, Dani locked her legs around his thighs to keep him from pulling away. She wasn't ready to let him go yet.

"Not yet," said Dani hugging him to her. She loved the warmth and feel of his body against hers. "I've missed you."

"I'm glad, because I've missed you," said Greg moving to his back and pulling Dani with him.

"This is going to be a Christmas to remember,"

smiled Dani wistfully, running her fingers through the coarse hairs on his chest. "It's our first Christmas together in two years."

"I don't know how to say this," said Greg propping himself up on his elbow, "I have some bad news for you. Please don't get too upset. Stay calm and keep an open mind."

"I can handle anything as long as we're together. Nothing is going to spoil our holiday. There is absolutely nothing you can say to ruin this moment," she stated boldly kissing him.

"Mark is arriving here in about an hour. He's staying through Christmas. He's booked in the room across the hall."

"So, I was wrong," said Danielle punching the pillow and then laying back on the bed. She stared bleakly up at the ceiling. "Why, pray tell, is he coming here? My favorite persona and I get to break bread together at Christmas. This is a mean and cruel joke. God is testing me. That's it. This is a test. Doesn't Mark have a family somewhere? Why isn't he going home to St. Louis to spend Christmas with his parents? Why do I have to share you with him? It's not fair. We are going to drive each other, not to mention you, insane."

"Calm down. There's something you don't know. Mark's parents were killed in a car accident last Christmas driving down to Dallas. This is Mark's first Christmas without them. I couldn't let him spend it alone. He needs us. What kind of friend would I be if I weren't here for him when he needed me most? He's always been there when I needed him."

"I'm sorry. I didn't know about his parents. He never said a word to me about this when I saw him last year," stated Dani casually.

"It won't be as bad as you think. Honey, he's my

best friend. I would really like for you two to get along. After a while, he starts to grow on you."

"Like a fungus I'm sure. Why isn't he spending the holiday with Rolonda? I thought they were getting along really well."

"Not anymore. She wanted a serious relationship and Mark ran the other way, which is status quo for him. I can't wait until he finally meets his match. I hope he finds someone just as sarcastic and unyielding as he is."

"Are you sure there's not something going on between the two of you I should know about?" asked Danielle smiling sheepishly at him.

"Are you kidding? I would never sleep with a tramp like Mark." He winked, rolling over on top of her.

"You slept with Debra," mumbled Danielle half under her breath. She couldn't resist the barb.

"Dani," said the warning voice. "Don't go there. Let's make a deal. We will not discuss past liaisons. I won't ask you any questions about your past and you won't ask me any. Deal?"

"I don't have much of a past. You're the one with the ex-fiancé, not to mention the stalker you had before her."

"You would bring that up. I'm going to take a shower. Care to join me? I'll wash your back if you wash mine." He got out of bed and held out his hand to her. She caught it and he pulled her to her feet. She laughed as he swung her up in his arms and carried her to the shower.

After a long hot and steamy shower they dried each other off and got dressed. Danielle sat at the bureau brushing her hair.

"Just think of it as your most memorable Christmas ever. Please be nice to Mark. I'll make sure he stays in his respective corner of the ring if you will, so you two need not come to blows. I never could understand the animosity between the two of you. At one time I thought you and Mark had the hots for each other. You know, one of those love–hate relationships."

"Hardly." She laid the brush down and came to her feet. "That is the most ridiculous thing I have ever heard you say. Mark loathes the ground I walk on and the fairy tale he thinks I live in. I'm not exactly his type."

"True point, but I wish the two of you could bury the hatchet and be friends." Her eyes narrowed. "Okay so maybe that's stretching it. How about being civil?"

"I can handle civility. I think. I'm making no promises if he starts with me. I will try to be nice to him this weekend. After Christmas, all bets are off."

"Good enough," said Greg dropping a kiss on her pouting lips. "All I'm asking is you give it a try."

Danielle breathed a sigh of relief when he finally dropped the subject. Mark Sanders was a subject she did not want to delve into. Every time she saw Mark, she felt guilty. He reminded her of a night she wanted to forget.

She tried to talk Greg into leaving her behind while he picked up his friend, but he was having none of it. He pulled her out the door behind him.

Danielle didn't go willingly, but she went with him to the airport. Her holiday was not going anything like she had planned. This was supposed to be a special weekend for the two of them.

They were waiting at the gate, when she spotted Mark. Greg waved to him and Dani saw his gait slow, when he saw her. Pasting on a smile, she watched him and Greg exchange warm greetings.

"Am I seeing things or is this a mirage? I guess if it was a mirage it wouldn't be Danielle I'd be seeing," Mark teased.

"Cut it out. This is a no mudslinging weekend. It's

Christmas and we are all going to spend it together. Are you hungry?"

"No, but I could use a drink. The plane got in a little late, so I'd better go check in at the hotel first. This is definitely going to be an unusual Christmas," said Mark under his breath, while opening the car door for Danielle.

"I wholeheartedly agree, Doc." Danielle climbed into the car and slammed the door shut in his face.

Three whole days with Mark Sanders, what did I do to deserve this? I can do this. I have to do this. Greg and Mark are best friends. I have to accept that. God give me strength, patience, and a sense of humor, because I am definitely going to need all three to deal with Mark's sarcasm and witty repertoire.

They were seated at the bar in the hotel lobby when Greg's beeper went off. Uncomfortable at being left alone with Mark, Danielle watched Greg go up to his room to answer the call.

"I won't bite, Danielle. You are perfectly safe with me," said Mark trying to put her mind at ease. "Relax."

"Mark, I hate this charade we're playing." She nervously took a sip of her frozen margarita. Her hand shook slightly as she set the glass back on the table.

"I know it is, but we have to do it. Have you changed your mind? Do you want to tell Greg about us? Do you want to ruin our friendship? Do you want to lose him forever? He would never forgive either one of us. If you decide to tell him, we'll both lose him. Is that what you want?"

"That's not what I want, either. You are his best friend. He needs you in his life. I just feel guilty about it."

"Don't. It was my fault. You were lonely and missing Greg. I knew what you were doing and I didn't care. I wanted you. I took unfair advantage of you. I never had any illusions that you cared anything about me and it was just sex for me. I know you were trying to get back at Greg by going out with me. You wanted Greg, not me," he said honestly. "I wanted you because I knew I couldn't have you. I wanted sex, Dani, nothing more. Call it a moment of temporary insanity," he whispered. "I admit, that I am a little attracted to you, but I know your heart belongs to Greg and his belongs to you. I will not let you destroy his happiness or yours. I love Greg like a brother and I don't want to see him hurt by this. We have an agreement, Danielle. Neither one of us will tell Greg or anyone else about this. This is our secret. We made a mistake and because of that we have to live with the consequences of that mistake the rest of our lives. We shared an almost wonderful night together. We can't let one mistake destroy our lives. You don't have to avoid me or worry when I'm with Greg because I would never tell him that I lusted after his ex-fiancé. You and Greg have always belonged together. This is the last conversation I want to have about that night. We have to get past this and get on with our lives. Some things were just not meant to be. You and Greg were meant to be. Let yourself enjoy it and be happy. I'm happy for you guys. "

Danielle stared at Mark in surprise not knowing what to say. She knew he meant every word he said.

"Thank you. I'm glad we had this chance to talk. I don't know what I would do if I lost Greg again. He means everything to me. He wants a truce between us and I think it's time we gave him one. I don't want to bicker and banter with you anymore."

She watched him take a sip of his rum and coke. He sat the glass down and looked squarely at her.

"Agreed. A truce it is. I envy Greg. He seems to have everything he ever wanted, his career and a woman who loves him very much. Sometimes I look at you and Greg and wish things had turned out differently. I'm just glad things are working out for you.

He's pretty excited about being a daddy," said Mark changing the subject. "I hope that works out for you guys."

"Me, too. Yes he is excited. We've gone through a lot to get where we are right now. I just hope we manage to walk down the aisle before we mess things up again."

"I think you're over the hump this time," he winked. "Hey you shot him and he's still here. What does that tell you?" They both burst out laughing and that's how Greg found them.

"I leave for ten minutes and come back and there's no blood anywhere. I'm in shock. Will miracles never cease? You will never believe what's happened?" smiled Greg.

While they were having breakfast on Friday morning, Greg got a call and excused himself from the table. When he returned, he was smiling.

"It's over. The guy suing my client agreed to our last offer. I'm having the papers couriered over to him the day after Christmas and I am going home." He pulled a smiling Dani off the barstool and into his arms. "If you can delay your flight until Monday night. I'll fly home with you both."

"That's great news. Now I can at least start planning a wedding. So when do you want to get married?" asked Danielle hugging him.

"As soon as it can be arranged," laughed Greg returning her hug and planting a hard quick kiss on her mouth.

"There's no time like the present. I have an idea," said Mark smiling. "It's perfect. Let's get out of here. Don't ask. Just follow me. Trust me." He winked.

She and Greg exchanged worried glances, before blindly following Mark's lead. Trusting Mark Sanders was not something Danielle took lightly.

Mark drove them downtown to the main court

house. He told them today was their wedding day. He was tired of waiting around for them to tie the knot. He informed them that the waiting was over and they were getting married today if he had to drag them kicking and screaming in front of the judge.

Danielle and Greg exchanged dubious looks. Mark told them in Georgia there was no waiting period for a license or to get married.

Greg and Danielle discussed it for about a half an hour and agreed to get married today. They followed Mark to the window to register. They were disappointed when told by the clerk they were booked up with marriage appointments through the New Year.

To cheer her up, Greg reminded Danielle to get busy planning her wedding. She would get the wedding she wanted after all, including the long white wedding gown.

This appeased her somewhat, but she was also tired of waiting to marry the man she loved. She prayed nothing would interfere this time.

Chapter 20

Danielle remembered Betsy's sister lived in Atlanta. She called Betsy to get her number and called Tara to introduce herself. Her cousin invited her over to her house for lunch.

She took a cab to Tara's place to give Greg and Mark some male bonding time. The area of town was nice and beautifully landscaped.

Tara's townhouse was beautiful. She felt the warmth of the place when she walked inside. Tara was tall, dark and slender. Her brown hair was cut short and stylish. It was obvious she and Betsy were sisters. They looked a lot alike.

The hardwood floors gleamed as she invited Danielle inside and welcomed her with open arms. Tara heard all about her from Betsy and from her mother.

Danielle took in the stylish living room decorated in black and white. Like Tara, everything was neat and tidy. The overstuffed black leather couch looked inviting, as did the matching recliner. Black and white curtains hung over white wooden blinds. There were black marble inn tables on both sides of the couch. An Oriental-style rug protected the floor from the couch and tables.

They sat and chatted easily about family and careers. Tara was a reporter for the local television station. She had numerous awards displayed over the fireplace and on other walls.

During their conversation, she told Danielle she was going home to Rusk for Christmas. She was staying through the New Year.

She offered Danielle the use of her townhouse stating that no-one should have to spend Christmas at a hotel. Danielle was hesitant at first, but soon warmed to the idea. She would actually be able to prepare Christmas dinner, or at least a part of it.

The townhouse was a two story brick with two bedrooms, two baths and a two-car garage. She gave her the keys and told her to have a Merry Christmas. She was flying back out of DFW, so they could get together then for Danielle to return the key.

Danielle snuck off while Greg and Mark went down to the hotel bar. She went grocery shopping, and then drove Tara's car to the townhouse to get everything ready.

She sat the groceries on the counter with a smile. She inhaled the heady aroma of homemade cornbread dressing. As promised, Tara made the dressing for her. She had also left Danielle recipes for pecan and sweet potato pies.

She placed the glazed honey baked ham and the Cajun turkey in the refrigerator, rolled up her sleeves, and put on the apron. As pecan pie was one of Greg's favorites, she wanted to surprise him with it. Her last attempt at making one was a failure. The inside was soggy and the pecans were almost burned to a crisp. She prayed for a success this time.

Okay, I hope I don't mess this up too bad. Even I

can follow a recipe. If they come out terrible, I can say I tried.

She made both pies and placed them in the oven to bake. She walked back into the living room and smiled at the twinkling Christmas tree and the packages she placed beneath the tree.

She peered down at her watch and decided it was time to call the hotel. She left a message for Greg at the front desk.

Pack enough clothes for two days, including my presents, have Mark do the same, and meet me at 5:00 P.M. at 25B Vista Street.

The pies were ready and at least looked edible when the doorbell rang. She was smiling when she opened the front door. She waved them inside, and they looked around in puzzlement.

"Welcome to our Christmas retreat, boys. This is where we are spending the holidays, not in some formal hotel room."

"We're not in Kansas anymore Toto," replied Mark, whistling as he stepped inside with his bags. "This is some place. Who does it belong to?"

"It belongs to my cousin, Tara. She went home to East Texas for the holidays and was kind enough to invite us to stay here. With the assistance of Tara and two restaurants, we have a Christmas feast."

They both stared at her speechless and then looked at each other. Both men seemed temporarily at a loss for words.

"I didn't know you could cook anything but pork chops and green beans," Mark said setting down his bags.

"One of my many hidden talents. Mark your room is to the left." Danielle lightly slapped her forehead at their puzzled looks. "Oh forgive me that's the back yard. Surely you don't want to be in the doghouse yet.

What I meant was upstairs to your left. Greg our room is the first door on the right."

While Mark went to put his things in his room, Greg followed her into the kitchen. Untying the apron from her waist, he laid it on the counter.

"I can't believe you did all this. You are one incredible lady. I love you." Her heart soared. She would never tire of hearing those three wonderful words.

"I love you, too." Danielle smiled, throwing herself into his arms. She pulled his head down and kissed him.

Lifting her in his arms, he twirled her around the room. Setting her on her feet, his mouth covered hers in a tender kiss.

"Hey you two, not in the kitchen. Normally I wouldn't mind, but I'm starving." He looked in the refrigerator and took out the ham. "This looks delicious. You did a hell of a job on such short notice, Counselor. I hope it's as good as it looks."

They both rolled their eyes at Mark, but neither commented. He was as tactful as always, but they were both used to it.

Later that night they sat around the television, eating popcorn and watching old Christmas movies. By the end of the movie, they were all reciting bits of *It's a Wonderful Life*.

Danielle said goodnight and left the guys downstairs watching sports highlights. She showered and got into bed. She drifted peacefully off to sleep.

Later, Greg showered and eased into bed next to Danielle. He spooned his body to hers and she moaned in her sleep. Catching his hand, she moved it from her waist to her breast. Greg was a bit surprised when she moved against him seductively.

He quickly rolled away from her and grabbed a condom from his wallet. He moved back to her and nibbled her neck.

"Dani," he whispered against her neck. "Are you awake, sweetheart? If not, you are having one hot dream right now."

His voice stirred her from her dream world. She rolled onto her back and pulled his head down to hers.

"I was having the most delicious dream. No," she said planting tiny kisses on his chest, "I want the real thing."

About an hour later, they were both exhausted and sated. Danielle snuggled against his warmth and they both fell asleep.

The next morning, they awoke to a white Christmas. Danielle caught Greg shaking presents tagged with his name. He was like a little boy in a candy store.

Smiling to herself, she went back into their bedroom and snatched up her camera. She took several shots of him before he noticed her.

He waved her over to him. She sat down beside him on the floor and gasped when he stripped the camera out of her hands. He took several shots of her, before setting the camera aside and rolling her onto her back.

"Merry Christmas, sweetheart." His lips brushed hers gently. "You'll have to thank your cousin for me. I'm glad we're not in the hotel."

"Merry Christmas my love. I'll be sure to thank her for all of us." She pulled his head down to hers and their lips met and clung.

"Not again. Do you two ever let up?" Mark asked plopping down on one knee, next to the tree. Dani and Greg sat up smiling, but not before stealing another quick kiss.

"Never. We can't keep our hands off each other," said Greg, kissing her again. "Isn't it obvious? We have a lot of lost time to make up for."

"I think you guys covered most of the lost time last night," Mark shot back smugly. "These walls are paper thin."

Danielle's face turned crimson as she glared at Mark. He would have to be ungentlemanly enough to mention it.

"Can you be any more crass?" His eyebrows rose suggestively. "Forget I said that. Merry Christmas to you to, Scrooge."

"We'll try to keep it down tonight," winked Greg, smiling at Dani. She elbowed him in the ribs. "Ouch!"

"Merry Christmas guys, and thanks for sharing it with me," said Mark sincerely. "It means a lot to me to be here with you both. It helps to ease the pain. Now, what I want to know is which presents are mine?"

Laughing, they all opened their gifts. Danielle gasped when she opened her first gift from Greg. He took the large pear-shaped diamond engagement ring from the box and placed it on her finger.

Tears sparkled in her eyes as she stared down at the ring. It was magnificent. She held up the ring to the light.

"It's beautiful." She wiped the tears from her cheeks. "I don't know what to say. Am I dreaming or is this really happening this time?"

"I think it's long overdue." Greg got up and kneeled down on one knee. "Danielle Roberts Masters, will you marry me?"

"Yes," she smiled through her tears. "I would marry you tomorrow if we could arrange it. I love you."

"All this mushy stuff. I think I'm going to be sick," said Mark rolling his eyes at the happy couple.

"You are sick," agreed Greg tossing him a package. Mark caught the gift. "Open a present and pretend we're not here."

"The ring is beautiful, Danielle. Congratulations guys, again. I'll tell you right now, I'm not buying you guys any more wedding presents. I have the crystal wine glasses you wanted the first time. I have the crystal candleholders you wanted the second time. I don't think I need any more crystal." Danielle and Greg rolled their eyes at Mark. "This time, you get a gift certificate to the store of my choice."

"This time," smiled Greg pulling Danielle into his arms, "we will make it to the altar. You will be my wife." His mouth captured hers in a tender kiss.

"Enough already. Get a room. Here have a present." Mark pressed a present in both Greg and Danielle's hand. "Dani, yours was last minute. I didn't know you would be here. You can exchange it if you don't like it."

He bought her a red sweater and gave her a silver spoon for the baby she wanted. His gift brought tears to her eyes. Danielle smiled through her tears and thanked him.

Mark bought Greg season tickets to the Mavericks. Danielle bought him season tickets to the Cowboys.

Greg bought Mark the new set of golf clubs he desperately wanted. Danielle bought him a monogrammed lab jacket.

Taking a deep breath, Danielle took out her cell phone. She had put off calling home long enough. Dialing her parents' number, she gripped the telephone. She wasn't sure what kind of reception she would receive from her father. He was so unpredictable.

"Hello," said the laughing voice. She could hear her father's voice in the background talking to someone.

"Aunt Karen, hi. Merry Christmas," said Danielle smiling into the phone. "Sounds like you guys have company."

"Dani, Merry Christmas to you, too. As a matter of fact, we do have company. How is everything going with you and Greg?"

"Not the way I had planned, but I have no complaints. How's Dad? How did he take my disappearance?"

"Better than we thought. He wasn't very surprised. As a matter of fact, he's standing right here. I'll let you ask him yourself."

"Merry Christmas, sweetheart," said Jack. "I hope your Christmas has been everything you wanted it to be."

"Merry Christmas, Dad. It's been wonderful. I'm sorry I left the way I did. I should have told you I was coming here."

"I had a feeling you were going to do just that. I understand why I went. Tell Greg, Merry Christmas for me."

"Grandpa! Grandpa! Look what Santa brought me." Danielle stared at the phone in her hand puzzled.

"Dad are you there?" she asked puzzled. "Who was that? Is there something I should know?"

"Hold on a minute," said Jack distracted. She could hear him talking to someone. "Say hello to Aunt Danielle."

"Hi Aunt Danielle. Merry Christmas. It's T.J, remember me?" Danielle sat down quickly in the chair. "Where are you? Mom wants to talk."

"Merry Christmas, Tony," whispered Danielle. She gripped the phone and happy tears came to her eyes. Another of her Christmas wishes had come true. Janelle was in Dallas. This was more than she could have hoped for.

"Dani. Merry Christmas. I hear great minds think alike. Tony and I arrived in Dallas the same day you left. I think Jack is still in shock."

"Merry Christmas, Janelle," said the strangled voice. Dani cleared her throat. "I'm so glad you came. Is this a short visit or are you there to stay?"

"I'm not sure yet. I guess that depends on a lot of things. Listen, Jack wants to talk to you. I'll see you when you get back to Dallas."

"To say the least, I was speechless, when I came home and found Janelle and Tony here," explained Jack. "She'll meet the rest of the family at lunch in about an hour. I'm trying to talk her into staying permanently. Maybe you can help me convince her when you get back. When are you coming back?"

"Greg and I are both flying in Monday night. We'll drop by on the way from the airport. I've got to go Dad. I love you and I'll see you soon. Merry Christmas."

Greg came over and kneeled down in front of her. He took the phone from her still fingers and hung it up.

"What happened?" Greg was tense as he watched her reaction. "What did he say to you to upset you?"

"He didn't say anything to upset me. Janelle and Tony arrived the day I left. Greg, my sister has come home. I didn't think I'd ever see her again after they way we parted."

"Are you sorry you came?" he asked holding his breath. Their eyes met and held as he waited for her answer.

"No," she answered quickly and truthfully. "Don't ever think that. I am where I want to be," she said, smoothing the wrinkles from his forehead. Her lips brushed his and he pulled her into his arms. "Janelle and I have a lot of time to make up for, but so do we. This is our time."

Danielle announced dinner and they all went out to the dining area off the kitchen. Holding hands, Greg said the blessing.

"Thank you God for this meal we are about to receive. Thank you for Dani and for Mark. And for Dani and Mark finally making peace." Mark squeezed her hand. "Bless our family and our friends who can't be with us today, but are here in spirit. Bless those who have, and those who have not. Thank you for sending Janelle home. Please let us have a joyful Christmas and a safe journey home. Amen."

"Amen," they chorused.

The meal was every bit as delicious as it smelled. Greg and Mark had second helpings of almost everything.

After dinner, they made her go into the living room and relax while they cleaned up the kitchen.

Danielle turned on the radio and lay down on the couch. She sang along with "Away in the Manger" and drifted off to sleep.

When she awoke, she was covered with a blanket. As she sat up, she saw a snowball go sailing past the window.

Getting to her feet, she sauntered over to the window. She laughed at the sight of Greg and Mark having a snowball fight. They were like two kids playing in the snow. Picking up her camera, she walked to the door and took several shots of them.

She blew a kiss to Greg and broke his concentration. Mark chose that moment to strike and a snowball hit Greg in the chest. He immediately regained his concentration and prepared for retaliation.

Danielle was headed back inside when a snowball hit her bottom. She turned accusing eyes at Mark only to find Greg was the culprit. Setting the camera aside she made a snowball and threw it at Greg. Now the battle was really on.

Danielle said a silent prayer of thanks later that night as she lay in Greg's arms. This had been a truly wondrous Christmas. She had Greg, and her sister was home where she belonged. She had not been sure she would ever see Janelle again. Even if it was only for a visit, she was there now, and that in itself was a major accomplishment.

Then there was Mark. He tried so hard to hide his sadness and loneliness. He had an 'I don't need anyone attitude,' but she knew it was only an act. He was in his own private hell shouldering the blame of what happened to his parents.

He also took the blame for what almost happened between them. They both knew the fault lay with her. She deliberately went after him. He never would have gone after her if she hadn't made the first move. She crossed the line and he had the good sense to stop things in the nick of time.

Danielle prayed for him to meet a nice woman and not chase her away with his attitude. She wanted him to experience the kind of love she and Greg shared.

Maybe if she introduced him to Janelle they could help each other heal. They both pretended to be so tough. She would have to think about inviting them both over for dinner to see if there was a connection.

She would of course have to do it without her father's knowledge. Mark was not exactly one of his favorite people and he would throw a fit if he knew she was even considering it.

"I've been thinking about something." She rose up and rested her elbows on Greg's chest. Their eyes met.

"Uh oh, that usually means trouble. Pray tell, what is weighing so heavily on your mind when you should be exhausted and sleeping?"

"Mark needs to meet a nice woman and settle down. I have just the woman in mind for him. With a little push in the right direction."

"Don't even go there," warned Greg reading her mind. "You said yourself Janelle has had a rough time of it. Mark is my best friend and I love him dearly, but I know him. He's gun shy about any kind of commitment. He also has a thing about dating women who have kids. He doesn't want the responsibility. Putting the two of them together would be a huge mistake."

"We could invite them both to dinner and see what happens. There is a possibility there will not be a love connection."

"What if there is?" he challenged. "What if they hit it off? Honey, he's got issues. Would you really wish him on your sister?"

"He's not a bad guy. They both have issues. I'm

convinced the love of a good woman can change any man."

"And what fantasy world are you living in? How many glasses of wine did you have tonight? Don't interfere. I don't think Mark or Janelle would appreciate it."

Danielle fell silent, but she was not finished by a long shot. She would invite them over for dinner and she would give them both a nudge in each other's directions. What was the worst that could happen?

The morning after Christmas, Danielle and the guys cleaned up the townhouse before they dropped Mark off at the airport. He flew back early Monday morning.

Danielle waited at the townhouse for Greg to conclude his business. Once everything was finished, they flew home together.

Chapter 21

They arrived at DFW airport at 7:05 P.M. After waiting for the luggage, they took the shuttle bus to the parking lot where Dani had parked her car.

It was about 7:45 when they finally pulled up at Dani's parents' house. She was so excited she hopped out of the car the minute it stopped. Catching Greg by the hand, she dragged him with her to the front door.

A smiling Karen instantly opened the door for them to enter. She hugged Danielle and then Greg.

"Welcome home. Come on in. I want to hear all about your trip," said Karen with her arm around her stepdaughter.

"We had a wonderful time." Danielle held up her finger and showed off her engagement ring. "It's official. We are getting married as soon as we can reschedule."

"That's wonderful," Karen said, catching her hand to inspect the ring. She hugged Dani and Greg. "I'm so happy for you guys. There will be a wedding in two weeks. Leave all the preparations to me."

"We accept," Danielle laughed. "How are things going here? Is everything okay? Where's Janelle?"

"She's upstairs putting Tony to bed. Go on up. He's

in the room across the hall from your old room. Janelle is occupying your old room."

Greg followed her up the stairs without comment. She knocked briefly before entering Tony's room.

"Aunt Dani." Tony hopped out of bed and ran to her. Kneeling down, she hugged the smiling imp wearing Spider-Man pajamas. "Mommy's making me go to sleep, but I'm not sleepy yet." He yawned, covering his mouth with his hands.

Janelle got up from the bed and turned around to face them. Danielle smiled at Greg's gasp. He stared from Dani to Janelle and back again.

"Who's he?" whispered her nephew, pulling on Danielle's pant leg. "Why is he looking at Mommy like that?"

"This is your Uncle Greg. He's the man Aunt Dani is going to marry. Say hello. He's looking at your mom strangely because she and I look so much alike."

"You're supposed to look alike if you're twins," came his reply as he shrugged his shoulders. They all laughed at his honest reply.

"Hi Tony, it's nice to meet you." Greg kneeled down and held out his hand to Tony. The little boy shyly took it.

"Greg this is Janelle Corinthos. Janelle this is my fiancé, Greg Thomas." They exchanged hellos and shook hands politely.

"I'll go down and chat with Karen, while the two of you talk. Your time is up the minute Jack gets home." He kissed Danielle's cheek before leaving the room.

"Let's go across the hall to my room and talk," suggested Janelle. She leaned down and kissed her son goodnight.

Danielle followed her from the room. They went into Dani's old bedroom and closed the door so they wouldn't be disturbed.

"I'm glad you came," smiled Danielle. "I didn't

think I'd ever see you again. Dad must be ecstatic you're here."

"That's putting it mildly. He was pretty excited. Don't get the wrong idea about me being here, Danielle. I only came because I had no place else to go. The Corinthos have blackballed me from New York. I lost my job and was evicted from my apartment. No hospital in New York will touch me now. I honestly don't know how long I'll be staying," she said.

"The important thing is you're here. I'd like a chance for us to get to know each other. I'd also like to get to know my nephew. I do have one other favor to ask. Greg and I are getting married right here in two weeks, more or less. I'd like for you to attend our wedding."

"I can't make any promises. I have a problem with you spending time with Tony. I don't want him to get too attached to you or Jack. When we leave here it's only going to cause him more pain. He's had enough pain in his young life. Greg is not what I expected. He's gorgeous and doesn't appear to be stuffy at all. I expected you to be marrying a blue blood. Greg's not, is he?"

"No, he's not. Our upbringing is pretty much like night and day. I had all the advantage he didn't have. He's worked hard to get where he is and I'm very proud of him. We've been together on and off for about five years. We've come close several times to walking down the aisle, but never made it to the finish line. This time we will."

"I'm happy for you. I can see the two of you love each other very much. I hope things work out for you."

"Thanks. We'll talk more later. I'd better go downstairs and play referee. If Dad's home, I'm sure he and Greg will find something to argue about."

Janelle followed her down the stairs. They found Greg in the den with Jack and Karen. Greg and Jack were having a heated discussion about a baseball strike, which had happened a few years earlier. Greg was for the players and Jack the owners, which wasn't a big surprise.

"So what you are saying is that no matter how much money the games bring in, and how much the owners raise the ticket prices, the players should not get a piece of the pie!"

"A piece of the pie!" argued Jack, glaring at his soon to be son-in-law. "If it were up to you they would get the whole pie!"

"Why not? They are the ones out there playing and sweating! They bring in the crowds and they are the ones getting injured!"

"Gentlemen! Gentlemen! I personally could care less! The strike was over years ago. This is a moot point. Besides, it's football season now."

"I agree with Karen. I like football better, too. Those are the real men. They will play during a thunderstorm. They are the ones who shouldn't have a salary cap," stated Janelle, surprising all of them.

"True," agreed Jack and Greg simultaneously. They looked at each other unbelievably. They had actually agreed on something.

With that thought in mind, Danielle quickly called it a night. After saying their goodbyes, they left and headed to Greg's house.

Greg brought in the luggage while Danielle collapsed on the sofa. Greg massaged her bare feet and ankles.

"Dani, there's something I have to tell you," said Greg staring at her intently. "When I moved back to Dallas, it was for one reason only, to make you my wife. I have loved you forever it seems," his hand caressed her soft cheek. "My plan was to get you back no matter what."

"You got me. There is no place I would rather be

than right here with you. I love you. You give meaning to my life. I don't know what I would have done if you hadn't come back home." She laughed. "I probably would have come after you."

"Would you really?" His eyes searched hers for the truth and he found it staring back at him. She was very serious. He could see the unconditional love shining in her eyes. "There's something I have to ask you? If things had turned out differently and Lexi was my daughter, would you have been able to deal with it? Could you have loved her like she was your own child?"

"I loved her before I found out about you and Becky. You being her father would only have made me love her more." As she spoke the words, they both knew in her heart they were true.

Love shone brightly in his dark piercing eyes as he smiled down at her. At this moment, he loved her more than he thought was possible.

The week flew by for Danielle. She was swamped with work, wedding invitations, decorations, and floral arrangements. Luckily for her, her dress and the bridesmaid dresses were already in the possession of the wedding party.

She had dinner twice with Janelle and Tony at her parents' house. Janelle still hadn't decided what she was going to do. She was still in hiding from the Corinthos and their group of attorneys and private investigators.

Danielle knew it was only a matter of time before they tracked her to Jack's door. She wanted her sister to be prepared for them legally.

Jack said he would represent Janelle if it came to a court battle. He filed all the necessary paperwork to let her ex-husband know where she was, but conveniently had it lost in the system by someone who owed him.

Greg was in the middle of dictating a letter, when Tara buzzed him to let him know Jack Masters was there to see him. Puzzled, he turned off the machine and went to open the door.

"Hello Jack. Come in," said Greg stiffly waving him in. "Knowing you, this is not a social call. So what do you want?"

"I know you are a busy man, so I won't take up too much of your time. I want you to take a look at this document and sign it for me."

Greg watched him take out an envelope and hand it to him. Still curious Greg took it and waved for Jack to take a seat. He opened the envelope and stared angrily at its contents.

He tried to calm himself before he spoke. This shouldn't have come as a surprise to him. He should have been expecting this, but it still angered him.

"You want me to sign a prenuptial agreement," seethed Greg. "After all this time, you still think I'm after Dani's money? Jack, I should feel insulted by this, but I'm not. I should have expected something like this from you. Does Danielle know about this?" He watched Jack flush under his close scrutiny. "Well that answers that. Maybe I should tell her what you have been up to. What do you think she would say, Dad?"

"She would probably be furious with me," he admitted, "but I am doing this for her own good. I am a very wealthy man and Danielle is my heir."

"Are you forgetting you have another daughter now? What about Janelle? Does she not rate part of the loot?"

"They are both my heirs as is my grandson. I am looking out for my family's best interest. Danielle is my daughter and I am only looking out for her best interest. I know you say you love her, and so do I. I am protecting my child. Don't stand there and tell me you wouldn't do the same thing? Do you have a problem with signing that document?"

"No, Jack, I don't have a problem with you protecting your daughter. I have a problem with you and your superior attitude. You have never given me a chance. I was never good enough for your little girl. Like you, I wasn't born with a silver spoon in my mouth. Nothing was given to me on a gold platter. Unlike you, I have had to work and scratch for everything I have ever gotten. You were a struggling law student when Jared found out about you. He shared every penny of your father's money with you. A father who was ashamed even to acknowledge your existence. Instead of understanding my struggle and relating to it, you belittle me for it. You didn't like me from the start and you only tolerate me now because of Dani, but you know what? I don't give a damn what you think about me anymore. I know I am ambitious and driven, but I had to be to get where I am today. I am through trying to earn your respect. I don't care if you never like me. Danielle and I love each other and you are going to have to deal with it. We are getting married and there's nothing you or anyone else can do to stop us. Leave the papers and get out of my office," hissed Greg coming to his feet and walking to the door. "I'll see you at the wedding, Dad." Yanking it open, he held it open for Jack to leave.

"Without those papers, there will be no wedding. I will make sure of that. I will make Danielle understand this is in her best interest."

"Good luck with trying to cancel this wedding. If you mention this to Danielle, you will push her away. Are you prepared to lose your daughter? Don't force her to make a choice. I'm afraid you won't like her answer," sneered Greg slamming the door shut behind his future father-in-law.

Frustrated with what little work he had accomplished, Greg took off early and headed home. He reflected on everything that happened to his family in the past ten years. It seemed like everything bad that happened was always centered around one person, Leo.

Leo had caused the entire family too much pain and humiliation of which to keep track. He broke into Danielle's house and tried to rape her. What would happen next was anybody's guess? It was time to face his brother. Greg had put it off long enough. He knew it wouldn't be pleasant, but it had to be done.

Greg stood outside the jailhouse for several minutes before making up his mind to go inside. He hadn't seen or talked to his brother since the night he attacked Danielle. Anger had kept him away. He had put this confrontation off long enough.

He got out of his car and walked into the jailhouse. After going through all the metal detectors he was on his way. Visiting hours were almost over, but the guard recognized Greg and let him in to see his brother.

As the guard led him down the hallway, his stomach tightened in knots. He wasn't quite sure what he was going to say, but he thanked God there would be bars separating them.

"You have twenty minutes before all the prisoners are shipped off to Huntsville," said the guard stopping in front of Leo's cell. "If you need me, holler."

"Thanks again," said Greg watching the guard walk away. He turned at last to face his brother. Their eyes locked in a battle of wills. Greg took in the bright orange jumpsuit and resigned himself to the fact Leo was going away again.

"What are you doing here big brother? I wouldn't think this was your scene. What do you want?" asked Leo lounging on the bed. "Did you come to see how the other half live or to seek retribution for your girl-friend?"

"Maybe a little of both. I want answers and nothing less than the truth will suffice. Why did you go after Danielle? Do you hate me that much?" asked the emotion-filled voice.

"Yes!" Leo sprang off the bed and pounced on the bars. "I hate both of you that much," he hissed through clenched teeth. Greg was taken aback by the hatred in his younger brother's eyes. "Greg the wonder boy. Greg can do no wrong. You don't know how sick and tired I am of hearing 'why don't you be more like Greg' or 'Greg would never do something like that.' If anyone compares me to you one more time, I will probably kill someone. I am sick to death of being in your shadow, of being your 'little' brother. You are the golden child and I'm just the bad seed."

"And whose fault is that? You go out of your way to hurt people and to alienate them. Do you have any idea how much pain you've caused Mama? You self-ish brat! She was lying in a hospital bed with a stroke and you didn't bother to come see her. She not only gave you life, but she refuses to give up on you. She thinks there is still some good in you. She believes you have a soul worth saving. I don't."

"You are the reason I went to prison. You were so busy with your uptown girlfriend and planning your damn wedding you didn't devote enough time to my case. Yet let me go down. You did this to me!"

"I am sick to death of the 'me me song.' Grow up. You blame everyone for your problems but yourself. You did it to yourself. You are the one to blame for this whole mess. I didn't ruin your life. You ruined it. If there is anyone to blame here it's you."

"You could have kept me out of the hellhole, but you didn't. You let me go to jail. You didn't try hard enough!"

"You are wrong Leo," he shot back. "I did every-thing I could for you. They wouldn't listen to anything I had to say. You were already on probation when you robbed the liquor store. I didn't do this to you. It's time for you to take some responsibility for your actions."

"While I spent three years of my life in jail, you never gave me a second thought. You went on with your perfect life like I never existed. You never even came to see me. You were glad to see me go down!"

"Yes I was," admitted Greg for the first time aloud. "It was time you learned a lesson about responsibility and paying for your crimes. You couldn't keep robbing and stealing and expect to keep getting away with it. You had to learn the hard way. You have done a lot of things I don't agree with, but I still considered you my brother until now. When you went after Danielle, you lost me as a brother. To attack the woman I love is un-forgivable. Did you know she shot me because of you? She put a bullet in me thinking it was you coming back to rape her. You have caused this family so much pain and grief I will be happy to have you out of our lives for good. I hope they lock you up and throw away the key because you are where animals like you belong. When and if you happen to make it out of here alive this time, don't bother coming home because you won't have a home to come to. We don't want you. You no longer have a family."

"I don't need you! I still have Mama. She won't give up on me the way everyone else has! She loves me! I'm her baby!" Leo went back to the bed and dropped down onto it. "Have a nice life, brother."

"My brother died the day you went after the woman I love. Goodbye Leo, we are finished." Greg shook his head sadly as he turned and walked away.

He got in his car and drove. At first he had no idea where he was going, then it dawned on him there was one person who would understand his pain.

Using his key he let himself in. The heady aroma of dinner filled the air. He followed the smell out to the kitchen where he found his mother.

"Hi Mom." He kissed her cheek and hugged her. She returned his warm hug. "Oh Mom, where did things go so wrong with Leo?"

Catching his face between her hands, she looked deeply into his troubled eyes. There were tears in both their eyes.

"I just came from the jail." He paused and took a deep breath. Greg didn't try to wipe them away as they rolled down his cheeks. "I never knew he hated me that much. What did I ever do to him? What did I do Mama?"

"Greg, none of this is your fault. I stopped blaming myself for Leo and Marie a long time ago. I raised all of you with the same moral values. I tried to instill in all of you right from wrong. What Leo did has no reflection on us. I know it hurts, but in time, the pain will lessen. Your brother did some unspeakable things, but he is still your flesh and blood. He is my son and I can't turn my back on him. He needs me."

"I need you. Travis needs you. Leo doesn't need anyone. He hates me. He tried to rape Danielle. How can I forgive him for that? How can you?" They sat down at the kitchen table.

"What he did was wrong and vengeful. He wanted to hurt you and he wanted to hurt Danielle, but he is still my son. He is still your brother. I cannot and will not turn my back on him. Son, I understand how you feel. You're hurting and you feel betrayed by him. Your anger is justified."

"You taught me love and forgiveness, but I can't forgive him, not this time. This time he went too far. He has pushed me away for years and now he's finally succeeded. I can't deal with him anymore. Maybe one day I will come to terms with him, but I don't see it happening anytime soon. You can't fix it this time, Mama, so let it go."

"I will, Greg, for now, but just remember," she said squeezing his hand, "we can't pick and choose our family. They are ours for life."

Chapter 22

Test results a few days before the wedding confirmed Janelle was Jack's daughter and Danielle's twin sister. It only confirmed what Danielle already knew in her heart. She welcomed Janelle with open arms. Jack took them all out to celebrate. Danielle, Jack, and Karen did everything they could to make Janelle feel like she belonged.

The test results also softened Janelle's attitude tremendously. She became more at ease with her new family.

Tony didn't understand what the celebration was all about. He had already accepted Jack and Karen as his grandparents and Danielle as his aunt.

Danielle had come over to join Karen and Janelle for lunch. She was headed out the front door to go back to her office, when the phone rang.

"I've got it! Hello, Masters residence," she said, setting her purse on the hall table. She instinctively picked up the pen and note pad on the table.

"Hi," said the friendly male voice. "I'm looking for Jack Masters. Is he there by any chance?"

"No, he's not. He's in court all day today." She took

the cap off the pen and was poised to take a message. "May I take a message?"

"Tell him Richard Grayson called. I was his college roommate. Let him know I called and I'll give him a call later tonight. He owes me a favor, and when I'm in town I intend to collect. I'll be in town this weekend and I'd like to get together with him."

"Got it," said Danielle jotting down at least part of the information. She dropped the pad and pen. "I'll give him your message." She hung up the phone. Danielle wrote the date and time at the top of the note and left it on the table. "Aunt Karen, I left a message for Dad on the hall table!"

She went back to the office to finish up the loose ends on the case on which she was working. As usual when she was working, she lost track of time. When her assistant stuck her head in the door to tell her she was leaving, however, it made her aware of it.

She logged off her computer and dashed out of the office. Danielle was meeting Greg at his house for dinner.

She let herself in and went in search of her fiancé. She found Greg in the den. He was sitting on the sofa talking on the telephone.

Dropping her purse on the coffee table, she sat down on his lap. She brushed his lips with hers and leaned back against his chest. She waited patiently for him to get off the phone.

"I'd love to get together, Richard." He put his hand over the phone. "Honey, can you get me a piece of paper?"

Danielle tensed hearing the name. She did not like the uneasy feeling washing over her as she brought him a notepad.

"How about lunch on Saturday? I'll bring my fiancé so you can meet her." He paused. "Sounds good. We'll see you then." He hung up the telephone and kissed Danielle full on the lips. "Hello beautiful."

"Hello yourself," she smiled. "Who was on the phone?" Hating herself for thinking it, she had to ask.

She knew how her father felt about Greg. *Would he do anything to keep them apart? How far would he go?*

"My old boss, Richard Grayson. He's coming to town this weekend and wants to get together for dinner. I hope you don't mind that I accepted for us."

Danielle closed her eyes. Her worst fears were just confirmed. It couldn't be just coincidence, her mind screamed.

Grayson said Jack owed him a favor. Did that favor have to do with him hiring Greg? Did her father take him away from her? Either way, I have to be sure.

"I know this is going to sound strange, but tell me again how you were hired by Grayson and Fuller?" she asked uneasily. She held her breath waiting for his reply.

"It's weird really. I was thinking about leaving after our break-up. When I received the letter from them in the mail, it seemed like a sign. I have no idea who recommended me for the job or how the firm got my name. I went to Oregon and interviewed with Richard Grayson and George Fuller. A week later, Richard phoned me and made me an offer I couldn't refuse."

Danielle felt the knot in her stomach tighten. She knew exactly who had recommended him for the job. Jack. Jack had wanted Greg out of her life, so he had his friend offer Greg a job in Oregon. Because Jack knew Greg and Danielle were not getting along well, he also knew she wouldn't go with him under the current circumstances.

"Do you have any idea who recommended you?" she asked rubbing at her now throbbing temples.

"Honey, I don't care. At the time, it was for the best.

We needed some distance from each other. We both did a lot of growing up in our time apart. It made me realize what was important in my life. It brought me back to you and to my family. Who ever did this, did us a favor. Sweetheart, why are you so curious about this all of a sudden? What's going on?"

Dani's anger was building, thinking about what her father had done to them. *Maybe if Greg had stayed, we could have worked out our problems. How dare my father play God with our lives? I can't let him get away with this. I have to face him.*

"I have to go," said Danielle picking up her purse and keys. "There's someone I have to see." She turned to face Greg. "I know who recommended you for the job in Oregon and I know why. Richard Grayson and my father were college roommates. Mr. Grayson called the house as I was leaving to let Jack know he would be in town this weekend. I took the message. Now I think I should go deliver it personally to my father. I don't appreciate being manipulated and it's time he knew." Danielle slammed the front door behind her.

Greg stared at the closed door. It took him only a few seconds for her words to sink in. When they did, he opened the door to go after her.

Jack had recommended him for the job in Oregon. He knew the reason. He wanted to get him away from Danielle. Greg was ambitious and Jack was positive he wouldn't pass up a prestigious law firm like Grayson and Fuller. Greg blindly took the bait and was reeled in.

From the look on Dani's face, he knew Jack had finally stepped over the line with his daughter. There was no way out of this one.

Okay Dani, you have a ten-minute head start on me. When you get through with your father, it's my turn.

* * *

Danielle was furious when she barreled into the house slamming the door behind her. She marched into the den looking for her father.

Angry and disappointed, she found the room empty. Walking back into the living room, she ripped the note off the pad and waited.

She was pacing back and forth, when the kitchen door swung open and Jack and Karen came through it. Jack was carrying a sleeping Tony in his arms.

"Dad, we need to talk," said Dani ripping up the note in her hand. "I took a message for you earlier today. I wanted to deliver it personally."

"I'll take Tony upstairs," suggested Karen taking the sleeping child out of his grandfather's arms.

"Who called and why are you so upset?" Jack asked watching his wife disappear at the top of the stairs. "What has Thomas done now?"

"It's not what Greg's done. It's what you've done," seethed Danielle barely keeping her voice down. "Explain to me how you and Greg's old boss were college roommates. Tell me it's just a coincidence and you didn't have your old buddy Richard Grayson offer Greg a job in Oregon as a favor to you," she finished. She watched the color leave Jack's face before it returned in a rush. She let the ripped message fall to the floor. "Richard is calling you back tonight. He'll be in town this weekend and wants to get together with you. Imagine my surprise, when I walked in on Greg having a conversation with this same person. How could you do that to me?"

"I can explain," he said moving toward her. "You and Greg were a train wreck waiting to happen. The relationship was doomed and you and I both know it."

"I don't know anything of the sort. Greg and I had our ups and downs, but we always worked things out. This was none of your business!"

"I was trying to help you get on with your life.

Danielle, you were miserable, and so was Greg. You had broken your engagement. You were not even seeing him anymore. I didn't want to see you hurting anymore. I thought if Greg left town, you would get on with your life and forget about him."

"So you decided to take temptation out of my way. Is that it? Remove the forbidden fruit so I wouldn't think about him. You sent the man I love away! You tried to play God with our lives! You had no right to do that!"

"I'm your father! I love you. When you hurt, I hurt. I was trying to help you. You told me it was over with you and Greg."

"And how many other times had I told you the very same thing? I love Greg Thomas. I have always loved him and I probably always will. There is nothing you can say or do to change that. You can either accept the fact that I'm marrying him and be happy for me, or you will not be a part of my life. If you do anything else to come between Greg and I, I will never speak to you again! I am through listening to you! I lost Greg once because I put you before him! It will not happen again. Greg comes first in my life now! Don't make me choose between the two of you!"

"Jack! Danielle! Lower your voices," Karen warned coming down the stairs. "What on earth is going on down here?"

"I'm leaving," Danielle said glaring at her father and then turning away. "I'll make other arrangements for my wedding since it's apparent my husband will never be welcome here."

"Hold it right there young lady," said her step-mother sternly. "I want to know what is going on and one of you had better start talking." She looked from Jack to Danielle. The doorbell rang, while Karen was waiting for an explanation. "Don't either one of you move a muscle," she warned going to answer the door.

"Greg. Hi. Come on in. Maybe you can shed some light on what's going on here."

Danielle went to stand beside the man she loved. Hugging her to him, he dropped a kiss on top of her bent head.

"Are you okay?" he asked looking into her angry eyes. She nodded not trusting her voice to speak. "Have a seat Karen. I'll be happy to fill you in," Greg said, meeting Jack's glare.

An hour later, Karen with the help of Janelle worked a minor miracle. They were all on speaking terms again.

For Danielle, things would never go back to the way they were with her father. Her trust in him was gone.

He fell from the pedestal she had him perched on two years ago. Her blinders were removed the day she found out he was her real father.

Janelle talked to Danielle about a father's love and how lucky she was to have Jack. She told her about growing up without a father and how hard it was for her.

Greg was more understanding than Danielle. He put himself in Jack's shoes and wondered if he would go to the same extremes to protect his daughter. In the end, he told himself he probably would. He might even do worse.

With their wedding day fast approaching and Danielle still upset with her father, Greg decided not to mention the prenuptial agreement Jack wanted him to sign. He knew it would only cause more problems between her and her father. Greg reminded her that although Jack was behind the offer, it was his choice. He made the decision to leave.

When he tried to talk to her about it, he seemed to make matters worse. From her point of view, if Jack hadn't interfered there wouldn't have been a job offer out of town, and he wouldn't have left her.

Danielle was not ready to forgive Jack for his role in separating them.

For years he had wished she would stand up to her father, and now she had. He hated seeing her so upset about her strained relationship with Jack.

Chapter 23

Danielle wore a deep blue pantsuit. Her bobbed hair curved to her face and brushed her shoulders. She wore three-inch spiked sandals.

Greg was clad in a dark gray business suit. His tie was loosened and casually draped around his neck.

After the rehearsal at the Masters Estate, Jack ordered white stretch limousines to drive them to the restaurant. Danielle maneuvered for Janelle and Mark to ride with her cousin Jeff and his girlfriend, Alissa.

Greg again warned her that she was playing with fire. She made no comment as she watched Mark take Janelle's arm and help her into the limo. Neither of them missed the look that passed between them.

Danielle was glad Karen found a babysitter for Tony. Janelle needed tonight. She looked stunning in a black pantsuit. Her long dark hair bounced on her shoulders and down her back in a mass of curls.

Karen reserved a private room at one of the most expensive restaurants in town for the rehearsal dinner. The entire bridal party would be there, along with both of their immediate families.

Danielle and Greg sat at the head of the table at the restaurant. She smiled in satisfaction as she watched

Janelle and Mark converse with each other. She also noted the frown on her father's face. She would have to warn her sister later about their father's meddling.

The meal was incredible and consisted of shrimp cocktail and lobster-stuffed mushrooms as appetizers, followed by a house salad with vinaigrette dressing. The main course was a juicy steak, grilled shrimp, and steamed vegetables. The restaurant supplied beverages of their choice. Everything was delicious, and for once everyone was getting along.

Danielle spent the night before the wedding at her parents' house. She did sleep like a log, but woke up with butterflies in her stomach. Tony and Jack brought her breakfast in bed, of which Tony proceeded to eat most of it.

Jack was a wonderful grandfather. Tony followed him around like his shadow. He thought the sun rose and set in his new grandpa, just as she knew her son or daughter would.

After breakfast, Danielle showered and went downstairs. The house was noisy and crowded. There were people everywhere. Some were arranging chairs in the living room, whereas others covered tables with tablecloths.

The florist was discussing the arrangements with Karen, and the two singers practiced their duet. The champagne fountain was already set up, but not yet running.

Jack had turned the largest downstairs bedroom into the bride's room. He had brought in several floor-length mirrors and had added a bigger vanity area so the bridesmaids and the bride wouldn't have to take turns applying their make-up.

Danielle slipped into the temporary brides room and smiled as she closed the door behind her. She went over to her dress hanging from the ceiling. The dress was the most beautiful creation she had ever seen. Her hand gently touched the soft satin.

It was a traditional white satin and lace with fitted puffed sleeves, a deep v-neck covered with white lace, and strands of pearls sewn into the material outlined the neck. The top was fitted, but it flared at her hips and reached the floor and beyond. The train was long and covered in pearls. The back was low cut with four delicate strands of pearls connecting to the material just above the satin bow.

It is finally happening. This is our day. Thank you God for giving us another chance. If you see fit to bless our union with our own baby, we will love and cherish him/her. If not, we are open to other options as long as we are together.

"I thought I might find you here," said Janelle coming into the room. "You are going to make a beautiful bride."

"Thank you." She smiled at her twin sister. "I'm so glad you're here. It means the world to me." They embraced warmly. No more words were necessary as they both fought back their tears of happiness.

A few hours later, Danielle was back in the room surrounded by her two bridesmaids, her matron, and her stepmother. She was a bundle of nerves as she watched Liz, Alissa, and Betsy get dressed.

Their dresses were beautiful strapless red silk creations. The dresses hugged each of them like a second skin and stopped just above the knees. Their matching short-waisted long-sleeve jackets lay on the bed. They also wore matching red pumps. The bouquets for them were red and white carnations. Karen and Liz helped Danielle into her dress and zipped up the back. Karen then draped a white beach towel around her shoulders.

"Dani, go change into your camisole and slip before Anton gets here. She handed the garments to her along with a robe. "He'll be here any minute."

"Girls, it's Anton the magician," whispered the soft sugary sweet voice. "Is it safe for me to come in?"

Before anyone could move, he flitted into the room. He wheeled in a large suitcase behind him.

Anton was clad in a long sleeved white ruffled shirt, black leather pants, and black leather boots. His head was bald and he wore a hoop earring in each ear.

"You must be the bride. Honey, what are you waiting for to change? Go. Go. While you do that, I'll see what I can do with the rest of the wedding party." Danielle left the room giving Karen a worried look. "Honey, that lipstick is not right for you." She heard him say to someone as she closed the door behind her.

When she emerged minutes later Anton was combing Alissa's hair. He finished and applied a red lipstick to her pouting lips.

"Magnificent. You look like a million bucks. I told you that was the wrong shade of lipstick for you." He turned to face Danielle. "You're up next sweet thing. I'll have you looking like a million bucks in a jiffy. Have a seat."

Twenty minutes later, true to his words, she was indeed transformed. Her gray eyes were tinted with several blends of purple. A single line underneath each eye and one stroke of mascara to her naturally long thick lashes accentuated her eyes. The light stroke of blush he applied to her flushed cheeks was barely noticeable. A light coat of red covered her small heart-shaped lips. Smiling into the mirror, her eyes sparkling with joy.

He had also worked a minor miracle with her hair. It was brushed into a French roll, with a few loose tendrils to soften her features. He positioned the crown of the veil perfectly inside the French roll. The comb attached to the back of the veil was pressed into the back of the French knot to hold the veil in place.

After a few adjustments, he stepped back smiling. Danielle came to her feet and turned around to face everyone. The oohs and ahs made Anton smile with pride.

"You look beautiful, Dani," said Karen wiping her tears. "Anton you've earned a bonus today."

Anton left the room beaming. With the help of everyone present, Danielle stepped into the wedding gown. They helped her pull the gown up and into place without messing up her hair or dislodging the veil.

"I agree with Aunt Karen. You look sensational," said Liz hugging her. "You are going to knock Greg off his feet."

There was a brief knock before the door opened and Victoria came sailing into the room looking gorgeous as ever. She was clad in a dark purple silk dress.

"Honey, you look gorgeous," said Victoria hugging her. "Wait until you see your groom. I don't know where the term *tall, dark, and handsome* came from, but Greg is all that and more today. Your mother would be so proud of you."

"She already is," smiled Danielle, meeting Karen's loving gaze. It took Karen only a few moments for what Danielle said to sink in. When it did, tears came to her blue eyes.

"Ladies, it's time for you to line up outside. Danielle, Jack is waiting outside for you. Be happy," said Victoria hugging her again.

"Can you ask him to wait outside for a few minutes? I'd like some time alone with my mother."

They all filed out of the room hugging her and wishing her well. Once the door closed behind them, Danielle held out her hand to Karen. Smiling through her tears, Karen took it.

"You have always been my mother, it's just taken me a little longer than it should have to realize it. I love you, Mom," said Danielle wiping at her tears. "You are my mother in all the ways that count. You

always have been. Karen, you unselfishly stepped in
when my mother died and took care of me. You were
always there at plays, gymnastics, and recitals. Knowing the truth about me, you loved me like I was your
own child. I will never forget that. You made me realize you don't have to give birth to a child to be its
mother. You gave me faith and hope for the future. Because of your love and strength, I can deal with whatever the future may bring. I love you, Mom."

"I love you, too. I've waited so long to hear you call
me Mom. I had given up on ever hearing those words.
I knew there was no way I could ever replace Barbara,
but I did so want to be your mother, Danielle."

Laughing and crying, they went happily into each
other's arms. There was no doubt in Dani's mind she
had made the right decision. Pulling back slightly,
Karen dabbed at Dani's eyes.

"Anton did such a wonderful job, we don't won't
to ruin all his work." She kissed Dani's cheek. "Be
happy sweetie."

Greg nervously paced the room. Peering down at
his watch, he moaned and sat down on the bed.

"Give it a rest, Greg," advised Mark straightening
his tie for the fifth time. "You are starting to give me
a headache with all that pacing."

"What's the matter, Doc?" laughed Travis slapping
Mark on the back. "You seem almost as nervous as the
groom."

"Yeah Mark," laughed Jeff. "Have you ever been
this close to a wedding altar before? I can see why
you're sweating. Guys I think he feels the noose tight-
ening around his neck as well."

"I hate weddings," said Mark nervously. "Why can't
people just go to the damn JP and get this over with.
It's cheaper and it's simpler. If I ever get married . . ."

he trailed off. "What am I saying, I'm never getting married. Can you picture me with kids in a minivan?"

"An SUV works just as well," teased Jeff, smiling and winking at Greg. "As the saying goes, 'there is a lid for every pot'." They took in the dark look Mark was giving Jeff. "Maybe not. Who in their right mind would marry you? It would take a saint just to put up with you."

"Or a sinner," Travis added laughing. "I don't know any woman with the kind of 'patience' it would take to put up with Mark. This is all a moot point because he has to date the same woman at least twice before he can even have a relationship. To my recollection, you've done that once, maybe twice."

"I don't know," Jeff threw in, "I saw the way he and Janelle were hitting it off last night. Maybe there's hope for him yet."

"We were talking," defended Mark uneasily. "Don't make more out of it than there was. It goes against my rules to date women with children."

"There's an exception to every rule," said Greg meeting his friend's eyes. Greg noted the flicker in Mark's eyes at the mention of Janelle. He knew the interest was there, but his friend was too stubborn to admit it.

They all burst into laughter and Mark glared at each of them. Ignoring them, he loosened his tie and unbuttoned the top button of his shirt.

Greg laughed out loud at Mark's shaky hands. His friend was actually sweating. He knew Mark was afraid of matrimony, but he didn't realize how much until now. This made Greg more relaxed.

"Guys, it's time to take your places," said Gabe poking his head in the door. "The music is about to start."

"Congratulations," said Jeff extending his hand to Greg. "Make my favorite cousin happy."

They all offered there congratulations as they left the room, until Greg and Mark were the only two left.

"Well, this is it friend. In a few minutes you are going to be an old married man," joked Mark. "I wish you and Danielle nothing but the best, my friend," said Mark sincerely. "Now let's get this over with as quickly as possible. I'm sure your new father-in-law is not too thrilled to have me under his roof. I can probably count myself lucky he didn't shoot on sight."

"Thanks," said Greg as they embraced warmly. "We'd better go before Jack sends out the posse after us."

"Honey, you are up next," said Jack peeping his head in the door. "You look so beautiful. I am so proud of you. I could not have asked for a better daughter than you. I love you," said Jack misty eyed.

"I love you too, Dad," whispered Danielle hugging him. "I don't always agree with you, but I do love you."

"I'm sorry about what happened with Greg. Maybe I was wrong about him. He's a very lucky young man. I hope he makes all your dreams come true. I love you, sweetheart. Be happy." They embraced again. "If you change your mind you can still slip out the back way," teased Jack wiping the tears from his eyes, "I have the keys right here." He jingled the keys in his pocket.

"Not a chance," said Danielle. "I've been waiting for this moment for four long years." Picking up her bouquet of red and white roses, she was ready. "Nothing is going to spoil this day for us. I'm ready." He held out his arm, and she took it.

She let Jack slowly lead her down the aisle. Looking straight ahead, her sparkling eyes met Greg's.

The sight of him took her breath away. He looked incredibly handsome and picture perfect in his black tuxedo. Victoria was right. He was indeed tall, dark, and handsome.

His eyes shone with love and pride as they settled on his beautiful bride. She looked like a fairy princess floating down the aisle toward him. Danielle never looked more stunning than she did right then. He would remember her like this the rest of their lives.

Smiling he mouthed the words, *I love you*, as Jack placed her hand in Greg's. His hand tightened on hers and he brought it to his mouth.

Her eyes were misty, but she was determined not to cry anymore. She didn't want all her pictures to show her with red eyes.

"Today we are gathered here to witness the marriage of Danielle Elizabeth Roberts Masters to Gregory Allen Thomas," said Reverend Pryor opening his Bible.

Danielle and Greg were both fighting to keep their tears of joy at bay during the ceremony. When the minister pronounced them man and wife, Danielle turned to face her husband. She caught his other hand and beamed up into his smiling face.

"I love you with all my heart and soul. I have always loved you and I always will. I promise to love, honor, and cherish you the rest of our lives. It's been a hard and rocky road for us, but we finally made it. I have learned a lot from being with you and being without you. It has made me a better and stronger person. From this day forward, I promise to put you first in my thoughts and my actions. You are my life, my future, my husband."

Danielle smiled through her tears as Greg took his handkerchief out of his pocket and dabbed her eyes. His own eyes were misty as he smiled back at her.

"Danielle Elizabeth Roberts Masters, I have loved you from the first moment I saw you. Yes, we have been through a lot in the past four years. I think it has made us both stronger and smarter. I promise to love and cherish you the rest of my life. I will forsake all others for you and because of you. You are my life and my future. I will also put you first in my thoughts and actions. I know what life is like without you in it, and I never want to go back there. I love you, Dani, with all my heart and soul, and I always will."

Greg raised the veil slowly to reveal his wife's beautiful, smiling face. His mouth captured hers in a tender kiss.

"After four years of waiting, I think you can do a little better than that," laughed Mark urging him on. "Give her a real kiss."

Laughing, his head lowered again, and this time in a kiss that curled Danielle's toes. Her arms went around his neck and she returned his passionate kiss.

"Ahem," coughed the minister. Greg raised his head, but not before kissing her again. "May I present to you Mr. and Mrs. Gregory Thomas."

Laughter and applause filled the room, followed by an *Amen* that sounded distinctively like Greg's mother.

Breaking apart and arm in arm, Danielle and Greg walked down the aisle. The rest of the wedding party followed them.

The next half hour was spent with the photographer. He took every pose imaginable. When he finally finished, Dani thought her face was going to crack from smiling so much.

"Congratulations, Mrs. Thomas," said Greg brushing her lips with his. "You look magnificent. Are you happy?"

"I'm ecstatic, Mr. Thomas." She kissed him. "You clean up pretty good yourself. I might actually be able to take you to the country club," she teased.

"Congratulations, you two," said Mark, hugging Greg first and then Danielle. "I wish you both all the best."

Jack held out his hand to Greg and, without hesitation, he took the peace offering. Taking the envelope out of his jacket pocket, Greg handed it to him.

"Signed, sealed, and delivered," said Greg. Puzzled, Dani stared from her husband to her father. Greg put his finger to her lips. "Don't ask. It's not important," smiled Greg silencing her with a kiss.

"I just wanted to be sure," said Jack ripping the envelope in half. "Take good care of my little girl."

"Congratulations guys," said Karen hugging Danielle and then Greg. "I wish you all the best. I'm so glad it's finally over. We can all breathe easier now."

"Thanks, Mom. Thank you for everything. You did a wonderful job. The house looks beautiful. Everything looks beautiful."

"My dream finally came true for the two of you. I'm just so happy," cried Mrs. Thomas hugging both of them. "Praise the Lord. It took you both long enough, but it finally happened."

The rest of the day was a blur for Danielle. She vaguely remembered her and Greg cutting the wedding cake. She and Greg danced the first dance to "Here and Now" by Luther. Next she danced with her father and Greg danced with his mother, and then with Karen.

"May I have this dance?" asked Mark holding out his hand to Danielle. She caught his outstretched hand and let him lead her to the dance floor. "You look enchanting."

"Thank you." They circled the dance floor. "Mark, I want you to know you are welcome at our home anytime. I don't want you and Greg to drift apart. Good friends are hard to find and often hard to keep. I want you to be a part of our lives."

"I'm glad you feel that way. I guess this means we won't have to arm wrestle for which nights I have your husband." They both laughed as they danced.

Amid well wishes and congratulations, she and

Greg slipped upstairs to change clothes. Their bags were already packed and loaded in the white stretch limousine waiting for them.

Greg planned the honeymoon as a surprise for Dani. She had no clue where they were going, but since she was told to pack for a warm climate, she assumed it was somewhere in the Caribbean. Their flight was due to leave for destination unknown in about an hour and a half.

Karen called all the single women to gather around the stairs for Danielle to throw the bouquet. Turning her back, she gave it a toss. When she turned around again, Janelle was standing away from the crowd holding the bouquet and looking down at it as though it would bite her.

Meeting her sister's sympathetic gaze. Janelle tossed the bouquet again and one of the other girls caught it.

When Danielle looked back again, her sister had disappeared. She scanned the room looking for her with no luck.

"It's okay Dani. It was an accident," said Greg kissing her cheek. "Okay guys. Line up for the garter toss. This includes you Mark," said Greg calling to his best man before he could slip out of the same door Janelle had.

Mark reluctantly came over to join the other single men. Greg tossed the garter. Danielle and the rest of the crowd burst out laughing when it landed around the corsage on Marks lapel.

"Can you be a little more accurate next time Thomas?" frowned Mark removing the offensive object. He held up the shiny red garter and all the men took a step back. Shrugging, he slipped it over the sleeve of his tuxedo and exited the room.

"We are out of here," said Greg leading her down the stairs. "Say goodbye." Laughing Greg swung her up into his arms and carried her away.

Epilogue

After two unsuccessful in vitro procedures, Danielle and Greg decided to give it one last try. Eight months later, on August 28, Gregory Allan Thomas II and Hope Karen Thomas were born five minutes apart at Parkdale Memorial Hospital. Proud parents Danielle and Greg were beaming with joy at their tiny miracles.

A Husband and Father's Tribute

To my wife, my best friend, and the love of my life.
People like us search for the stars above,
So hell bent and set in our ways, we sometimes
   hurt the ones we love.
It takes an act of God to make our minds unswirl,
Minds clear, our love is now etched forever in
   our little girl.
Be there only one or if there were none,
Till death do us part our love will shine forever
   as bright as the sun.

More of the Hottest
African-American Fiction from
Dafina Books